"I've Been Dreaming of Seeing You Again. . . ."

Sam didn't ask why—she didn't need to.

"It probably would have been better if you hadn't."

"I don't believe that, and neither do you," Drew said.

He was right. Standing close to him, she was suffused with bliss. For a moment, she thought nothing could possibly be better than the way she felt right now. Then he kissed her, gently, testing, and she saw how foolish she had been. She was only beginning to understand the meaning of feeling good.

He touched her face, as if to reassure himself. "You know, I was almost convinced that you were a figment of my imagination."

"How do you know I'm not?" she asked, almost unsure herself.

"This is how I know."

He kissed her again, not tentative but hungry this time. Sam stopped thinking, stopped breathing. She existed only in his embrace, and she wanted it to go on forever. . . .

FOR RICHER, FOR POORER

FOR RICHER, FOR POORER

LEAH LAIMAN

POCKET BOOKS

New York   London   Toronto   Sydney   Tokyo   Singapore

This book is a work of fiction. Names, characters, places and
incidents are either products of the author's imagination or are used
fictitiously. Any resemblance to actual events or locales or persons,
living or dead, is entirely coincidental.

An *Original* Publication of POCKET BOOKS

POCKET BOOKS, a division of Simon & Schuster Inc.
1230 Avenue of the Americas, New York, NY 10020

ISBN: 0-671-86482-3

First Pocket Books printing June 1994

10 9 8 7 6 5 4 3 2 1

POCKET and colophon are registered trademarks of
Simon & Schuster Inc.

Cover art by Punz Wolff
Stepback art by Diane Sivavec

Printed in the U.S.A.

❧ 1 ❧

Sam Myles knew even before it happened. The crowds, on their feet in the stands, shouting over the deafening roar of the engines, didn't know. The drivers, moving in a pack around the dirt track, nudging each other's fenders, trying to break away from the herd, didn't know. But as the gold and red D'Uberville Turbo Eight banked on the turn with just three laps to go, Sam knew it was going to happen. There was no point in getting on the horn to try to change things. Pete Wojek was a good driver, but, as Sam had told him many times before, he didn't know squat about mechanics. And he wasn't about to listen to Sam shouting instructions into his headset, especially with the smell of victory overpowering the odor of burning rubber.

Sam watched as Pete found the slot, dropped the hammer, took it to ninety-six hundred revs, and popped the clutch. The D'Uberville streaked into first

1

place—for about fifteen seconds. Then, as it flashed past the pit, Sam heard the heart-stopping crack of a thrown rod. The engine seized, the wheels locked, and the car spun, slamming into the Valvoline sign painted on the wooden retaining wall. The car rolled backward, lost in the flying dust left in the wake of the competition streaming by. The yellow flag went up; Sam felt, more than heard, the collective gasp of the spectators, and it was hard to keep the panic at bay. But then, miraculously, the car rolled out of the dust cloud in one piece, stopping not three feet from the pit. Pete popped the web strapping from the window and crawled out, pushing the car the remaining few feet to the pit. Sam was under it even before it stopped, hoping against hope, but knowing the inevitable. As far as this race was concerned, it was over for both of them.

In the grandstand Drew Symington was already picking his way through the throng, gently pulling along his fiancée, Bethany Havenhurst, like a father with a recalcitrant child. He was too excited to pay much attention to Bethany's complaints, but that didn't stop Bethany from voicing them.

"Why do we have to go down there?" she wailed. "It was bad enough sitting up here with all those beer-swilling lowlifes, but at least we were in the shade. Down there it's so . . . dirty!"

Drew stopped a minute to let her make up the arm's distance between them. She was a study in misery, and Drew felt something akin to sympathy, fully aware that the supposed ordeal he was making her bear was delirious joy for just about everybody else in the place. He knew he shouldn't have brought her.

After all, mixing it up in the bleachers of the Oakdale Fairgrounds on Superdirt Sunday wasn't exactly up her alley. On the other hand, he'd gone with her to the Jean-Paul Gaultier fashion showings in Paris, and the pushing and shoving to get close to the models on the runway was a lot scarier than anything they'd find here. The difference, of course, was that Bethany could accept a splash of champagne on her dress, but the thought of stepping on spilled beer horrified her. And of the five thousand people sweating in the makeshift bleachers around the dusty red-dirt oval below them, he could safely guarantee that not one of them was related to any of the royal houses of Europe. In fact, most of them probably worked for his father, at the D'Uberville Motor Company in Oakdale.

Drew looked at his fiancée: slate-gray eyes shaded in designer sunglasses; wheat-blond hair slicked back and tied at the nape of her neck with a Chanel bow; her matching white cotton piqué sundress, just a little number from the Chanel boutique, which had probably set her father back about the same amount as a month's salary for the guy in the aisle, pushing past her immobile size-six figure. Drew started to laugh.

"What?" said Bethany, taken aback. "What the hell is so funny?"

Seeing she was getting upset, Drew struggled for control.

"I'm sorry, honey. It's just that you look so . . . perfect. You're the only person I know who would go to a stock car race in a white dress, sit in the middle of a sweaty crowd with the thermometer pushing one hundred, and still look like a vanilla ice pop straight from the freezer."

"Is that supposed to be a compliment?" asked Bethany, a little unsure.

"You bet it is," laughed Drew. "Indulge me some more. Let's take it to extremes and see if you can withstand the grime of the pit."

Bethany knew he was teasing her now, but it didn't matter. At thirty-two, with his longish black hair, dancing blue eyes, and patrician good looks, Andrew Symington was hard to resist. They had been engaged for six months, and even though the Havenhursts weren't exactly peasants and paupers, Bethany knew that as far as the upper echelons of Woodland Cliffs society were concerned, she had made the catch of the decade.

She smiled to belie the complaint in her words as she grudgingly followed in the path he made for her with his elbows.

"Fine, if you must. But I really don't see what brings you to these places at all. I mean, it's not like I don't appreciate racing. Monaco is fine. And, of course, we always know everybody. But this—"

Drew interrupted, "They don't race D'Uberville Classics at Monaco, and in case you've forgotten, I've got a family interest."

Bethany, of course, had not forgotten. It would be impossible to separate Drew from his heritage, the D'Uberville Motor Company. The company was the raison d'être for the entire region, where the DMC plant employed a good seventy percent of the population. It had been built by the vision of one man, Drew's father, Forrest Symington, and the money of one woman, Drew's mother, Mathilde D'Uberville. And as much as she loved Drew for himself, Bethany was not likely to forget that as the only son and principal heir of Forrest Symington and his wife, Mathilde D'Uberville Symington, her fiancé was in line for an inheritance roughly the size of the gross national product of any number of small nations.

Jean-Claude Renoir was perhaps even more aware than Bethany of what the Symington family was worth. In fact, Jean-Claude had made quite a study of the Symingtons, especially their scion, Andrew. Had Bethany not been so intent on keeping her eye on the future and off the melting crowd, she might have noticed Jean-Claude's keen interest in their progress as he followed at a discreet but constant distance. Like them, Jean-Claude did not look as if he belonged in this arena. He was dressed smartly and expensively: black Egyptian cotton shirt, tan Armani trousers, woven leather espadrilles with no socks that proclaimed, as much as his Gallic profile, that he was not American. He was handsome in an offbeat way, with a hardness in his eyes and at the edge of his mouth that made him look possibly dangerous, and therefore all the more attractive. He didn't look like the kind of person who would be interested in stock-car races, and indeed, he was not. His only interest in being at the Oakdale Fairgrounds—indeed, his only interest in being in America at all—was Drew Symington. As Drew and Bethany made their way to the pit Jean-Claude gave up his pursuit and turned toward the exit. They would make his acquaintance soon, but not yet. Not until Jean-Claude had put his plan in motion, had set the trap, and was ready to spring it.

By the time Drew and Bethany had made their way to the pit Pete had removed his helmet and goggles and was trying out explanations on the pair of legs that stuck out from under the paralyzed D'Uberville.

"I had the guy dead to rights, I swear it."

"The only thing that's dead is this engine" came the reproach as Sam tossed a wrench at Pete's feet.

Pete deftly jumped out of the way, shaking his head, almost bumping into Drew, who held out his hand and introduced himself.

"I'm Drew Symington, and I just wanted to congratulate you."

Pete looked at him hard, trying to ascertain if this was some kind of a joke. He knew the name. Hell, anyone within a hundred miles of Woodland Cliffs/Oakdale recognized the Symington name. But the chance that a Symington would be approaching him at a dirt track to congratulate him for a lost race seemed pretty slim. Pete's eyes were drawn to Bethany as Drew introduced his fiancée, and then he knew Drew was for real. Anyone engaged to this lady in white would have to be a blueblood. More out of habit than hope, Pete worked his white-toothed smile, ran his fingers through his curly brown hair, and wondered if maybe they'd come to the wrong place. After all, in case they hadn't noticed, he hadn't even finished.

"The race doesn't matter," said Drew. "You took it into the red trying to get ahead of the pack—that's why it blew. But it's a great car. I saw you in the qualifiers. You made the pole in record time. And I checked your stats with the officials. Not only was it the fastest run they'd ever had, it was the cleanest. We make good cars at DMC, but we don't make them like that."

Pete laughed. The guy had a bank account in the stratosphere, but his feet seemed, remarkably enough, to be on the ground.

"You're telling me," Pete said. "This baby was built from the ground up. It's a classic D'Uberville DMC X600 chassis, but everything else is new and improved."

"I can see that," Drew acknowledged. "Would you mind letting me in on some of your secrets?"

"They're not mine," Pete admitted reluctantly. He indicated the legs still wriggling under the car. "You'd have to talk to my ace mechanic, Sam Myles."

Drew smiled in anticipation as Pete obligingly knelt down and shouted to Sam to get out from under there, only to be met by a barrage of loose bolts flying in his direction.

Drew was taken aback. "He's not too friendly, is he?"

"Well," Pete began, but Bethany had had it. She grabbed Drew's arm with an engaging smile and enough force to let him know she meant business.

"Darling, you saw your car. Now I think it's time we let these people get on with whatever it is they do. Your parents will be waiting. Have you forgotten they're having guests at the estate for dinner?"

"No," Drew replied. "I tried to forget, but I couldn't. But you're right. We'd better go."

He turned to Pete. "Thanks, but I'll take a rain check on that introduction. Maybe your Sam Myles will be in a better mood next time we meet."

Pete grinned. "Maybe."

The two men shook hands. Without thinking Pete stretched out his hand to Bethany, but her involuntary shudder made him withdraw it immediately and rest it on the hood of the dirty car. Instead he gave her a dazzling smile, then told Drew he tended bar at Bamboo Bernie's when he wasn't racing. He'd be there anytime Drew wanted to talk cars. With a huge sigh of relief Bethany led the way off the field, happy to be taking her man back to the lush environs of Woodland Cliffs, to territory she could control and understand.

"Look." She chuckled proudly, indicating her still-immaculate dress. "Still no spots."

"You're a treasure, sweetheart," said Drew, with only the barest hint of sarcasm.

Pete watched them walk away arm in arm and broke into a loud guffaw. The rich bitch wouldn't touch him, but, moving close behind her as they'd turned to go, he'd left his mark: a full red-dirt handprint that waved to him with every upper-class wiggle of her small, round behind. Still laughing, Pete turned his attention back to the car and Sam.

"Get out here, babe," he called. "I think you've made yourself one important fan."

Sam came out from under the D'Uberville cursing softly, and wondering what the hell Pete had to laugh about. They'd been over it a thousand times; there were certain things you just couldn't do in a stock car, and one of them was run her into the red and expect to get away with it. But Pete wasn't listening. He was pulling at the wet bandanna that Sam used as protection from the August sun, freeing a cascade of copper-colored curls that fell around a face so delicate that even streaks of grime couldn't hide its beauty.

Drops of boiled transmission fluid steamed from

8

her coveralls as Pete began to wipe the smudges off her face with the damp rag, gently teasing, "God, you're sexy when you're mad and dirty and talk like a grease monkey."

Sam—nobody called her Samantha except her mother—grabbed the bandanna out of his hand. A small dust cloud erupted as she slammed it into the ground, her emerald eyes turning a darker jade with the force of her anger.

"Damn you. You do this every time. You know I know more about cars than you or any of your pit-stop pals. But instead of listening to me, you push the goddam envelope until it tears. Then, when I tell you what you did wrong, you patronize me and pretend I'm the same as any other cute little bimbo who likes to talk cars with the big boys. Well, I've had it. You don't drive them right, I don't build them. It's that simple."

A quick zip and Sam was out of the coveralls, no longer the anonymous mechanic, but a five-foot-nine head-turner dressed in shorts and a T-shirt, the sun glinting gold in her fiery hair as she stalked out of the stadium, completely unaware of the sensation she created. Pete knew better than to follow. He'd had experience with her temper, and he knew if he confronted her now, he wouldn't have an icicle's chance in hell of winning the encounter. But if he gave her distance, she'd cool off. Then he'd get some flowers, play little-boy-lost, turn on the charm, and get back in her good graces. What's more, if he did it with just the proper hint of despair, she'd end up giving him more than he had any right to expect. He deserved her anger. She had been right; he had been wrong. It was going to take a hell of a lot of work to get the D'Uberville back on the track. But that didn't really matter. Because Pete Wojek knew that if there was one thing that Samantha Myles loved more than him, it was fixing cars.

At the moment Pete was pretty far down on the list of things Sam loved. They had met in high school, because even then Pete had been into drag racing and Sam had been into anything on four wheels. Pete's first interest had been in getting Sam into the back-seat. But once he'd seen a sample of her skill with a wrench, they'd spent more time under his car than in it. Still, it was her choice, not his. Pete's blood had boiled from the minute he saw her, and even though he recognized her talent, he would have preferred to have one of the guys work on his car while he worked on Sam. For a long time Pete was just the owner of a car Sam wanted to rebuild. But Pete was relentless, and eventually the charm had worked. Or so he liked to think. To this day he wasn't absolutely sure if what had convinced Sam it was time to go all the way was love of Pete or the D'Uberville Classic they were doing it in.

It had always been that way. From the time she could walk and hold something at the same time, she had toddled after her father in the garage with her play tools, saying, "Me fix, too." They'd all thought it cute at first. But by the time her younger sister Melinda was born when Sam was three, her only interest in dolls was to remove their body parts and stick a wrench into their hollows to "make go better." By the age of eight, when most little girls were playing with dolls and having tea parties, Sam had stolen the wheels off Melinda's tricycle and made her first car. Melinda had cried, and her mother had spanked Sam. But her father had been impressed, no question about it. Harvey had no sons. Sam was the only one who would share his American love of speed and the automobile. From that point on, Harvey Myles had started taking Sam to the races, and there was no turning back. It didn't matter that her mother got angry, that her father laughed, that the other kids mocked her. Samantha Myles knew one day she'd build a car that others would dream about.

Sitting in the reception area outside of Forrest Symington's office, Melinda Myles looked at her watch and knew that the race would be over by now. She wondered if Sam had won, then remembered it would be Pete driving, not Sam. But they were always Sam's cars, and out of loyalty she thought about them as her sister's wins, knowing that Sam did, too. She would have been at the Oakdale Fairgrounds today, celebrating—she hoped, by now—with Sam, while the driver groupies threw themselves all over Pete, thrusting their little autograph books and their big chests into his face. She marveled that it never seemed to bother Sam. It would have made her crazy if women did that to her boyfriend—if she had a boyfriend.

Right now, all Melinda wanted was a job. The employment agency had called her that morning, explaining there was an emergency. One of Forrest Symington's private secretaries had quit without notice after she had been forced to put in ten hours on the third Saturday in a row. The amount of work that was obviously required didn't daunt Melinda. She had graduated from Miss Driscoll's Secretarial School three months before, and this was the first interesting possibility she'd had. If she didn't get this, she'd be talking to the foreman on the line tomorrow, trying to join her father and her sister, and that was the last thing she wanted. She'd done well in high school, gotten top grades at Miss Driscoll's, typed ninety words a minute, was a demon on the computer, all so that she wouldn't have to spend a life with dirt and grease so imbedded in her skin and under her nails that her hands, like Sam's, would never be quite clean. She'd hoped to avoid the auto industry altogether, but that was kind of hard to do in the Oakdale/Woodland Cliffs area. Working for the CEO and owner of the D'Uberville Motor Company would do nicely. She had to stop and remind herself that she had yet to get the job. She clasped her hands together to keep them from shaking as she heard "Next," and the door opened, leading into Forrest Symington's inner sanctum and her future.

Forrest liked what he saw. Chestnut hair, hazel eyes, fair complexion, and a figure that wouldn't have embarrassed a centerfold. He smiled and waved at her to sit down while he glanced at the résumé the employment agency had supplied. She was young, inexperienced, but smart, that was clear. And the only other contender he had been able to see on such short notice was a matronly grandmother who had the stern demeanor of a high school Latin teacher.

"Can you start tomorrow?" he asked, not looking up at her.

"What?" She was caught off guard.

"Can you—"

"Yes, no problem." She had heard; she wasn't going to make him ask twice. She dared to look him in the eye. He was handsome, silver-haired, older, but not as old as she had expected. His eyes were a steel gray, and she could see how they could command attention; but right now there was a twinkle in them, and she thought he had the warmest smile she had ever seen. She hoped he would use it often on her.

"Surprised it was so easy?" he asked, disarming her.

"Yes," she admitted, not knowing whether that was the right answer or not.

"Well, everything is going to be much more difficult from now on. Are you prepared for that?"

"Absolutely," she replied fervently.

"Fine. Monday at eight-thirty."

"I'll be early," she said.

"Be prepared to stay late. Monday. Tuesday. Maybe every day."

"My life is in your hands," she dared to joke, and she was rewarded with the dazzling smile again.

"Actually, it will be in Catherine Morton's hands."

"I'm sorry?"

"Catherine Morton. She's my assistant. You'll be taking most of your orders from her. She's on vacation now, but she'll be in tomorrow. I didn't want her to be overwhelmed on her first day back, so I'm doing the hiring for her."

"Oh, I see," Melinda answered, hoping he didn't detect the disappointment in her voice. She should have known it was too good to be true. Girls like her didn't start out at the top. It would have been a dream come true to be at the right hand of the top man, especially this particular top man, but she'd take what she could get and be happy for it.

He reached out, shook her hand. "Thank you"—he looked down at her résumé and finished—"Melinda."

He put a gentle hand on her shoulder as he walked her to the door. She didn't believe this job was going to be as difficult as everyone said. And if it was, she didn't think she'd mind in the least.

"Monday," he said as he closed the door behind her, then quietly to himself, knowing she was beyond hearing, "You look just like your mother."

Jean-Claude Renoir didn't bother to wait for Drew and Bethany to leave the stadium. He knew where to find them when he wanted to find them. He went to a nearby coffee shop to wait. The timing had to be right. He was aiming for an entrance somewhere after the second or third cocktail of the evening. He'd done his research well. He wanted the fortress vulnerable but not decimated. Any earlier and Mathilde would be wary, on guard. Any later, she wouldn't be functioning. He took a sip from the cup the waitress placed in front of him and grimaced at the poor imitation that, in America, passed for coffee, and he longed for the heady French brew he was used to drinking. It was a small sacrifice to place on the altar of his vengeance. Knowing it was useless to complain, he pushed the cup aside, making room for the Gucci leather saddle-bag that served as a small suitcase. He unzipped it and from the side pocket pulled a crumpled issue of *Society* magazine. It fell open on the same page to which it had been turned a hundred times. For the hundredth time Jean-Claude gazed at the engagement

picture of Bethany Havenhurst and Andrew Symington. Beneath their smiling portraits was a glowing
announcement of their impending nuptials and their
intent for eternal happiness. Jean-Claude studied it
for a moment, his face and his heart turning to granite
as he whispered to himself: "Never."

❧ 2 ❧

"Anybody home?" Melinda shouted excitedly as she let herself in through the back door.

"In here," came the response, and she raced through the kitchen and into the small living room of the simple cottage that had been the Myles home since before she was born. Harvey was on the plastic slip-covered couch, as she knew he would be, beer in hand. Melinda plopped down beside him, a huge grin on her face as she took the remote control and turned off the TV.

"Hey," complained Harvey, "the news was going to have highlights of today's race."

"Weren't you there?"

"Yeah," said her father, "but you weren't."

"It doesn't matter. I know what happened. I heard it on the radio. Sam lost. Pete totaled the car, and she's going to be pissed as hell for a week. Then she'll get over it and build him another one. Just like she always does. They'll show it at eleven, too. Anyway, I've got news of my own."

"Okay, let's hear it," Harvey said, catching a little of her excitement. She hadn't said anything earlier when she left the house, except that she couldn't go to the race and she wasn't going to church, even though she was dressed for it.

"Mom, get in here," called Melinda, wanting the double whammy of telling both parents at once.

"This must be good," laughed Harvey as Diane made her way in from the bedroom, towing the vacuum behind her.

Melinda stood up, the plastic making a popping noise as it unstuck from her skin. Melinda cringed every time she saw the sofa, never mind sat on it, knowing that in homes all over Woodland Cliffs people sat on creamy white sofas with no covers and no fears of leaving grease stains. But today it didn't matter. She had a job. It was just the first step, but soon, she was convinced, she'd have a place of her own, and plastic sofa covers would be irrelevant. After the call had come from the employment agency this morning she had said nothing to her parents. She'd gotten their hopes up before, and she didn't want to disappoint them again. Besides, she didn't want to jinx it by talking about it. Obviously, she'd been right. The charm had worked. She cleared her throat to make her announcement.

"You are looking at the new private secretary to the chief executive officer of the D'Uberville Motor Company."

"What?" Diane dropped the vacuum hose and sat down.

Harvey beamed, hugging and congratulating his younger child. "Good for you, honey. I knew you'd do it."

Diane seemed shaken. "When did this happen?"

Melinda explained about the emergency and the call from the employment agency, about her nervousness and her silence for fear she'd have only bad news to report. But for a change, it had gone in her favor. In fact, it had been almost effortless. She would never have believed a man like Forrest Symington could be so easygoing, friendly even. Oh, she knew the work would be hard, and it would probably be a lot tougher working for him than being interviewed by him, but she didn't care what anybody said; she looked into his eyes just for a minute, and she'd guess he was a pretty gentle man.

"What are you making?" asked Harvey, ever practical.

Melinda was embarrassed to say she hadn't even asked, she'd been so excited about getting the job. But it couldn't be worse than the nothing she was bringing home now.

Agreeing, Harvey gave her a hug, then turned to Diane. "Isn't this great, honey?"

Diane hadn't spoken for a long time, and Melinda turned to her, expecting her mother's approval.

"You can't take that job," said Diane, grim.

Melinda looked at her mother in shock. Harvey, misunderstanding, started to explain. "She's right, honey. It doesn't matter what she gets, it's going to be better than starting on the line. Whatever she makes now, she'll work hard, and it'll go up. Right, Melinda?"

"Of course," Melinda agreed, accepting her father's

18

interpretation of Diane's hesitation, even though she knew it didn't sit right.

"I wouldn't care if you were making a million dollars," Diane went on, confirming Melinda's suspicions. "It's not a good job for you."

Harvey, persisting in misconception, continued his argument, but Melinda cut him off.

"Why, Mom? I think it's my dream come true, so why don't you want me to take this job?"

"You can do better."

Before Melinda could say anything, Harvey exploded, finally understanding that he didn't understand.

"Are you crazy, Diane? You make me come up with seven thousand dollars to send Melinda to secretarial school so she won't have to work on the line. You won't even let her do day work there 'cause she might chip her nails and her hands won't look pretty enough to pick up a phone. You let her turn down two offers because they're not high-class offices, and I get to keep footing the bills. And now, when finally it all pays off and she gets an offer from the classiest guy in the state, you say no! What the hell is she holding out for? The president of the United States is not going to be looking for a secretary in Oakdale anytime soon."

Diane was cornered, and she knew it. She looked away from both of them, picking up her vacuum cleaner, heading back to the bedroom and her chores, knowing it was a retreat but trying to make it look like a concession.

"It's still cars, but do what you want."

Melinda watched her mother close the bedroom door behind her and heard the vacuum cleaner start to hum. She turned to her father. Harvey shrugged.

There were lots of things about Diane he didn't understand, but she was a good wife.

"It's okay, honey. You did good. Mom'll see."

Melinda hoped so. Because no matter what anyone said, she wasn't giving up this job. She called Sam, wanting an antidote to her mother's negativity. She knew her sister would be as thrilled as she was—*because* she was. That was one thing the sisters shared: excitement for the other's successes. She was disappointed when there was no answer at either Sam's apartment or her garage. Knowing her mother was upset, although she had no idea why, Melinda went in to the kitchen to start dinner, telling herself it didn't matter. Nothing mattered except that starting tomorrow, on her first day of work, the rest of her life was going to be different.

Dinner at Belvedere, the Symington estate, was always a formal affair, and by the time Jean-Claude Renoir arrived the senior Symingtons were already dressed in evening attire. Mathilde, as usual, looked exquisite. Her hair, still dark except for a pure white streak that only served to heighten its ebony gloss, was swept into an elegant coil, exposing her long neck and emphasizing her ramrod posture. Her gown was deceptively simple, a perfectly straight black silk column, hand-embroidered from bosom to floor with tiny black seed pearls. At Mathilde's throat hung a single star sapphire the size of a peach pit, surrounded by diamonds. Her earrings were of the same hue and shape, but smaller in size, all obviously chosen to reflect the blue of her eyes.

When Robert, the butler, entered the library to

inform them that there was a French gentleman at the door by the name of Jean-Claude Renoir, claiming to be a relative of Madame's, Mathilde was pouring her third martini. Forrest was still on number one, having arrived late from the office, full of his tedious news about hiring a new secretary. Relatives did not generally drop in to see Mathilde unannounced, but two drinks and relief at not having to listen to Forrest discuss business was enough to intrigue her. Before Forrest could question her judgment she told Robert to show him in.

There was no hesitation or doubt in Jean-Claude's step as he entered the library.

"Madame." He took Mathilde's hand and almost brushed it with his lips, then stood back and looked at her intently, no trace of modesty or embarrassment. *"Mais, c'est incroyable. Vous avez le visage D'Uberville. La beauté délicate de votre famille."*

"Vous connaissez ma famille?" Mathilde slipped easily and happily into her native tongue.

Jean-Claude took note of Forrest and excused himself in charmingly accented English. "Forgive me, sir, but your wife looks very like her mother. So beautiful."

Forrest took Jean-Claude's outstretched hand and shook it without indicating welcome. "Just how are you related, Mr. Renoir?"

Jean-Claude smiled; the very cue he needed as he launched into his monologue, well-rehearsed and delivered with just the proper combination of certainty and diffidence.

"Of course, you Americans might not consider us true relations, but in France the offspring of one's mistress must be considered part of the family. It is tradition, especially with artists as famous as my great-great-great-uncle, Pierre-Auguste Renoir."

At the mention of the impressionist painter Mathilde beamed. There had been rumors of some connection, although she could never quite place it in the family tree. She liked to think her artistic temperament was a legacy, and here she was about to get confirmation. Jean-Claude sensed, more than saw, her almost imperceptible nod to Robert, who appeared at his side bearing a cocktail on a tray. Mathilde sat on the peach silk sofa, indicating that Jean-Claude should sit beside her as she leaned toward him, trusting, ready. Jean-Claude felt the tug; the hook was secure.

"Jacqueline D'Uberville was Pierre-Auguste Renoir's mistress, although because she was married, and of good family, it was never discussed. They had a son, Pierre, whom Jacqueline passed off as the child of her husband. But it was common knowledge, at least in the Renoir family, that Pierre was Pierre-Auguste's son."

"But Pierre was the name of my grandfather's brother."

"Exactly," said Jean-Claude, and he thought, There goes the line.

"And what brings you to Woodland Cliffs?" asked Forrest, looking for the catch.

"I am an art dealer myself," said Jean-Claude. "I have delivered a very valuable sculpture to a Mrs. Dorothy Radcliffe."

This part was true. It had taken Jean-Claude a long time to make a connection in the area; he had had to call in a lot of favors with other dealers in Monaco. But he knew he would require at least some verifiable facts.

"I know Dorothy," said Mathilde, and Jean-Claude, feigning surprise, knew that she would be on the phone as soon as he'd gone to check him out. That was the sinker.

"Because of my field, and my name, I have tried to follow the history of our illustrious ancestor. Jacqueline D'Uberville was always a favorite of mine. So beautiful and elegant. I still have some portraits of her left to me in the family collection. You know, you look very much like her."

Mathilde beamed and asked Jean-Claude where he was staying in town. Jean-Claude explained that, regrettably, he intended to go to the airport tonight for an early flight back to Nice tomorrow. He had only wanted to meet Mathilde, to see her at least once, to fill in the gaps of his visual history. It had been worth the detour. Insisting he could impose no longer, he rose to leave, holding his breath, hoping he was making the right move—pawn threatens queen.

"But you have just arrived, you cannot leave. We have so much to talk about. I'd like to know more about the D'Uberville connection to the Renoirs. If you have no pressing business back in France, couldn't you stay with us a few days? I so rarely get the opportunity to speak French, and hearing about the family would be an added delight."

Jean-Claude smiled, certain now that his strategy was correct, and made his perfunctory protest. Mathilde insisted, as he knew she would. With a Gallic shrug marking his graceful acquiescence he tossed Robert his keys so that his luggage could be removed from his car. Pawn takes queen.

Unaware that she had been played, Mathilde beamed at Jean-Claude and indicated her empty glass, and Forrest poured. He refilled his own, then Jean-Claude's as well.

"Merci," said Jean-Claude, smiling. His work with the senior Symingtons was done. By the time Drew came home Jean-Claude would be introduced as his long-lost cousin. He brought his drink to his lips, surreptitiously glancing at his watch. He had left Drew and Bethany at the racetrack over two hours before. He wondered why they were not home. But he was patient. He had waited two years already. Two hours seemed like nothing.

To Sam, the same two hours seemed like an eternity. Angry at Pete, Sam had stormed out of the stadium, intending to go to the rundown shed that served as her garage. Never mind the D'Uberville that Pete had totaled. She had a car waiting for her, her final project for the design engineering class she was taking at the university. But, needing to work off the rage, she had walked at top speed a good five miles over to the mill pond. She stopped, breathless, not quite sure how she'd gotten there, but glad she'd come. It was peaceful and beautiful, one of the few places near Oakdale where the DMC factory works had not encroached. It was after six; but even though the sun was low in the sky, its heat had not abated. Sam felt a drop of sweat trickle down her neck, and more than anything she yearned for the cool, clear water of the pond to wash away the grime of the track from her body and the stress of the race from her mind. She looked around, certain she was alone. Then, quickly, she kicked off her sneakers, stripped off her T-shirt and shorts, and plunged into the water.

Sam floated, weightless for a while, watching clouds drift overhead. She let the ripples break over her body and thought about Pete. Resignation had taken the place of anger as she realized he almost couldn't help himself. He had pushed the D'Uberville beyond its tolerance, believing that man could master machine —the way he believed that man could master woman. And he was wrong on both counts. In a way, she couldn't blame him. In the little pond of Oakdale, Pete Wojek was a big fish. There was never a lack of young women, racing groupies, crowding around the stadium exits, ready to accommodate the handsome driver. To Pete's credit, he never paid much attention beyond signing a few autographs, occasionally on a proffered body part. But sometimes Sam wondered if she had ended up with Pete because everybody else thought he was so great. Not that there was anything wrong with him; far from it. He had a steady job to fall back on, and if he would just listen to her once in a while, he could even have a decent professional career as a driver. Still, although she tried to keep the feeling at bay, she knew there was something missing. And she knew what it was, too. He had no vision.

Pete liked driving, and he liked winning even more, but it didn't really matter. He appreciated Sam's ingenuity with a motor, but he considered it just "tinkering." He expected, as did just about everyone else Sam encountered—including her own family— that eventually they would settle down. Sam would work on the line until she got pregnant; Pete would tend bar at Bamboo Bernie's, maybe even work up to managing the place someday. They'd get a little house, have a couple of kids, barbecue on Sundays, save up to take the kids to Disney World one year, and maybe even go to the Caribbean themselves the next.

As Diana Myles frequently said to her daughter, "What's wrong with that? It sounds like a good life to me."

"That's because you don't expect enough," Sam always answered.

"I expect to eat, which is a lot more than some people can say right now. With the economy the way it is . . ."

Sam knew the routine by heart. But it didn't matter how many times she heard it; she never believed it. Because she had what they all lacked. She had a vision. She was going to build a car. Not a funky modified stock car for Pete or some other hotshot to race, but a real car for real people, more exciting and efficient than anything that had ever been placed on the market by any of the big companies in this country or any other. She didn't know how she was going to do it. But it was her vision, and she'd be damned if she'd give it up.

Sam forced herself back to reality, reluctantly leaving behind the comfort of a dream she'd had many times before. Treading water, she shielded her eyes from the setting sun and looked back to shore. Lost in her reverie, she'd drifted, and she could no longer see the place where she had hastily dropped her clothes. Still not anxious to leave the cocoon of the sun-heated water, she lazily swam in the general direction from which she had come. Reaching the sand, she stood for a moment, naked and dripping, a modern Venus emerging from the sea. She spotted her clothes a good fifty feet away and ambled languidly to get them, warm sun and gentle breeze drying her on the way.

Then she heard it. The sound of a car, approaching fast. Sam started to run, but she knew she couldn't make it as she heard the crunch of wheels on the gravel path grow closer. Ducking beneath the overhanging branches of a weeping willow, her slim body shielded behind the massive trunk, she watched as a brand new D'Uberville ZSX convertible pulled up short at the bank of the pond. Her heart began to beat faster as the driver got out and leaned on the hood. His straight black hair was windblown, and a wave fell over eyes so blue Sam felt she could drown in their depths even at that distance. She forced herself to pull back behind the tree, afraid of being seen. She knew this man, although he did not know her. She had seen his face in the paper countless times, had heard his family history repeated and had followed the daily occurrences in his life that were orchestrated for public consumption. But she'd never seen Andrew Symington in person before; and she had never, ever expected that his actual presence would cause such an intense feeling.

"Well, is this it or not?"

Sam jumped at the sound of a woman's voice, clearly in a state of absolute irritation. She had been so mesmerized by the sight of Drew Symington, she had failed to notice that there was someone else in the car.

"This is definitely the place. Come out here, Beth, look at it," Drew sighed.

Not bothering to hide her pique, Bethany Haven-hurst joined her fiancé.

"It certainly took long enough to find it."

"Don't be angry, Beth," Drew soothed, putting an arm around her. "I'd heard it was beautiful here. I just had to see for myself."

Unrelenting, Bethany let her manicured nails tap an impatient beat on the car while Drew turned his face to the setting sun and breathed in the flower-scented air.

A feeling of regret, of something lost, caught Sam unawares as she watched Drew calm his irate lover with a single kiss. The ice maiden warmed but did not melt as she let Drew lead her toward the edge of the woods. Sam had an irrational urge to rush over to them, slap Bethany's face, and take her man away. Angrily, she willed her heart to slow and told herself to stop being so foolish and face reality. She was hiding naked behind a tree, two strange people were walking toward her, and if she got caught, she would be completely humiliated in front of her boss's son and his supercilious fiancée. Indignant at the invasion of what she considered her private lair, Sam wondered what the hell they were doing there. Why didn't they just get into their overpriced car and zoom back where they came from?

As if Sam's thoughts had been telepathically transferred, Bethany grumbled, "Really, Drew, why are we bothering with this? Why don't we just go to your parents'? They're expecting us."

"It's cocktail hour. I'm sure they've got plenty of martinis to keep them occupied until we get there. Don't you like it here?"

"Oh, it's very pretty. But what's the point? It's not as though we could build a house here or anything. It's completely in the wrong area. We could never live in Oakdale, no matter how quaint and rustic. You know that."

Drew shook his head, but Sam wasn't sure if it was a gesture of agreement or annoyance.

"We're not looking at homesteads, dear. I told you, this is the site of the new plant."

"Then it will all be gone in a matter of weeks, won't it?"

"Exactly," said Drew sadly. "And that's the point."

The bile rose in Sam's throat. She couldn't believe what she had just heard. They were going to build a factory here. They were prepared to destroy heaven on earth for money in the bank. She was appalled, disgusted with herself for even considering for a moment that there might be some appeal to a Symington. She hated him at that moment and knew without a doubt that he deserved the woman by his side.

The woman by his side, on the other hand, clearly felt that she deserved better.

"Do you think we've had enough of this nostalgia for nature? It's just not worth ruining my shoes. Can we go now?" Bethany whined.

"Maybe you're right," Drew acquiesced reluctantly.

He turned to follow Bethany, who was already heading back to the car. Forgetting her own state, Sam watched them go with a mixture of relief and regret, anger and anguish.

It was then that Drew turned back for one last look

at the sun hovering over the horizon. Sam froze like a deer caught in the headlights of his bright blue eyes. He gasped. She was lit by the fiery glow of the setting sun, naked and beautiful as Botticelli's Primavera, emerging from a sylvan glen. Her hair was a copper flame that framed strong, perfectly aligned features. Its deep russet tones were reflected in the triangle that joined her long, golden legs. Her body trembled, and for a moment he wondered if she were real or the siren spirit of this wondrous place, come to haunt him for every wrong that had ever been committed against her earth. He stared, and her body stiffened. He looked into her eyes then and saw the defiance as she refused to cower or cover, refused to let herself be embarrassed by this interloper. He knew at that moment that she was human, that without a word she was telling him that she, in all her glorious nakedness, belonged; he did not. He looked back at Bethany, but she was already in the car, rubbing at her shoes, oblivious to the vision before him. Silently he started moving toward Sam, and suddenly her courage failed her. It took all her will not to scream and bolt, but she knew that the minute she left the shelter of the tree, Bethany would spot her. Nothing could be worse than the certainty that the designer-dressed bitch in the car would turn her into a funny story at the dinner table. She braced herself, not knowing what for. To her shock, Drew came closer, smiled, then stooped, picking up something from the ground. For a moment she was confused, wondering if he was playing some kind of game, stalking her, preparing her for some ultimate humiliation. But as he continued toward her she saw a flash of something familiar in his hand. He was carrying her clothing, holding it out to her like an offering to a goddess, his eyes full of prayer. Sam wasn't afraid anymore.

"Drew, darling. What are you doing back there? Will you please hurry up?"

Bethany's voice broke the spell. They had both forgotten she was there. Protective, Drew reached out to Sam, moving her back behind the tree, out of sight. A spark ignited at the place where his hand touched her shoulder. For a moment the fire flared, engulfing them both. Then he dropped the clothes at her feet and turned away, hurrying out from behind the tree just as Bethany was getting out of the car to find him. Sam heard but could not see as Drew hustled Bethany back into the car, muttering apologies. She heard the sound of the engine revving, the grinding of the gravel as the car sped off.

The air became still again, and Sam was more alone than she had ever been. She looked at the clothes at her feet, remembering suddenly that she was naked. She felt like Eve expelled from the Garden of Eden, but without her Adam. In seconds she was dressed again, but the acute sense of vulnerability would not leave her.

Needing some distance, she forced herself to laugh and think about it dispassionately. She had just been found hiding behind a tree in her birthday suit by the richest and best-looking man in the county. The whole encounter had lasted maybe three minutes, and they had never spoken a word. The odds on their ever meeting again were too minute to calculate; and even if they did, the chance that he would recognize her was pretty slim; and even if he did, she'd probably wish he hadn't, because the whole thing was pretty damn embarrassing. Laughing again, she headed toward home, feeling as though she'd been away a long time. But though she wouldn't admit it, even to herself, she couldn't quite shake the feeling of loss.

❧ 3 ❧

"I know, we're late," Drew said, with the smiling tone of a child who knows he will not be punished, as he ushered Bethany into the sitting room.

Drew stooped to give his mother a peck on the cheek, and it was clear that his looks, as well as his wealth, were inherited. Bethany preened a little, knowing that soon this same seed would be planted in her.

"He's been very tedious," Bethany added without rancor, hoping for sympathy from her future mother-in-law. "First we had to sit through those awful races."

"Why, Bethany," Forrest interrupted, fully aware he was goading, "I thought you liked car races. At least, you did before you got engaged."

Bethany gave the old man a veiled look, trying to gauge if he was just teasing or if there was a more pointed quality to his remark. It didn't matter; she could not afford to rise to the bait.

"Of course," she said, smiling brightly. "With the right people, in the right place, any activity can be enjoyable. Today definitely did not qualify on either account."

"Then perhaps we can make it up to you by being *aussi amusants que possible,"* said Jean-Claude, coming forward from the corner where he had stood politely from the moment they entered, waiting for someone to take notice. How typical, he thought, for the rich to ignore anyone outside their known circle. But he was used to that, and just as used to making himself known when necessary.

In Drew's case, Jean-Claude was wrong. Drew had seen him, but his unfailing sense of priorities had led him to greet his mother first, out of respect as well as affection. He was already making his way over to introduce himself to their guest by the time Jean-Claude had made his erroneous assumption. Bethany, on the other hand, fixated as she was on making the proper impression on her soon-to-be in-laws, had been completely unaware of the stranger until he had spoken. Now she scrutinized him under veiled lashes as Mathilde introduced him as a dear cousin. Jean-Claude, certain he was now home free, had no trouble delivering the full force of his most charming smile. His sharp Gallic features were softened by dark hair curling around his face, and Bethany was not entirely immune to the courtly kiss he placed on her outstretched hand.

Unsuspecting, but naturally curious, Drew started to question the family ties, intending nothing more than friendly conversation. Jean-Claude, anticipating difficulties and wanting more than anything to grind his heel into that handsome, arrogant face, inwardly reared, but he forced himself to maintain his perfect composure.

Addressing himself to Bethany, even though it had been Drew who asked the question, Jean-Claude said, "But I think your afternoon has been boring enough without my adding to the tedium." At that, Bethany laughed, feeling an instant kinship with this gallant Frenchman. Recognizing a dull barb aimed in his direction, Drew might have answered, but Mathilde was drawing him toward the door.

"Go change, children, we're all waiting," Mathilde said with her lyrical accent, deflecting the possibility of even disguised conflict.

Relieved, Jean-Claude resumed his seat and promised himself he would be more careful with what he said. The mother was easy with a drink or two in her, which he was certain could always be arranged. The girlfriend was not insurmountable. He smiled to himself, enjoying the pun. But the men were not as easily charmed as the women, and the son, in particular, was clearly nobody's fool. He would have to take care. He'd planned too long and worked too hard to blow it all with a careless word. For now, they must all accept him as cousin Jean-Claude, family friend. Later they would know the truth.

Dinner might just be more interesting than usual, Bethany thought as she hurried off to the guest suite she occupied whenever she came to Belvedere. Even though her family lived only on the other side of Woodland Cliffs, the demands of social life at the Symingtons', as dictated by Mathilde, required several changes of clothes at the ready. When they had first

started going out, a lot of time had been spent going
back and forth between the two estates. It had marked
a turning point in the relationship when Drew had
told her she might just as well pack a bag and stay all
weekend.

Bethany had known that first weekend would mark
the course of her life, and she had planned it with
painstaking care. Her clothes were sexy enough to
attract Drew's attention, but her choice of designers
impeccable enough to appeal to his mother. She had
drunk just enough champagne to put a flush in her
cheeks and make her warm and compliant, without
giving the least hint of being unable to control her
pleasures. She had left her flannel pajamas at home,
choosing instead a nightgown of sheerest blush char-
meuse with lace insets over the bosom, revealing all
while appearing to uncover nothing. And since that
first night, when Drew had knocked discreetly on her
door after the household slept, she had spent most
weekends at Belvedere and not bothered to bring a
nightgown at all.

By the time they had announced their engagement,
everyone on both sides seemed fairly pleased with the
arrangement. It was, unquestionably, a match that
enhanced the social standing of both families.
Bethany knew that didn't matter to Drew, but she also
knew that it was of enormous importance to his
mother. Not that Mathilde could influence her son so
readily. But even though Drew professed to love her in
a kind of abstract, matter-of-fact way, Bethany
sensed, though she hoped that Drew did not, theirs
was a cool love, without the fire or fervor of a deep-felt
passion. That was fine with her; she would rather live

without and live in style. But she wasn't sure how Drew would feel if he ever stopped to think about it.

Fortunately, he didn't. Having inherited his father's love of cars, he was already working his way through the ranks, in the manner of the heir to the throne. In all probability he would always be more enthralled with an afternoon at some crummy race, watching homemade cars raise clouds of dust in suffocating heat, than with anything Bethany could offer him. Given what she was getting in exchange, that was fine with Bethany, and she didn't want anyone raising questions in Drew as long as it was fine with him.

Still, as she changed, she couldn't help thinking of the smoldering look in the Frenchman's eyes when he looked at her.

"Jean-Claude," she breathed to herself, liking the sound. "I wonder what you would do if you could see me now," she added, checking herself in the mirror, her body voluptuous in a strapless lace bra and matching panties.

"More than a kiss on the hand, I think." She laughed as she wriggled into her dress.

"Stop that. Just remember it's Andrew Symington on *Fortune* magazine's list of the wealthiest men in the world, not Jean-Claude the Frenchman," she scolded herself, stifling any hint of hot temptation. There was too much at stake, and her position was just a little too precarious, to take any chances.

Bethany knew Mathilde recognized her value, aware that the Havenhurst line, although not nearly as wealthy as the Symingtons, was well-stocked with distant cousins named Vanderbilt and Rockefeller, strong ties to the real American aristocracy. It was

Forrest she had to be careful of. Bethany might be shallow, but nobody had ever accused her of being stupid.

"Your father doesn't like me," she had said to Drew, shortly after they had become engaged.

"He just thinks you're spoiled. Which you are."

"Me? What about you? Your family is richer than mine. A lot."

"I know. But your father inherited his money. My father had to make his."

"By marrying your mother."

It was common knowledge that Forrest Symington had financed his car company with his wife's fortune and then graciously named it after her family.

Drew, not in the least sensitive, laughed. "Don't think that wasn't work."

He was not far off the mark. Forrest had come north from a dirt-poor town in Georgia at the age of sixteen with not much more than the clothes on his back. He had made his way to Detroit and worked his way up in the ranks of the Chrysler Corporation, learning everything he could about cars, and even more about business. But the most important lesson he had learned was that he could turn his good looks to advantage with the young ladies of Grosse Pointe; and, hiding every bit of the rube he had been under self-taught layers of manners and refinement, he had become a reasonable escort, if not an altogether acceptable suitor, for the daughters of the new American aristocracy.

Forrest had met Mathilde D'Uberville at the coming-out party for one of the Ford girls. She was visiting from France, and he knew immediately, even before he had been told about the family château in the Loire Valley, that hers was an authentic nobility. She was fragile and lovely, genteel in a way that was inborn and could never be learned. Applying himself to the task as he had never done before, Forrest set his sights on wooing and winning Mathilde. Was it love or expedience? He never bothered to ask. But within a year, overcoming the objections of her family and the shock of Grosse Pointe society, they were married.

It was clear that in spite of the bride's credentials, the newlyweds would never completely ascend the Grosse Pointe hierarchy. But that mattered not at all to Forrest. He had greater dreams. Armed with his knowledge and Mathilde's inheritance, he took his new wife to another place and set about creating a dynasty of his own in a kingdom of his own making in Oakdale, Illinois. And it was Mathilde who established a regal society with herself as the queen in nearby Woodland Cliffs, so near and yet so far from the working-class people who were turning her great fortune into an even greater one.

For Jean-Claude, dinner that evening turned out to be a bonanza, a real family affair, with not only Drew and Bethany in attendance, but also Drew's sister, Sarah, and her husband of six years, James Fielding. By the time Drew and Bethany had returned, Mathilde and Jean-Claude were happily chatting in their native French, with Sarah and James able to keep up their part of the conversation. Only Forrest, having never learned more than a term or two of endearment in his wife's tongue, was left out, but it was clearly as much by choice as by circumstance. While the years had been kind to Mathilde's looks, they had done nothing for her mind, and Forrest had long since found her tedious in any language.

Drew was uncomfortably but beautifully ensconced in a dinner jacket, while Bethany wore a short brocade Christian Lacroix pouf that might have looked silly on anyone less perfectly proportioned, but which, on her, enhanced long, shapely legs and an ample bosom. They barely had time to greet the newcomers before Robert announced that dinner was served. The gentlemen offered their elbows to ladies other than their mates, as decreed by custom and Mathilde, and they headed into the formal dining room, where a white linen–clad table, bedecked with enough silver and crystal to stock a bride's registry, shone under a towering chandelier.

With Jean-Claude jumping to escort Mathilde— freeing Forrest to forgo a ritual he disdained and barrel over to his place at the table on his own— James moved to Bethany, and Drew happily put his sister's hand on his arm. The affection between them was obvious, even though those who knew them wondered how they could possibly be from the same family. Two years older than Drew, but without much to occupy herself after finishing school in Switzerland, Sarah had drifted around the Continent, getting involved with a Eurotrash crowd until her father had cut off her bank account to bring her home. She looked nothing like her brother, favoring her father with her blond hair and fair complexion, but she was pretty enough and didn't lack for attention from the eligible young men in her crowd. The surprise of it was that she had actually fallen in love with the "right" sort of man, at least as far as Mathilde was concerned.

Forrest was just as happy to have his daughter married and out of trouble. He rewarded the couple by giving James an advisory post and a seat on the board of directors of DMC, and by building them a new house not too far from Belvedere.

Only Drew had reservations, and it was the one point of contention between siblings who got along remarkably well.

"He's after your money," Drew had said when Sarah had confided that James had asked her to marry him.

"How can you say that? His family is very important," she protested.

"You sound like *maman*. Just because his relatives came over on the *Mayflower* doesn't mean he isn't a gold digger."

"Are you telling me you don't think anyone could love me just for myself?"

"Of course not. I'm not talking about you. I'm talking about James. You're wonderful. He's the one with the problem."

But any reference to his opinion just upset Sarah, and once the two were married, Drew kept his thoughts about his brother-in-law to himself.

James was too smart to get on the wrong side of the heir to the manor, but he knew where he stood. Without making an issue of it, he safeguarded his position by becoming the doting son-in-law, courting Mathilde almost as much as he had her daughter, treating Forrest with just the right combination of affection and deference, and biding his time. He knew if Drew fell out of favor, Sarah would get all, and if that day ever arrived, James stood to gain a lot by being by her side, supporting whatever position her parents took. It would have helped if they had had a child, and they were working on it. But six years of trying had done nothing but take the spontaneity out of their lovemaking, to the point where James did his duty at home, but his pleasure, ever so discreetly, he sought elsewhere.

None of these issues arose at the dinner table, which, by Mathilde's decree, was reserved for witty, noncombative conversation. James made it a point to compliment all the ladies, each of whom was, indeed, exemplary in her own way. It always amazed him to find that centuries of wealth, a fortune in clothes, and a really good hairdresser could compensate for any imperfections. Sometimes he wondered if maybe it was those little flaws that attracted him to the women he paid. But not tonight. Tonight was for being charming and erudite, for playing family politics. With Jean-Claude, recognizing in James a fellow gamesman, and just as intent on striking the perfect note, the women reaped a bonanza of attention that for them made the dinner quite a merry affair.

Unlike James or Jean-Claude, Drew had nothing to prove. Since he was always honest, everyone knew exactly where he stood, like it or not. In his own way he was close to all of them, and that's why all of them could see that tonight he was somewhere far away.

To Mathilde it was just ill manners, and she called him on it. *"Cheri,* come back to us. You seem a million miles from here."

"Not that far." Drew laughed, being completely honest. In fact, he was only about forty miles out of town, on the edge of the sylvan glen where he had seen a wood nymph with flaming hair. He had been trying to figure out if what he had seen was a mirage. Not that he wondered if the woman was real; he knew there had been a wordless encounter with an unclothed person behind a tree. But was it possible that she could be as incredible as he remembered, or was her beauty a figment of his imagination, a fata morgana created by the desert of his soul? He wanted to tell the world that he had had a vision, but at the same time, he knew that to speak of it would be profane.

Trying to save the moment, Bethany ruined his dream.

"We would have been back much earlier, but we stopped by the site of your new plant." She smiled winningly at Forrest. "It's the perfect spot."

Forrest was pleased. Nothing engaged him quite so much as his business, and he found it particularly gratifying that his only son seemed just as interested as he was.

"It is perfect, isn't it?" he exulted. "There's plenty of space, no encroaching civilization to complain about noise or odors, and best of all, that lake is the perfect repository for emissions."

Drew cringed inwardly at his father's euphemism for using the lake as a waste dump. He wondered where the wood nymph would swim when the plant was built.

"It's a good location," he started diplomatically, "but it does kind of seem a shame to ruin its pristine beauty."

"Nothing is as beautiful as the color of money, son," Forrest guffawed, and the others laughed with him. Only Mathilde stiffened a little at the crudeness. James, noticing, tempered his amusement.

"A new plant will certainly give the people of Oakdale something to look forward to. There's a recession going on. They could use the work," James said.

Mathilde nodded approvingly. Helping the people was an acceptable goal; making money in the process was just something you took for granted but didn't speak about. But the conversation was getting too specific, too close to the unpleasant world of business. With consummate skill Mathilde graciously turned it around, delivering an anecdote about someone in their set, amusing but not too catty, just the right tone to take them to dessert.

Usually when Mathilde steered the group away from any topic that might seem remotely relevant, Drew was annoyed. Tonight he was grateful. For him, dinner passed in a haze. He smiled, replied when necessary, but the part of his heart that remembered the woman was locked off, protected by an iron gate of will. After dinner was the difficult part, the time when he was expected to walk his fiancée through the gardens, his arm around her, her head on his shoulder. It was almost a relief when Bethany suggested they retire, even though he knew that the dark of the bedroom would bring other hazards.

As was their habit, he and Bethany said their good-nights to the family and made their way to separate rooms. Usually he gave her a half-hour; then he would quietly slip into the guest suite and join her between the guest sheets. He wondered what she would make of it if he simply failed to show up. He could pretend he had fallen asleep from exhaustion and apologize in the morning. But Bethany wasn't about to let that happen. More aware than Drew realized, she could sense that something had happened, that Drew was distant and withdrawn, though he hid it well. She didn't know why, but she knew enough to nip it in the bud. She stripped off her clothes and looked at herself naked in the mirror. She liked what she saw, but Drew had seen it before. It was a long time since she had bothered with sexy nightwear at Belvedere, but perhaps that was just as well. She'd need a little more ingenuity to attract attention.

She went to the closet and surveyed the clothes that Odile, the maid, had unpacked for her that afternoon while she was out. She was going riding tomorrow while the men went to their tedious offices, and Odile had thoughtfully laid out her riding gear. Bethany smiled. Why wait for tomorrow? She pulled on her leather boots and slipped into her black velvet riding jacket. Taking the crop for effect, she made certain the coast was clear and tiptoed down the hall to Drew's apartment in the west wing.

Drew was half undressed, still pondering what to do, when the door opened. Startled, he looked up, and the effect was all that Bethany could have wished for. She stood in the doorway, backlit by the faint glow of the hall light, blond hair falling over her eyes, the black velvet of her jacket straining against her ivory skin, revealing a deep cleavage and the curve of her breast. From under the jacket her long white legs emerged, losing themselves in knee-high leather boots. When she moved the folds of the jacket opened to reveal a hint of intoxicating secrets between her legs. Tapping the crop on her thigh, she was a vision of black and ivory, hard and soft, light and shadow. Her lips, painted a deep purple-red, slashed the chiaroscuro landscape, and when she planted them on Drew's mouth, grinding her velvet-covered torso into his bare chest, he knew he could not protest. She pushed him back on the bed, and, dropping her jacket and the crop, but leaving her boots in place, she climbed on top of him. Taking his hands, she placed them over her breasts and began pumping slowly. With that, the image of the afternoon's encounter that Drew had been secretly cherishing fled, as if in the face of a sacrilege. When it was over Bethany lay breathing softly in his arms, her costume long since discarded. Drew, spent and satisfied, laughed at himself for ever questioning where his true desire lay. But as he closed his eyes, the last thing he saw before he fell asleep was the face of the enchantress in the woods.

In a guest room down the hall Jean-Claude Renoir couldn't sleep. He should have been pleased; so far his plan had gone even better than he had hoped. But lying in the enemy's lair gave him no comfort. Rising from the rumpled bed, he went to his suitcase and, digging into its deepest compartment, pulled out a worn manila envelope. Emptying the contents on the bed, he leafed through a sheaf of tattered newspaper clippings, yellow with age. He didn't bother to turn on the lamp beside his bed; the light of the moon was enough. He didn't really need to read the words. They were embedded in his memory from countless perusals on countless nights like this. He closed his eyes, and still he could see the headline in *Nice-Matin:*

"Jeune Dame Morte sur la Grande Corniche"; and in *The International Herald Tribune:* "Bride Killed by Hit-and-Run." He rubbed his fists into his eyes; a single tear escaped. Angrily he wiped it away. He'd cried enough. The time for tears had passed. Now was the time for revenge.

4

While the Symingtons enjoyed their elegant repast Sam sat in front of a flickering TV, sound off, hoisting a pair of chopsticks from a cardboard take-out container of Chinese food. Totally indifferent to what she was seeing, with only a passing interest in what she was eating, she finally gave up, zapping the television to blankness and tossing the almost-full portion of sesame chicken into the garbage. She thought about calling Pete, even picked up the phone, as she had already done twice this evening, hoping that a dose of Pete's lusty reality might shake her from the lingering haze of her twilight encounter. But, as she had done twice before, she hung up without dialing, unable to face the inevitable recriminations that would come before they made up, and the macho posturing that would come after.

The doorbell rang, and she went to answer with a mixture of relief and trepidation, assuming Pete had decided to be the first to move this time. When she opened the door and Melinda breezed past her, she grinned and sank onto the sofa beside her sister. She could feel herself relaxing, certain that in a few moments she'd be turning her tale into an amusing anecdote, freeing herself from the mystery of the unspoken moment with a man she'd never meet again.

"I guess it's not too late, or you wouldn't look so happy to see me," said Melinda, sharing the joy the two sisters usually felt on meeting.

"It's never too late for you," answered Sam, meaning it.

"Oh, yeah? What about the time I came over after I broke up with Hank, and then Pete walked out of the bedroom wearing a towel standing at attention, wanting to know what was taking you so long."

"Well, Pete's not here, and he's not coming."

"Oh, I see. Another fight."

"I guess you could say that. We didn't actually fight, because I wasn't actually speaking to him."

"I heard about the race. I'm sorry about the car."

"Me, too. And it was his own damn fault."

"Well, at least Pete's all right. You'd feel a lot worse if something had happened to him."

"I'm not sure about that. Maybe then he'd learn his lesson."

"Oh, come on. You don't mean that. You can't care more about your car than you do about Pete."

Sam thought for a moment, as if, indeed, she were weighing the choices. Melinda looked at her aghast, then gave her a playful punch as she realized she was being teased.

"Sometimes I wonder if you know how lucky you are," she said, eyeing Sam.

"How lucky am I?" Sam played along.

"Well, first of all, you've got a great guy. Pete is gorgeous, and fun, and exciting, and best of all, he's got a steady job—and it's not in a factory."

"Like bartending is better than working on the line?"

"I think it is. At least he's got somewhere to go. Everybody knows Bernie thinks he's great and is going to let him manage the bar when he moves to Florida. Who knows? Pete could even end up with a place of his own. No assembly worker is ever going to get a piece of DMC—unless he can save up enough to buy a used D'Uberville."

"Yeah, I guess you're right."

"Of course I am. Best of all, Pete really loves you. All those bimbettes coming on to him at the track, and he's only got eyes for you. What more could you want?"

"A lot," Sam said softly, as much to herself as to Melinda.

Melinda knew Sam had dreams. From the time Sam had been old enough to tell her little sister stories, she was regaling her with tales of her impending fame and riches. She was going to design a new car and build a huge company from the ground up, just like Forrest Symington, and Henry Ford before him. When she was young Melinda had believed Sam, and they'd made happy plans together about buying fabulous estates right beside each other, traveling to Europe with an entourage of children and nannies, having romances with royalty who somehow never seemed to figure much into the picture with the estates or the children. But they'd both grown up since then. As much as Melinda prayed that all her sister's dreams would come true, she wished Sam would be a little more practical. In spite of Sam's aspirations, her talent, and her will, all of which she had in abundance, it was still highly probable that an apartment of her own was all the estate that Sam was going to get, and Pete was as close to a prince she was likely to meet.

Melinda didn't bother saying any of this to Sam; she'd heard it all before, not just from her sister, but from her mother as well. In fact, in a funny way, Diane Myles blamed herself for Sam's all-consuming ambition. She had met Harvey in high school, and when they graduated there was never any doubt that they'd both work on the line. College wasn't even a consideration, and they knew if they wanted to get married, they'd both have to bring in an income. It was taken for granted in Oakdale that a job on the assembly line at the D'Uberville Motor Company plant could see you through from cradle to grave. You never got rich, but you never starved either, and the company credit union would help you make a down payment on a house and give you a good deal on a car. For kids like Harvey and Diane, early marriage, work on the line, kids, and eventually retirement, all under the watchful eye of a paternalistic company like DMC, seemed about as good as you could expect in life.

But Diane had pushed it. While most of her girlfriends quit when they became pregnant with their first children, Diane wasn't ready to cut the family income in half. There were still things she wanted to have, places she wanted to go, that would quickly recede from her grasp if Harvey was the only breadwinner. She was offered a leave of absence a month before Sam was born, but she insisted she could handle it, and she stayed on the line until, unexpectedly, she'd gone into labor three weeks early. They had made it to the hospital in time, but Diane never forgot that Sam had almost been born in an automobile factory. She had heard that unborn babies could sense things from the outside, that they could hear music and voices, feel anger and anxiety. If that was possible, then that's what had happened to Sam. Somehow, breathing in the metallic air of the plant, Diane had delivered to Sam in utero a case of auto affinity that could never be shaken. For Diane it was confirmation that she had overreached, a sin that was being visited upon her daughter in the form of vaunting ambition that was sure to end in the death of dreams.

It kind of pleased Harvey to see his daughter aim for goals he could never even imagine. But it irritated and even frightened Diane to see Sam "wasting" her time on design engineering classes at Woodland University and spending every extra penny she earned on cars, cars, cars. What good would it do her? She'd end up marrying Pete and working on the line until she had her kids like the rest of them. Better to have no unrealistic aspirations than to watch them wither in the drought of reality and leave nothing but an arid dissatisfaction that lay like a layer of fine dust over your entire life. Diane knew that Pete encouraged Sam to build those racing cars of his, but once they settled down, Diane hoped they'd both realize that this little hobby was too expensive and dangerous for people like them. And even Harvey, who got a great kick out of having a daughter who knew more about cars than any of the guys, figured the best Sam could hope for was saving a lot of money on repair of the family station wagon. Sam knew they all loved her, that they wished her well, but still it disconcerted her to realize that there was no one in the world, not one single person, who shared that faith that she had in herself. And once in a while, on nights like tonight, it made her wonder if maybe they were right and she was wrong.

Seeing Sam looking so miserable, Melinda knew it was time to change the subject.

"Listen, talking about you, you, you all the time is getting pretty boring," she joked. "Could we talk about something really important for a change?"

"Sure. Like what?"

"Me, me, me."

Sam feigned an immense yawn. "Not that old sorry subject again."

Melinda stood up, pretending to be insulted. "Well, if you're not interested in my news"—Sam perked up—"I'll just head out," Melinda went on.

Before she could take two steps, Sam had wrestled her sister back onto the couch.

"Wait a minute. Did you say news? As in something I don't already know?"

Melinda grinned but said nothing.

"Okay, spit it out," demanded Sam. "Don't make me beg."

Melinda preened a little, anticipating her sister's reaction. "I got a job."

"A real one? A good one?" Sam asked, excitement rising in her voice. Sam knew that Melinda had been looking ever since she'd graduated from Miss Driscoll's, and they'd all been praying she'd be able to stay off the line.

Melinda grinned and nodded. Wiggling her manicured nails in her sister's face, she announced, "No dirty hands for Mr. Forrest Symington's personal assistant."

"What? Are you kidding? You're working for the man himself?"

"Well, actually, I think I'm sort of the personal assistant to his personal assistant. But he interviewed me himself."

Sam hugged her sister. "This is great. No, I'm understating the case. It's fantastic, wonderful, stupendous."

Melinda nodded in agreement. "I think so."

"What's he like?"

"Nice, real nice. Handsome. Distinguished. Kind of perfect. Scary."

"Why scary?"

"I could mess up, you know?"

"You won't mess up. He wouldn't have hired you if he didn't think you could do the job."

"The truth is, he wouldn't know. He didn't ask me any questions or anything. He just looked at me, glanced at my résumé, and asked if I could start on Monday. Can you believe it?"

"Sure I can. You have competence, capability, and class written all over you. And you must have wiggled your butt at him."

Melinda laughed. "Give me a break. The guy is twice as old as I am and way out of my league. Besides, he didn't even give me a chance. I was in and out of there in three and a half minutes."

Sam gave her sister another hug. "I'm sure you'll do great. It's wonderful, Melinda. I'm happy for you. I really am. Mom must be overjoyed. Finally one of her girls grows up to be a lady."

Melinda shook her head. "That's what's so strange. Mom didn't want me to take the job."

"Are you kidding?"

"No. She got all upset, said I could do better. I think her exact words were 'It's still cars.'"

Their mother's loathing for DMC was the stuff of family legend, but they'd all assumed it was confined to working on the line. More than once they'd heard how she'd almost given birth to Sam on the factory floor. Recounting the tale elicited amusement from Harvey, but from Diane there was disgust. But there was confusion as well. For Diane had gone back to assembling cars a few months after Sam had been born and had stayed on the line until she became pregnant with Melinda. To hear Harvey tell it, he'd made it clear to his young wife that she wasn't obliged to go back to work, but she couldn't seem to stay away. Knowing full well she was biting the hand that fed them, Diane pooh-poohed the very idea that she would choose to be a factory worker if it hadn't been absolutely necessary to make ends meet. DMC was fine for Harvey, and she couldn't help it if Sam was infected with the auto virus. But she intended to do everything in her power to bleach that blue collar white for Melinda.

Sam shook her head. "Don't worry about Mom," she comforted Melinda. "She's just having a knee-jerk reaction to DMC. There isn't a single graduate of Miss Driscoll's school for wayward white-gloved secretaries who could do better than assistant to Forrest Symington."

"Assistant to his assistant," Melinda corrected.

"That's good, too," said Sam reassuringly. "You're happy, right?"

"I'm happy," affirmed Melinda.

"Then we're all happy. Even Mom."

* * *

Diane Myles was not happy. She knew she'd sounded idiotic when she had told her daughter she should not accept a job that to any other person would have seemed ideal. She felt bad about raining on Melinda's parade and wished she could have just congratulated her and wished her luck and said how proud she was of her. Melinda was the good girl, always cooperating in whatever dream Diane had had for her baby. And logic dictated that working for Forrest Symington, the richest and most powerful man in the county, had to be the fruition of all those dreams. But to Diane it was the culmination of her worst nightmares. And she couldn't even explain why.

After they'd all gone to bed—earlier than usual, to escape the closeness of a room made airless by a mushroom cloud of tension—Diane had lain in bed listening to Harvey's measured snores, trying to quiet the noisy panic in her thoughts that kept sleep at bay. She had heard Melinda emerge from her own room and quietly move around the kitchen, getting a glass of water, opening the refrigerator, closing it again. She knew her daughter well and knew that she herself was the cause of Melinda's restless agitation. She wanted to get up and go to her, apologize, tell her everything would be all right. But she didn't feel that way, and she was afraid that if she confronted Melinda now she would only make things worse. She heard Melinda leave the house and knew that she must be going to see her sister, to get from her the comfort that Diane could not give. In a way, she was grateful that her children had always been close, were always there for each other. But at the same time a jealous suspicion rose inside her, knowing her children would talk about her, and cluck their tongues, and wonder what made Momma so nuts sometimes.

She got out of bed, not even bothering to be quiet, knowing nothing would disturb the dead man's sleep of her exhausted husband. She dressed and took the car keys from the pocket of his pants, left, as always, where he had taken them off, on the floor at the foot of the bed. She told herself she needed air, just a ride along Route 22 with the windows opened, to cool the heat of dismay that was building inside her over-worked imagination. She'd be back, refreshed and ready to repair yesterday's frayed feelings, before Harvey even woke up.

Diane drove along the two-lane blacktop that led away from the tract houses of Oakdale, willing her mind into a blankness to match the moonless night. She approached the turnoff to Woodland Cliffs, fully intending to continue along the highway, bypassing its winding streets dotted with gated estates. But scarcely ten feet past the exit the car swerved into a half-U, straightening on the exit, then slowing onto the flower-planted boulevard that announced entrance into an elegant environment, light years away, though only a few miles distant, from her own shabby community. Diane felt not in control, as though the D'Uberville sedan was negotiating the maze of un-named streets on its own, like a horse returning to its home stable in spite of the admonishing kicks of an unwilling rider. She didn't remember applying the brakes or turning off the lights, but somehow, with-out fixing on an address, she had arrived. No num-bers were needed to specify location here, for the mansions, half hidden by stone walls and towering hedges, announced their identities by names spelled out in wrought iron over forbidding gates. Diane knew where she was, knew that from the moment she had risen from the bed she shared with Harvey this had been her true destination: Belvedere, home of Forrest Symington.

Idling in front of the filigreed gates, Diane could see the stately white-columned home, floodlit against the dark sky, a sumptuous tableau of architectural drama and obvious luxury. A crystal chandelier spilled its warm glow through the arched leaded-glass windows that framed the carved wooden door. Although it was quite a distance from the curb down the cypress-lined drive to the mansion itself, Diane felt certain that she could discern figures in evening dress passing through the foyer from one wing of the house to the other. For a moment rage overcame her, unreasonable and unrelenting. She wanted to ram the gates of the illustrious Forrest Symington and his wife Mathilde D'Uberville, crashing her D'Uberville sedan—still under loan and technically owned by DMC—into the master himself. Instead she leaned against her horn, letting out a lengthy, angry blast that set dogs to barking. Then, as flashlights illuminated the paths of security guards moving in her direction, she pressed her foot to the floor and sped off, horn still blaring her anguish into the night.

〰 5 〰

"Samantha," someone whispered in her ear. No one called her Samantha except her mother. But this was a man's voice. Sam struggled to wake up as he whispered again, "Samantha," half entreaty, half reproach.

She opened her eyes. He was there, standing at the foot of the bed, whispering her name like a litany. He was even more beautiful than she remembered from the mill pond, his dark hair still falling over one eye, lit by the moon shining through the window behind him.

He reached his arms out to her, saying again, "Samantha."

His body glowed, and she saw the ripple of perfectly proportioned muscle over a wide expanse of chest and realized that now he was the one who was naked, and she was fully clothed. She was confused for a moment, unable to remember why she had gone to bed dressed, but thankful that she wasn't in her customary night-time garb of torn T-shirt and sweat socks. But she never questioned why he was there, naked as a god. It seemed only right that it be so.

"How did you find me?" she murmured, her pleasure and gratitude at his accomplishment obvious. "I thought we'd never see each other again."

"You should have known better," he gently admonished. "This was meant to be."

Her heart raced. "Yes, it seemed that way to me, too. But how could you . . . We come from different worlds. . . . You were with another—"

His finger on her lips silenced her. He smiled, a radiant grin that banished all doubt. "Don't ever question destiny." He was right. She knew it. There was nothing more to say.

"I want you," she confessed.

"And I *need* you," he responded.

Magically her clothes disappeared, and she felt his hands moving over her, under her, into her. She wanted to say his name, "Andrew . . . Drew . . ." but his mouth covered hers with kisses, taking her breath away, and she felt herself rising and falling in a fog of excitement and desire. She was drowning in his very presence, and suddenly she felt that she needed to surface or die.

"Aw, Sammy," he said, "I knew you couldn't stay mad at me." Like a stone the haze dropped from her faculties. She was fully conscious now, pushing at him, her languid body now rigid with rejection, forcing him off her.

"Dammit, Pete," she shouted, "what the hell do you think you're doing? Get off me."

Pete rolled away, groaning, "What's the matter now?"

"What do you think? I'm not real crazy about being raped while I'm asleep."

"Raped? What are you talking about? You held out your arms to me. You said you wanted me. You were very, very sexy." He rolled over to her again, trying to snuggle his way back into her good graces. But she sat bolt upright, leaving no soft spots unprotected, clearly having none of it.

"I was sleeping. Anything I said was in a dream."

"Oh, really? What exactly were you dreaming about? Or should I say who? It was pretty clear *what* was going on."

Sam remembered, felt the heat rush through her body, and was grateful that the dark hid her blush. "I don't remember anything except waking up and finding you pawing me," she covered, pulling down the torn T-shirt she was wearing after all to hide anything that might stimulate a comeback from Pete. "How did you get in here anyway?"

"I still had a key from when you asked me to come over last week and change your shower head."

"Okay. You can leave it on the dresser on your way out."

Pete was already pulling on his clothes. He looked angrier than she had ever seen him. She thought he might also be in a little bit of pain by the way he gingerly pulled his zipper over the still tumescent bulge between his legs.

"What is with you, anyway? I'm sorry about the goddam car. I was trying to win a goddam race. That's what I do. Build 'em faster, they won't break."

"I don't have to build them faster, you just have to drive them better."

He turned away, limping toward the door, and she

felt sorry for him for a moment, feeling his agony. She almost called him back, wanting to relieve him. He was, after all, her lover. But something held her back. She couldn't make love to him, not right after being with Drew Syming . . . She stopped herself, forced herself to remember it had been a dream. Pete was reality. But instead of making her feel more sympathetic, it just made her bitter, and she called out, "Don't forget the key," but he had already slammed out the door.

Alone, Sam sat in bed for a moment, rubbing her eyes, trying to knead away the last vestiges of morphean confusion. She looked at the clock and realized she had to get moving. She had promised to pick up her father on the way to the plant, and he would be livid if he had to punch in his time clock even one minute late. She showered quickly, scrubbing her head with soap, pulling on her clothes, not bothering to dry her gleaming curls. She raced out the door but paused for a moment, looking back into the bedroom. She saw him then, as he had been before, naked and beautiful, beckoning her back to the unmade bed. For a moment she had to keep herself from running to him, he seemed so real. She pulled the door shut, locking it with a definitive twist, as if she could lock out the image and forget the dream.

Pancakes were atonement. Melinda looked at the stack her mother had prepared and knew an understanding had been reached. Harvey was already wolfing down his breakfast when Melinda sat down at the table. She'd changed three times, wanting to look perfect for her first day on the job, and finally settled on a simple sleeveless black-and-white-checked dress, buttoned down the front with tiny pearl buttons, cinched to show off her tiny waist with a black patent belt. It was long enough to be demure, but she'd left a button or two open for a slight flash of leg so as not to look dowdy. On her feet she wore black patent ballet flats, and at her open throat a single strand of pearls, unabashedly fake, but highlighting the opalescent quality of her ivory complexion, flushed now with equal parts of excitement, anticipation, and plain old fear.

She wasn't hungry and would have turned away from the plate that Diane placed in front of her. But she knew that food was the peace offering, and to refuse it would be to spurn her mother's gesture. They wouldn't talk about what had happened the night before. They had all learned over the years that Diane had her reasons, which usually remained secret from the rest of them, and it would only re-ruffle smoothed feathers to question the motivation for previous disputes. When Diane cooked the quarrel was over, and to bring it up again would only risk more recriminations, followed by more silence and less food. When the girls were young, and Diane and Harvey argued over some unknowable subject, it wasn't unusual for them to come home from school and find no dinner. Once, after a particularly acrimonious quarrel, they had subsisted on cereal for every meal for a week. Eventually, to protect themselves from their mother's peculiar manifestation of her anger, they'd all learned to cook—even Harvey had his specialties—and Diane was permitted her retreat without undue upheaval of the family schedule. But even knowing that her withholding of services meant little to her grown family, Diane couldn't help herself. When her anger abated her apron went on.

Melinda was spared her mother's scrutiny of the progress on her plate by the arrival of Sam, who burst through the door, dressed in her assembly line uniform of shapeless overalls. The bandanna she used to tie up her hair as a safety measure at work was around her neck, and with copper curls coiling around a face scrubbed clean as if to counteract the permanent stains on her clothes, she still managed to look incredibly beautiful.

"Wow, look at all those pancakes. Must have been a bigger crisis than I thought. But I'm glad to see it's all over."

"Please, Sam, don't start," Melinda pleaded. "I'm nervous enough as it is."

"Okay, okay." Sam grinned as she helped herself to a stack. "Anyway, you've got nothing to be nervous about. You look great."

A pinched look came on Diane's face as she looked at her younger daughter, knowing Sam was right. Melinda did look great. Too great. She always did.

"Don't you think your plaid dress might have been more appropriate?"

Melinda turned to Sam with the eyes of a supplicant begging for reprieve. Sam looked at Diane, saw what was coming, and hugged her plate, protecting her pancakes, three deep and drowning in syrup, from the long arm of their disgruntled mother.

"Leave her alone, Mom," said Sam between forkfuls. "It is not considered appropriate to wear a frumpy housedress that was handed down from your

Great-aunt Tess on your first day as the boss's personal assistant."

"Just his assistant's personal assistant," corrected Melinda, hoping to placate her mother and not to start her career at work with a scene at home.

"Let's go, girls," said Harvey as Diane snatched away his plate in an unguarded moment. He looked longingly at his plate for a moment as Diane mercilessly plopped it into the garbage; then he raised his eyes to his wife. But she wouldn't meet his gaze, and knowing it would only do harm to pursue it, he moved to protect his daughters. "Come on, Melinda, we'll drop you off."

"Just one more bi—" started Sam, until she felt her sister's elbow dig into her ribs. "Good idea," she amended, reluctantly laying down her fork beside the half-eaten pancakes as she got to her feet.

Diane watched as the three of them headed out the door. She had an urge to call out to her baby, to bring her back, but she knew it would only convince them that she was even crazier than they thought. Suddenly the door opened, and Melinda came running back in. Relief flooded over Diane as she threw her arms around her daughter.

"You don't have to go, Melinda. I'll call for you if you want, say you're sick—"

"Mom, I just forgot something." Melinda extricated herself from her mother's arms and went into her bedroom. A moment later she came out, kissed Diane on the cheek with an airy "Don't worry, Mom, it's a great job, I'll be fine," and raced out.

The scent of lilacs lingered in her wake, and Diane realized Melinda had returned to put on perfume.

With no one to see her and no need to explain, she sat down at the kitchen table and began to cry.

"Dear God," she prayed. "Please, please, don't let anything happen to her."

There were pancakes on the breakfast buffet at Belvedere—and sausage, bacon, muffins, and waffles, as well as a chef at the ready to make omelets of choice. Jean-Claude gazed at the display with faint revulsion, wondering how Americans could stuff themselves at this hour, longing for a simple baguette and a grand crème, the half-steamed-milk, half-dark-espresso coffee that the French favored for breakfast. The Symington men were already leaving the table, heading off to work, as Jean-Claude had hoped. The women, of course, were not yet awake, as Jean-Claude had expected. He needed time to sort his thoughts, work out his plans, the fruition of which would require the cooperation of the women and the benign neglect of the men.

He wasn't concerned. Although the mood had been congenial at dinner, and everyone had appeared cordial, he had already sensed a certain indifference when Mathilde had addressed her husband. While carefully complimenting all the women, James had displayed no real interest in any of them, including his wife, and Jean-Claude recognized in him the restlessness of a sexual wanderer. Drew was different, Jean-Claude knew: an aficionado of women, but definitely not a playboy; a magnet for female attention, but confident enough of his manhood to require no external reinforcement; striving for nothing, he seemed to achieve everything. But Jean-Claude sensed that he had been absent, somehow, from the evening. He had paid every required courtesy to his fiancée, and then some. Taking a nocturnal snoop through the halls, Jean-Claude had heard the unmistakable sounds of a woman reaching climax through Drew's closed door, and he was certain that the tender good-night scene Bethany had performed at the end of the evening as she scurried to the opposite wing was just for show. Still, Jean-Claude's Gallic sixth sense told him that if Drew was a man in love, it wasn't with his fiancée. All the better for Jean-Claude. Bethany Havenhurst figured prominently in his strategy, and after hearing her loud and insistent moaning the night before, and seeing Drew entirely unaffected the morning after, Jean-Claude knew how he was going to reach her.

❧ 6 ❧

When Melinda arrived at the executive offices of the D'Uberville Motor Company Forrest Symington was already locked in the conference room in a meeting. Melinda was introduced to his assistant, Catherine Morton, by one of the other girls. Wanting to start off on the right foot, Melinda had put on her warmest smile, stretched out her hand to shake, and said, "I'm Melinda. What do they call you? Cathy? Kate?"

"Catherine," had come the curt reply, and her hand had been ignored as Catherine launched into a litany of Melinda's duties, foremost among which seemed to be that she must never, ever, address Forrest Symington directly. If she had a question or a problem, Melinda was to come to Catherine, and it would be dealt with. Forrest hated to be disturbed by the girls who worked in the office, and it was Catherine's job to see that he wasn't. Melinda would have differed with her, having seen the twinkle in Forrest's eyes when he interviewed her. But she knew if she wanted the job, it was Catherine she had to please and no one else. Melinda had no doubt that Forrest had assigned Catherine the task of managing the office and protecting him from the minutiae of the clerical operations. But Melinda would lay odds that it was Catherine herself who had decided to guard her boss with an impenetrable fortress, when a simple shield would have done as well. It was hard for Melinda to believe that the man who had looked at her with such warmth would never, ever want to speak to her again.

But it didn't take long for Melinda to begin to wonder if perhaps Catherine had been right. There were days when she hardly saw the big boss. When she came in he would be in a meeting; when he went to lunch she would be in the Xerox room; by the time she left for the day he would frequently be gone already. On the rare occasions that they bumped into each other, his smile was as warm as it had been, and he always asked how the job was going. Melinda always smiled just as warmly and said how much she was enjoying the work, but it never went beyond that. It was Catherine who sat in the meetings and took notes, which Melinda later had to transcribe, staying late alone, after the others had gone.

Forrest's closest confidant seemed to be his son. Having returned from several years abroad, where he had gone to learn the foreign car market, Drew had as keen an interest in the business as his father. DMC was not only a cash cow inheritance for Drew, it was a psychic legacy as well. The American passion for cars that he got from his father and the European appreciation of grace inherited from his mother combined in

Drew to make DMC as essential an element of his life as breathing. From her vantage point, Melinda thought that the only person she knew who loved cars that much was her sister Sam. But the distance between Sam's expression of her ardor for cars and that of the Symingtons was—well, the distance between Oakdale and Woodland Cliffs, or Melinda's cubicle in the secretarial pool and Forrest Symington's executive suite.

"What do you do there?" Diane asked her one night when she returned home late as usual.

"Work," Melinda answered shortly. She'd fought so hard to take the job, she didn't want her mother to know how disappointing it had turned out to be.

"What kind of work? I mean, do you spend all your time with Mr. Symington?" She tried not to sound more than casually interested.

"Actually, I hardly ever see him," Melinda admitted. "He's got this personal assistant named Catherine Morton, and she makes sure that nobody ever gets to work with the boss but her."

"Well, if she's his assistant, I guess that makes sense." Diane tried to keep the relief out of her voice.

"I guess. I'd probably do the same thing if it were me. But still, after I met Symington I kind of thought the job was going to be really fun. With Catherine around, it's anything but."

"You know, honey," said Diane, trying to sound deeply sympathetic, "your helping with the rent is great, but we don't need the money that bad. If you want to quit and look for something else, it would be okay."

"Thanks, Mom. But I don't think I'm ready for that. It would be such a waste."

"No, it wouldn't. You'd have it on your résumé, so you could probably get another job in no time."

"I'll think about it," Melinda said, sensing it was important to her mother and not wanting to risk more silences and meals withheld.

Melinda excused herself and went to her room, exhausted from a day full of simple but hateful tasks. She remembered someone once telling her that if you don't know what to do, don't do anything. Things happen, the situation changes, nothing is the same, and before you know it, the decision has been made for you. Disgruntled, Melinda forced herself to do nothing, waiting restlessly for things to happen.

Things happen, Melinda thought as she held a wastepaper basket and turned her head away while Catherine Morton heaved her breakfast into it.

"I've got to lie down," Catherine gasped as she stretched out on the floor of the ladies room.

"You should go home," said Melinda. "You're really sick. Is there someone I can call to pick you up or something?"

"No, I'm fine," declared Catherine vehemently from her prone position at Melinda's feet. "I'll be all right in a minute." She dragged herself up, hanging onto the edge of the sink and Melinda's outstretched arm, stood for a second, then slumped over the basket, retching again.

"God, what am I going to do? Mr. Symington has an important engagement at the plant. I've got to be there."

"Well," said Melinda philosophically, "you can go and take the chance that you'll spill your cookies into his lap. That might be acceptable in some circles.

After all, former President Bush did it to the prime minister of Japan. Or you can go home and let someone else cover it for you."

Catherine tried to get up again. This time Melinda didn't offer to help, not out of meanness, just to convince Catherine she wasn't going to make it on her own. Catherine sank back down to the floor and looked at her, helpless. Things happen, thought Melinda, and the situation changes.

"Okay, Katy," Melinda said, knowing her superior was in no condition to challenge her, "this is what we're going to do. I'm getting you a cab, I'm giving the driver your address and an extra ten bucks to make sure you get in all right. Then I'm coming back in and telling Mr. Symington he's just going to have to make do with me taking his notes until you get well. How does that sound?"

Catherine nodded, as close to grateful as she could ever be, as Melinda reached out her hand and helped her off the cold floor. As a singular act of kindness to the woman who had shown her nothing but hostility at worst, indifference at best, she stopped Catherine before she stepped out into the harsh light of public scrutiny and wiped some vomit-tinged spittle from her chin with a damp paper towel. The situation changes, and nothing is the same, thought Melinda as Catherine smiled at her apologetically.

"There's a flu going around," said Melinda, actually feeling for Catherine in her weakened state. "You'll get over it and be back in no time. I'll hold the fort, don't worry." Nothing is the same, she thought, and before you know it, your decision has been made for you.

Forrest Symington was surprised, but definitely not displeased, when Melinda tapped lightly on his door and entered at his command. The smile with which he rewarded her faded somewhat when she informed him that she'd just sent Catherine home sick. For a moment he looked at her as though she'd lost her mind. *She'd* sent? On whose authority?

Melinda anticipated the unspoken challenge. "It was send her home or risk your shoes."

"I'm sorry?"

"She has the flu or food poisoning or something. It could have gotten pretty ugly."

"I see. Well, you probably did the right thing."

"I think so."

"I've got to meet with some of the executives and then make a statement to the workers at the plant in Oakdale this morning. She was supposed to take notes. You'll have to come in her place." Forrest frowned, not at all pleased by this change in routine, however necessary.

"I know," Melinda said as sweetly as a child. "I've already called for your driver. He'll be picking us up in five minutes."

He smiled again, that dazzling smile, and Melinda felt rewarded, as he meant her to.

"Can you take shorthand?" he asked as an afterthought. "I talk pretty fast, and I need you to write down anything anybody else says as well. Whether they're formally recognized or not."

Looking into Forrest Symington's eyes, Melinda felt suddenly brave, brazen even.

"You hired me. Didn't you read my résumé?" She could feel her eyelids batting, as if with a will of their own. She knew she was being outrageously coquettish. It was absurd and inappropriate, but she also knew, somehow, that he wouldn't mind.

Forrest burst out laughing. "Touché. As I recall, I did hire you after a very perfunctory meeting. And I must admit it was based more on a feeling than on a careful study of your secretarial skills. You looked like you could handle the job."

Melinda looked at him from under her lowered lashes, a small grin playing at the corners of her mouth.

"Okay, okay," Forrest chuckled, delighting in being discovered, like a small boy playing hide-and-seek. "I hired you because I liked the way you looked, and it had nothing to do with your clerical ability at all. Does that make me a sexist pig?"

"It makes you either a man with great instincts or one incredibly lucky son of a gun, because it so happens I have absolutely super skills."

The intercom buzzed. Without hesitation and with just a little daring Melinda perched on Forrest's desk, crossed her shapely legs, and picked up the telephone.

"Mr. Symington's office," she said, her voice clear, professional, with none of the playful bantering tone she had displayed to him. He looked at her appreciatively, liking what he heard as much as what he saw.

"Thank you. We'll be right down." She got up from the desk, all business now as she turned to him. "The car is here. Do you have your notes? Is there anything you want me to take for you?"

"I'm all set. Just get what you need, and let's go. And tell the rest of the staff you won't be back until after lunch."

She headed out, hiding her excitement, trying to look cool, as though this were the sort of thing she did every day. She couldn't wait to see the reactions of Harvey and Sam when they saw her on the dais with Mr. Symington. At least this would be affirmation to her father that the money he had grudgingly paid to Miss Driscoll was well spent. She hesitated at the door for a moment, wondering if she should mention that her family worked in the plant, but when she turned back his attention was already elsewhere as he gathered his papers together. She tried to formulate an opening gambit, but he wasn't even looking at her, and she knew whatever she said would be awkward and irrelevant. Almost everyone within a twenty-mile radius worked for Forrest Symington. In a sea of faces her father and sister would just be two more employees. She'd taken a chance today, being more informal than was proper so she could make an impression. He'd responded graciously, as she'd hoped—known —he would. But that didn't mean he was suddenly going to develop any personal interest whatsoever in her or her family.

He looked up at her, clearly distracted, already thinking about the remarks he was going to make to the workers, anticipating reactions, both negative and positive.

"Well?" he asked expectantly.

Melinda knew she had already said enough. "I'm ready." She smiled and held the door as he walked through, not looking back, knowing without telling her that she would secure his office and follow where he led, which she did.

By the time they descended from Forrest's twentieth-floor executive office suite to the street Drew was already waiting in the car. Although father and son worked closely together and were in constant contact throughout the day, they had decided, when Drew returned from Europe, that he would set up his headquarters on a lower floor. Understanding the subliminal significance of being at the top, both figuratively and physically, Drew had chosen to place himself squarely in the middle. There was no point in pretending he had to start on the bottom; everyone was aware that DMC was his to inherit and that he had every intention of presiding as its CEO when his turn came. But at the same time he wanted to be a part of the actual process, and to avoid, as long as possible, that rarefied atmosphere of privilege that would remove him forever from the day-to-day reality of what it takes to make a car. Somehow, from his vantage point on the eleventh floor, he seemed more accessible than his father at the summit. Employees on all levels approached him with their problems and felt unintimidated, offering opinions and criticism to which Drew listened with an open mind, dismissing some as interesting but inapplicable, accepting others as progressive and important, but treating both the imprudent and the wise with the respect and dignity he felt every human being deserved. The only thing Drew had not done since returning to his home turf was mingle with the auto workers at the various DMC plants. The visit to Oakdale today was to be his introduction to the men and women who worked on the line and actually built the cars that were planned in the executive boardrooms a few miles and a lavish life-style away.

Sitting in the front seat beside the driver, Melinda turned and glanced at the two men in back. It was clear that Drew was not entirely in favor of the announcement that his father was going to make to the gathered workers, but it was just as clear that the elder Symington was unprepared to listen to his son's objections. While not dismissing his offspring's exhortations out of hand, he insisted that Drew would have plenty of time to exercise his judgment when he acceded to the throne. But as long as Forrest reigned he would call the shots as he saw them. And if things didn't work out, as in any sovereignty, the son would be left to contend with the father's sins. Respect for his father, and the knowledge that he still had much to learn about the industry he would one day inherit, kept Drew from pressing his point. They lapsed into an uneasy, though not unfriendly, silence while Drew gazed out the window and Forrest, to Melinda's unrevealed discomfort, gazed at her.

The advance team had done its work. By the time the Symington entourage reached the floor of the plant, after a short briefing of the officials in charge, a small dais had been built near the entrance and several folding chairs had been placed in a row behind a sound-equipped podium. Melinda felt a thrill of importance as a small buzz grew around them the moment they came into the room. Several of the foremen came up to shake their boss's hand. He knew them all by name, asked after their wives, and introduced them to his son. Melinda scanned the room and caught sight of Harvey, who had already spotted her and was excitedly making his way to Sam, brimming with pride, pointing out his younger daughter, cool and pristine alongside the bigwigs, to anyone in his path.

"Hey, that's my Melinda with the boss there. Doesn't she look great?"

"She looks clean," said Sam cheerily, coming up to meet him, both of them laughing in recognition of Diane's major criterion for a good job. "Mom would be happy."

"You'd think so, wouldn't you?" echoed Harvey, a little unsure these days about how his wife felt about anything. "Come on, let's go over. She'll introduce us."

He took his firstborn's hand and pushed ahead. Suddenly he was brought up short as Sam jerked her hand back, refusing to move, still as a stubborn mule stopped dead in its tracks.

"Come on." He pulled, annoyed.

Sam stood her ground. "We can't go over there."

"Why not?" He looked at her, frustrated, uncomprehending, aching to be presented to the thing that passed for royalty in Oakdale.

Sam's heart fluttered, and her mind raced. What could she tell her father? That she had just noticed that Drew Symington was standing beside the old man. That she couldn't be introduced to him, because they'd already met. That even though he didn't know her name, they knew each other more intimately than anyone else in the world, and if he learned who she was, they'd lose all the precious knowledge that had been bestowed on them in a magic instant. She looked down at her grease-stained overalls, angrily pushing back a curl that had escaped the bandanna tied low over her forehead. In her mind she saw the moment of their encounter in that paradise lost: her, naked and majestic; him, enthralled and guileless. In the space of seconds they had unequivocally shared something, touched a chord, one in the other, that transcended every earthbound convention they might otherwise embrace. If she met him now, it would all be lost. Once he realized she was nothing more than an assembly-line worker in his father's factory, he'd regard her, at best, with disdain, at worst, with amusement. Identified, she'd become a funny, slightly ribald story. Anonymous, she would remain forever a precious dream. None of this could she say to her father.

"We'd just embarrass Melinda," she said instead. "She's doing her job. Let's just leave her alone."

"Melinda's not like that. She's not ashamed of us. We're her *family,* for Pete's sake."

"And Symington's her boss. Just like he's ours and everybody else's. Believe me, he couldn't care less about who she's related to."

"What's with you, missy? You got a pickle up your ass about something?"

"Nice talk, Dad. And you want to know why I think we might embarrass Melinda?"

Sam knew she was being unfair. Harvey would never be less than unfailingly polite to anyone he perceived as being above him in stature. He was a simple man, crude even, but he wasn't stupid. And for her to suggest that he would jeopardize his daughter's job by being boorish was not only unreasonable, it was cruel. Sam knew he was hurt, and she felt guilty. But there was no way she could ever let Drew Symington see her again, let alone be introduced to him. She wanted to apologize to her father, but she knew it would just encourage him to start on her again. She was saved by the keening of feedback as the microphone protested a close encounter with a too-loud voice. The foreman introduced the man who needed no introduction: their employer, their mentor, their king, Forrest Symington. Sam heard none of it. She was drowning in the eyes of the heir apparent, who looked in her direction but could not distinguish her from the formless mass of the body of workers who made him rich and ever unreachable.

The applause brought her back to the surface. People weren't just clapping, they were cheering.

"What did he say?" Sam turned to Harvey.

"Where've you been?"

"I missed it. Just tell me what he said."

"We're getting a new plant, girl. Oakdale's going to be booming again."

"Did he say where it's going to be?"

"I just told you. Here, around Oakdale."

"I mean where exactly."

"No. It ain't built yet. It's a little early for a map."

"We have to find out."

"What difference does it make? Anybody who needs a job isn't going to have any trouble getting there, believe me."

"That's not the point."

"What *is* the point?" Harvey wondered, completely baffled by the one daughter he thought he always understood.

Sam didn't answer him. She climbed on top of a chair and started to shout to everyone to quiet down. When that didn't work she climbed on the assembly table. Harvey looked at her in shock, convinced, for the moment, that she had gone completely crazy. One minute she refused to walk calmly over to her sister and meet the boss. The next minute she was standing on a table demanding attention. One minute she was afraid they'd embarrass Melinda with a polite introduction; the next minute she was embarrassing the whole damn place by screaming at everyone to shut up. He tried to talk her down, but she was shouting too loud herself to hear his quiet entreaties. He tried to pull her down, but she angrily shrugged him off, stomping out of reach and continuing her insistent call for order until at last the place was quiet, and all eyes were upon her.

For a moment she almost lost her nerve as she unintentionally caught Melinda's eye and could not escape the horror in her sister's face. She looked back at Harvey, mortified, pleading silently for her to stop making a spectacle of herself. Then she looked at Drew, and his eyes showed no acknowledgment, and she knew at that moment that not only did he not recognize her, but even if he did, it wouldn't matter. When it came to the profitable bottom line of the D'Uberville Motor Company, none of them mattered.

"Excuse me, Mr. Symington," she began, faltering a little but forcing herself to go on. "Where exactly are you going to build this plant?"

Forrest was taken aback. They had agreed not to disclose the location, aware that it might be somewhat controversial. He hadn't anticipated anyone putting the question to him directly. Recovering his composure without ever revealing he had lost it, he pasted on a smile designed to dazzle.

"We haven't come to a final decision on that yet. But rest assured it will be in the environs of Oakdale. The purpose of this new factory is to reinforce our commitment to the company and you, our DMC community."

More applause, louder cheers. Relieved disaster had been avoided, Harvey reached out a hand to help down his distraught daughter. Sam ignored it.

"Isn't it true that you have already contracted to build this facility at the mill pond?"

Forrest was still smiling, but the steel in his voice was unmistakable. "Several sites are being considered."

Sam turned to her colleagues. "He's lying. They're putting up the plant at the mill pond, and they're using the reservoir, which happens to be Oakdale's main fresh water supply, to dump their toxic waste."

There was a buzz on the floor. Forrest's eyes were shooting daggers at Sam; he had to regain control. He turned to Melinda, who had buried her head in her legal pad, furiously taking notes, praying he wouldn't notice the fire in her cheeks and hoping that if she didn't look up, it would all disappear. "Find out who that wise-ass is," he whispered hoarsely, his anger evident. Melinda prayed for the floor to open up and swallow her whole. Or better yet, swallow her sister. "Now!" Forrest underscored. Melinda gave a weak nod and pretended to move toward the foreman, as Forrest struggled to gain a post of calm in the eye of the gathering storm.

He was thrown, no doubt about it. He had no idea how this rabble-rouser got her information. Aware of the possibility of controversy, the site had been a closely guarded secret—especially from anyone having a connection to or interest in the Oakdale residents. He had discussed it with only a few top board members and a few family members, none of whom would have reason or desire even to speak to this loud and dirty laborer, let alone reveal corporate confidences. He would have to deal with her later. Right now he needed to regain the advantage and keep the crowd from turning hostile to a plan which he regarded as crucial to the profit margin for the next decade. He began to talk, slowly, quietly. Imperceptibly he dropped some of the upper-class cadences painstakingly acquired during his transition from the rank and file to the ranking lord. The more he talked, the more he sounded like the man he was, son of immigrants, plainly raised and plain-spoken. He reminded his workers, calling them his colleagues and friends, about the days before the D'Uberville Motor Company had come to Oakdale, when Woodland Cliffs was swampland and unemployment was twice the national average; when Oakdale children were underfed and poorly educated. Things were bad then. They were good now. They could be better.

While his father spoke, Drew watched the woman who had started it all. She was still standing on the table, and her face registered some of the dismay he himself felt at Forrest's words. She had spoken the truth, and those who were informed knew it. Although Drew was not so naïve that he didn't recognize the necessity of the net of confusion Forrest was throwing over the issue to avoid dealing with it, it made him extremely uncomfortable to have to acknowledge that this was the way business was conducted. Forrest was waxing eloquent, taking off his jacket and handing it to the foreman, rolling up his sleeves, molting out of the patrician patina that years of privilege had grafted to his person. In contrast, the woman, cocooned in her sack of dirty coveralls and colorless head scarf, seemed to acquire added gentility with Forrest's every lie. There was an elegance to her defiance that impressed Drew, in spite of the fact that she was clearly intent on causing DMC, to which he owed his past life and his future fortune, a lot of trouble.

Forrest was winding up his remarks, having painted a glowing picture of prosperity for generations of Oakdale residents, improbably but effectively including himself in the canvas.

"There's a recession on now, folks. We all know what that's about. We know what's happening to our brothers in Detroit who are getting laid off right and left. Let's not let it happen here. Let's keep building. Let's keep growing. *Let's keep working!*"

A cheer went up from the ranks. Trying to look as though she was following instructions, Melinda had been making her way over to Stan Harkin, the foreman. Now she stopped, relieved. Forrest had control of the situation. Sam would step down now, Forrest would be congratulated; maybe he'd forget about the disruption altogether. Melinda was wrong on all counts.

Sam was already forcing herself to be heard. "Wait a minute. Sure, we all want to keep working. But what good is it going to do us to have jobs if our children are being poisoned and our environment polluted? We have to live in Oakdale. The Symingtons don't. The management here is trying to sell us a bill of goods.

We might profit in the beginning, but no paycheck, no matter how big or how steady, is going to buy us what we need when we start losing our health and our children."

"What the hell's your sister think she's doing?" Stan asked Melinda as she shuffled up beside him, upset at the ever-worsening turn of events.

"Beats me," said Melinda. "But I wished she'd stop before she gets us both fired."

Stan had known them both since they were babies, when both their parents had worked on the line. He'd been the one responsible for getting Sam a spot working on the power train, a position usually reserved for the more experienced men. Sam had always been a hellion, telling the older guys what to do, but she'd gotten away with it because she'd always been right. Up until now.

"From the sound of it, she's aiming to put us all out of work," muttered Stan.

Apparently Stan wasn't the only one of that opinion. The catcalls were coming from all over the room.

"Sit down and shut up."

"Get that asshole out of here."

"Don't listen to her. She's full of it."

A chant was starting up, "Build the plant! Build the plant! Build the plant!"

The mood was starting to get ugly. Melinda looked at Stan, momentarily forgetting her own awkward position, afraid that someone might actually jump up and tackle her sister.

"Don't let her get hurt."

But Forrest had accomplished what he wanted. He wasn't about to lose his advantage by allowing a threatening mob to create a situation, even on his behalf. He was talking again, calming them down, belittling Sam's analysis, chuckling conspiratorially at how emotional girls could get; and knowing they wanted—needed—to believe him, he was assuring them he was on their side.

Forgetting that his daughter was a grown woman, Harvey was furiously demanding that Sam get off the table in the same tone of voice that he used to order her to go to her room. But though she tried not to antagonize her parents too much with her independent opinions, it had been a long time since she'd let anyone tell her what to do. On the other hand, she was always open to reason.

"You're right, of course, but you're not going to get anywhere like this."

Sam looked at the young man who had addressed her. He was on the table, not exactly standing beside her, but crouching within earshot so she was the only one who could hear him. She didn't know much about him except that his name was Jack Bader. He'd moved to Oakdale a couple of months ago and gotten a job on the line because he was related somehow to someone with seniority.

"They wouldn't listen to you anymore if you could prove you were the mother of God, or God herself, for that matter."

Sam liked this guy. Whoever he was, he had a good attitude. And she knew beyond doubt that he was right. Without another word he jumped to the floor and reached out a hand to help her down. There was a smattering of applause as she disappeared from her outpost, but the attention was now on Forrest Symington and the platitudes he was pronouncing for the benefit of the believers.

"If you want to fight it, I'll help you," Jack went on when they were eye to eye, "but you're going to have to do it from down here, not up there. And it sure ain't going to happen today. If I were you, I'd take the opportunity to get out of here."

"There's nothing I'd like better. All this groveling at the feet of our feudal lord is making me sick."

Jack laughed. "Don't sugarcoat it, honey. Tell me how you really feel."

Sam looked at Forrest exhorting the workers to rely on him as they'd always done. They were *family*. Her eyes moved to his real family, to Drew, who looked away from his father but not into the crowd, his face impassive. Suddenly she felt violated by their meeting and stupid for fantasizing that it had been anything more than a humiliating encounter.

"Symington is offering them a plan that's going to make him and his little brat rich, and us and our kids sick, and they're lapping it up. It's disgusting."

"I know it. And you know it. You're just going to have to convince them of it. But not here. And not now."

"You're right. I'm going. But let's talk later."

Jack nodded and gave her a little shove toward the door, just to get her moving.

Elbowing her way to the back, Sam attracted some hostile mutterings, but the heckling was kept at an undercurrent to keep from disturbing the smooth oratory from the podium. Once she'd reached the door she turned around again and saw that her co-workers were intent on digesting the pap that was being fed to them by their self-appointed paterfamilias. They were ignoring her now, pretending she'd never been there or raised a question.

Only Drew Symington was watching her, his eyes unreadable, unreachable. She was ashamed to feel an unexpected rush of tears stinging her eyes. She knew it was ridiculous to feel betrayed. Her own people were against her; why would this stranger, born to be her oppressor, feel anything but disdain for her position? If she was betrayed at all, it was by her own heart, her own mind, which had fabricated an illusion of sympathy from an accidental meeting with the enemy on the site of the unannounced battlefield. Mortified by her own weakness, both then and now, she swallowed hard, steeling herself, turning the dewy tears to an angry wet glare as she pushed out the door.

Forrest was finished. Although he'd made no acknowledgment, he had seen her go. The people were on his side, and there was no one to steer them in a different direction. Hands reached out to pump his, and he took them all, turning them over to his son one by one to reiterate his stand. Not yet ready to condemn the only truth-sayer in the group, Drew remained noncommittal, substituting his opinion with his customary charm, telling anyone who asked how good it was to be home and how much he was looking forward to getting involved.

Although Forrest, perfectly relaxed, seemed to be moving in a random direction, letting the proffered hands point out a haphazard path, he knew exactly where he was going. So did Melinda, and she cowered by Stan, fully aware of what was coming. In minutes Forrest was standing in front of the foreman, ignoring the secretary he had sent on his errand of discovery, and demanding the knowledge for himself.

"Who was she?"

Feeling Melinda shake beside him, Stan took pity on her and the family he'd known all his life. "Who?"

Forrest's anger was all the more frightening for its icy control. He didn't even acknowledge Stan's feeble attempt at feigned ignorance. *"Who . . . was . . . she?"*

Stan sneaked a look at Melinda. She gave an imperceptible shrug, half permission, half forgiveness. They both knew he would have to answer. Hoping to temper Forrest's response, he figured he'd begin with credentials before he got to the name. "Well, now"— Stan purposely put the bumpkin in his voice—"she's normally a good worker, real good. Been with us a long time. Don't know what got into her today. Maybe time of month, that sort of thing. But—"

Forrest cut him off. "It doesn't matter. I don't care who she is. Fire her. We don't need employees who are going to bite the hand that feeds them. Get rid of her. No notice, no severance. Out!"

Stan nodded. At least he'd managed to keep Harvey and Melinda out of it. Considering the circumstances, it would be best just to do what he was told and let it go at that. But Melinda couldn't let it go. She couldn't stand by and watch her sister lose her lifelong job because she had momentarily lost her head. She was afraid, but it didn't matter. They'd called it the Myles Militia when they were kids. You attacked one of them, you attacked them all. From somewhere inside her she mustered courage she didn't know she had and moved to close the ranks.

"You can't do that, sir."

Forrest looked at her, uncomprehending. Her eyes were defiant, but her chin was quivering, and in that moment he was reminded again how much she looked like her mother. It was enough to soften his bark to a growl.

"I'll chalk that remark up to the fact that you haven't had time to get used to the way we do things here. Generally, since it's my company, I'm the one who decides what can or cannot be done."

Melinda blushed, chastened. She hadn't meant to sound so pushy, but she was desperate.

"I . . . I'm sorry, I didn't mean that the way it sounded. Of course, you can do anything you decide. It just doesn't seem like such a good idea to me. Maybe I shouldn't have said anything."

Forrest's interest grew. She was definitely as spunky as her mother. "I suppose now you're going to tell me why."

"If you'll let me."

She said it in such a way that he got the feeling he wouldn't have been able to stop her if he wanted to. Somehow she would have found a way to tell him what was on her mind. He could see that for some reason this was important to her. He was surprised to find himself both curious and interested in what she had to say. Hiding a smile, he gave a perfunctory nod.

Melinda knew she was risking her own job for her sister's, but it seemed only right. The Myles Militia— victory for all or trouble together. It had always been that way, except now, if she failed, instead of ending up grounded for the weekend, they'd both end up dead broke with nowhere to go.

She took a deep breath. "Well, to begin with, if you fire her, you're going to have the union to contend with. Even Stan here says she's always been a good worker, so the only cause for dismissing her would be that she spoke her mind, and there are a couple of hundred witnesses to that. Now, even if the union let you get away with it, because of who you are and everything, the Constitution wouldn't. The first amendment guarantees the right of free speech, and I wouldn't put it past that woman to charge you with violating her civil rights. If you fire her. Which I don't think you should. It wouldn't be worth the trouble. And it would just get her more attention. And she'd get to make her accusations against you over and over again, even if they're not fair. Because I'm sure the media would pick it up, and she'd go on all the talk shows, and . . ."

She knew she'd already made her point and wasn't enhancing it by babbling on, but she couldn't stop herself. For a minute she was afraid she'd blown it, but then Forrest started to smile—not the stiff, polite grin he used to hide his anger, but the dazzler that charmed everyone in sight and made Melinda melt on the spot. She stopped talking.

"Miss Myles, I'd like you to go home now."

Melinda's heart sank. She had been so sure she had won him over. Obviously the radiant smile was just the shark baring his teeth before he went for the kill. She turned to go.

"Wait a minute." Forrest stopped her. "I haven't finished."

Melinda cringed. Not only was she being fired, she was going to have to face the added disgrace of a public humiliation. The Myles Militia down in flames, in trouble together. She blocked her ears internally, not wanting to hear the inevitable insults. All she wanted was to be out of there as soon as possible. But Forrest wouldn't stop talking, and phrases were breaking through her self-imposed soundproofing.

". . . meet you at the airport. The car will pick you up in forty-five minutes. Is that enough time?"

She'd missed something, that was clear. "I'm sorry, sir, could you repeat that?" She focused on his words, trying to keep her heart from racing.

He spoke slowly, deliberately, as if to a bright but very young child. He knew he'd surprised her, and it pleased him.

"I want you to go home and pack. Take enough for a week. I am leaving for a series of meetings in New York this afternoon, and I'm going to need some help. Catherine usually goes with me, but since she's sick I thought I'd have to do this trip on my own. But now I see that you'll be able to handle it very nicely. We will travel together so I can brief you on the way. The flight leaves at eight tonight, so that gives you a few hours. The car will pick you up at seven. I assume that gives you enough time."

The conductor in her heart tried to keep the music to a low hum. They hadn't yet successfully completed the overture; it was too soon to burst into song.

Melinda had to ask. "Are you going to fire her?"

Forrest was already somewhere else. "What?"

"The woman who interrupted you. Are you going to fire her?"

Persistent little creature, Forrest thought. "No. You're quite right. It's not worth the trouble."

Melinda barely heard Stan's whispered congratulations or Forrest's exhortations not to be late. Her heart was in the midst of a full-fledged aria, and it was hitting all the high notes with absolutely perfect pitch.

∂7∂

Pete was already mixing drinks at Bamboo Bernie's by the time Sam walked in. She'd been driving around for hours, trying to calm herself down, but to no avail. Usually being at the wheel meant being in control, which for Sam was always the most comfortable position to be in. But today, after storming out of the plant, she'd been unable to find peace either on the road or within herself.

At first she'd gone to the mill pond, hoping to preserve her righteous indignation at what was about to befall her beloved retreat. But no matter how hard she tried, she couldn't rid herself of unwelcome images—hands touching, eyes meeting, souls meshing—that drove her deeper into despair over her foolish fantasies. She was not so stupid or naïve that she could ever believe that life would award her a prize as glittering as Drew Symington. But that it was necessary to annihilate her dream by making him not only inaccessible, but antagonistic as well, was more punishment than she expected. She felt like Cinderella, having lost her shoe after dancing at the ball. But for her, no prince would bring it back, and she'd be damned if she would spend the rest of her life hobbling barefoot through a daily routine of loathsome chores.

Anger empowered her, and she got back into her DMC Roadster, lovingly turned into a four-wheel-drive trekker with her own two hands. She screeched backward over the gravel path and sped out onto the freeway singing "Stick to Your Own Kind," from *West Side Story,* at the top of her lungs.

Still singing under her breath, she stopped at the door of Bamboo Bernie's and watched Pete at work at the bar. She made herself concentrate on his strong arms as he shook a martini, and she lost herself in his affable smile as he poured for his customer. The song was right, she told herself. She should stick to her own kind. She willed Pete to look at her and confirm what she already knew.

He turned and saw her, walked out from behind the bar, took her in his arms, and kissed her hard on the mouth—an answered prayer. She stayed in his arms for a few moments, familiar and comfortable, feeling he really was her own kind. She was sorry they had fought, that she had kicked him out of bed, and she told him so.

Pete grinned. "A few days without it, and I figured you would be."

"What's that supposed to mean?" She cringed a little at his crudity, but, needing to confirm the lyrics of the song that still spun around her brain in an endless loop, she smiled benignly and made an effort not to be judgmental.

"It's always the same, babe. You get mad. I stay away. You cool off. You come home to daddy. Where you belong." He pulled her to him again. There wasn't much finesse in what he said, but there was truth. It was where she belonged. She pushed the remnants of *West Side Story* from her mind, and with it the last vestiges of her unarticulated yearning for the man she couldn't have and made herself believe she didn't want.

Sam put her arms around Pete's neck and buried her face in his shoulder. He held her close, and for a moment she felt safe again, back on familiar territory after a harrowing foray into the enemy camp. She made a conscious decision to put everything except her affection for Pete out of her mind. She wouldn't think about what he'd done to the car she'd built; she wouldn't think about being caught naked at the mill pond; she wouldn't think about DMC and their lying, destructive plans. She was only going to think about her and Pete and their future together. She pulled him a little closer, and he kissed the top of her head.

"I hear you've been pretty busy today."

Sam's head jerked away. Everything she wasn't going to think about came rushing back in.

"What did you hear? And who told you?"

Pete chuckled. "Some of the guys from the plant came in for a beer after lunch. Seems like I'm not the only one who gets you riled up for nothing."

"For nothing? I wouldn't exactly call polluting our reservoir nothing."

"Honey, these people know what they're doing."

He was being condescending, and she hated it. "Yeah, that's my point. They know they're setting out to kill us, and they're just not telling us."

Pete shook his head, wondering where she got her ideas. "Building a new auto factory in the middle of a recession and helping everyone in Oakdale get a job isn't what I'd call killing us. You're going to have to get with the program, sweetheart."

"You know, Pete, you're really starting to piss me off."

"Aw, come on, Sam, get off your high horse. You made a lot of people mad at the plant this morning. I had to do a lot of talking to convince them that you weren't out to queer the deal."

"Thanks for nothing. I was."

"Don't be an idiot. You live here just like I do. We've all known each other since we were kids. You don't need Mac and Jimmy and T.J. thinking you're some kind of traitor trying to take food out of their kids' mouths."

"I'm not. I'm trying to save their kids."

"Give me a break. Like you know more than Symington about how to build a car and where to build it."

"I do."

"Honey, it's getting silly. And if you don't quit messing with the boss, it could get dangerous. You've got a job. Be happy about it and just keep your mouth shut so maybe other people can get a job, too."

"You don't get it at all, do you? This is just like when I tell you something about the car. You figure I'm a woman, so I must be working with half a deck. You dismiss what I have to say. And then by the time you figure out I was right all along, it's too late. Well, it's one thing to let you screw up one of my cars. It's quite another to let DMC screw up our lives. I don't know what I can do about it, but I *won't* keep my mouth shut and just watch it happen. And if you can't handle that, too bad!"

She was out the back door. Pete considered following her. Usually when she got mad he just left her alone until she cooled off. But this time she didn't look like she was going to cool off anytime soon, and he was afraid she was going to get herself hurt.

As he headed toward the back, confirmation that Sam needed protection walked in the front. Pete stopped short as Drew Symington came toward him. Drew was smiling, already stretching out his hand, reminding Pete they had met at the track. Pete didn't need any reminding. He knew who Drew was; he just didn't know why he was there. Had he been following Sam? Was he here to fire her or threaten her or who knows what? He took Drew's hand, shook it perfunctorily, and dropped it. His voice was noncommittal, but his guard was up.

"What can I do for you, Mr. Symington?"

"Call me Drew for starters. Mr. Symington is my father."

He smiled, expecting some response from Pete, but none came. He'd been away a long time. He didn't realize the locals were so unfriendly. He assumed it was his name that was putting Pete off and countered with an increase in cordiality that far outdid the way he felt.

"I'm been meaning to come and see you ever since the race, but I just never got around to it. Since I was in Oakdale on business today I thought I'd try to connect."

Pete looked at Drew, wondering if he was for real. "On business?" He'd been in Oakdale addressing the factory workers, most of whom were Pete's friends, relatives, or customers, all of whose lives would be changed depending on what Drew and his daddy had to say. It seemed a little disingenuous to call it "on business."

Still getting no response, Drew forged on. "It's about your mechanic, Sam Myles."

Now it's coming, Pete thought. Obviously he'd been following Sam. But if he expected Pete to finger her, even if they were in the middle of a big fight, he was barking up the wrong flagpole. Drew was waiting now. Pete had to say something.

"Yeah? What about Sam?" He wasn't giving a thing.

"Well, when I saw you at the track you said it was Sam who had designed your car. I wanted to talk to him about it. Can you tell me where I could find him?"

Him? Pete was confused. If Drew had followed Sam here, he'd know she was no him. Or was this just another ploy to get him to lower his guard, like "on business"? Pete looked at Drew, who seemed friendly enough, but he couldn't really tell. Rich people had a way of looking like they were pouring tea while they cut off your head.

He couldn't take a chance. He'd bail out Sam, then let her know what happened, and maybe she'd get the picture. Maybe she'd even thank him for taking care of her in spite of herself, which was what he was always trying to do and which was always making her mad. Maybe this time she'd understand she could do a lot better with him than on her own. They could be a good team if she didn't always want things her way and make out like he was always wrong. She'd have to admit he did the right thing this time, keeping the Symingtons from finding her.

"Listen, *Mr.* Symington," he began pointedly. "I'll tell Sam that you were here, and if Sam wants to find you, you're not too hard to track down. But I wouldn't hold my breath if I were you. Sam's got a lot of secrets when it comes to building better cars, and Sam is not about to share them. Not even with you."

"You mean especially not with me."

Pete shrugged.

"Fair enough," Drew went on. "It was worth a try. Just tell him I'm interested. And tell him I don't steal ideas and I don't take without giving something in return. I'm in the business of making better cars just like Sam. Here's my card. If he wants to talk, he can call me anytime."

"Yeah, I'll tell *him* that," said Pete as he took the card and threw it by the cash register. Finally something had made Pete smile, but for the life of him Drew couldn't figure out what it was. With a terse good-bye he walked out of Bamboo Bernie's, certain that was the last he'd see of Pete Wojek, the race-car driver/bartender, or his elusive genius mechanic, Sam Myles.

Without thinking about it, Drew found himself driving to the mill pond. The morning's events at the plant had set the place firmly in the forefront of his mind. With it came the image of the woman he'd come to think of as his "sunset flame," because of the time of day he'd seen her, because of her copper hair, because of the torch that he carried for her, even though they would probably never meet again.

He smiled ruefully. There seemed to be quite a club forming of people he wanted to meet that weren't going to accommodate him. It occurred to him that in Paris, London, or Ibiza he never had trouble meeting anyone he wanted. He'd just tell someone his name, point out the person whose acquaintance he wished to make, and it happened.

But in Oakdale, where he would have thought his lineage could get him an introduction to the abominable snowman, nobody was interested. He sighed, then laughed out loud, accepting a lesson in humility he didn't really need. He didn't actually think of himself as being particularly important, and now it appeared he had been overestimating himself.

He sat on the hood of his car, idly skipping stones over the water and through the rushes. The woman at the plant had been right; it would be a criminal act to destroy this place. He got back in his car, deciding he'd better stay away, as if to punish himself for the traitorous concept with a self-imposed exile from Eden. Heading for home, he found himself hoping Bethany wouldn't be there, then sped up to get there faster, a reproof for the second disloyal thought within as many minutes.

Drew didn't have to worry about Bethany waiting for him. She had spent a highly profitable day engaged in a marathon event of her preferred sport: shopping at the exclusive Woodland Cliffs Galleria. Though summer had barely begun, the French designers were already shipping their fall fashions, and she'd been tête-à-tête with her favorite saleswoman in the Chanel boutique at Saks Fifth Avenue. It was not a simple matter of trying on clothes to see if you liked them. Not at all. At two to five thousand dollars for a little daytime number, and up into the tens for evening wear, buying Chanel was a privilege accorded only to the few and favored.

While the store had a few items in stock, most of the styles had to be specially ordered, and even then, Paris would only agree to send a limited number. They'd combed through the styles in the loose-leaf black booklet, picking out which ones they thought would suit her and adding her name to the growing list of women who were willing to spend an auto worker's month's wage for a skirt and blouse. Bethany had come early, but she was dismayed to see how many size sixes had already been appropriated.

It had taken a crisp hundred-dollar bill, proffered in appreciation for the time and advice to get the saleswoman to sneak Bethany's name to the top of the list. She'd left the boutique feeling empowered, and she intensified her vigor by finding an absolutely perfect slip of a Calvin Klein dress, a little nothing, really, but very, very sexy, on sale from $850 to $499. She'd needed strappy sandals to go with it, and a perfect straw hat with silk flowers holding back the crown— not on sale, and almost as much as the dress itself— but she still could pride herself on the economy of her afternoon.

Coming into the open plaza of the Galleria, her arms laden with expensive packages, Bethany felt celebratory. She considered putting on her new clothes and trying to track down Drew. She knew he'd gone to the Oakdale plant with his father in the morning, but there was a good chance he'd be home by now. As much as he loved the automobile business, he needed to be challenged, and Mr. Symington senior was not about to loosen the reins and let his son take over quite yet.

Sometimes, when she thought about Drew in relation to his own life instead of hers, she felt a little sorry for him. He was sort of like Prince Charles, looking to keep busy and feel productive, waiting for his mother to abdicate in his favor so he could find something to do with his life. On the other hand, how much sympathy did the future king really need? And as the pretender to the throne of the future queen, Bethany didn't really see a life of wealth and privilege and maybe a little sloth as being all that bad. But it was just another way that she and Drew were different. Even if he was home, he'd be poring over annual reports or papers on new design theories, and he'd resent her invitation to come out and play because it would just reinforce the knowledge that it was makework, that he really wasn't a very busy man.

Still, it was four o'clock, and she was in desperate need of a little champagne and caviar pick-me-up, and if she hit just the right note she might be able to cajole him into taking her to Petrov's.

"Some days everything goes right," Bethany said out loud as she blocked the path of the man in front of her.

He had been heading toward her but looking in the windows to the right and left, politely avoiding the faces of his fellow shoppers.

"Tiens, c'est Bethany!" Jean-Claude exclaimed with surprise and delight, the delight being genuine, the surprise completely feigned. He had watched her going into Saks from a distance, taking care that she not spot him. Then he had waited for her to come out, wondering, as the hours dragged on, if he might have missed her or she might have slipped out through a back exit. But at last she'd emerged, and he'd decided

it would be more advantageous to let her bump into him than vice versa. Her apparent pleasure in "discovering" him confirmed that he'd made the right choice as he gallantly took the packages from her, explaining that his mission that afternoon was to find a gift for his mother, and he was simply at a loss. She looked at him over the top of her sunglasses as if weighing something, and he wondered if perhaps the mother line was just too transparent. But a moment later she took hold of his arm. "I'm exhausted and desperate for my afternoon tea, but I'll help you if—"

He was way ahead of her. "You are *une ange.* I will take you to tea after. *Je promis.* With your advice, *ça ne prends que dix minutes.* Ten minutes, no more."

She laughed. "I think I can handle that. Now, what type of thing are you looking for, and how much do you want to spend?"

She led him to Tiffany's, a few doors down. As promised, within minutes they had settled on a pair of gold Paloma Picasso earrings, moderately expensive, chic, and just conservative enough to suit one's mother. They had laughed when the salesman, thinking that Jean-Claude was buying a gift for Bethany, tried to pitch them more romantic—and more expensive—pieces, giving Bethany a subtle once-over, and telling Jean-Claude that he had a woman who clearly expected and deserved the finest, in return for which, he was sure, Jean-Claude would be amply and suitably rewarded. Jean-Claude had explained, rather dolefully, that the gift was for his mother. He only wished that Bethany were his to bestow gifts upon.

Locking eyes with her for just a moment, Jean-Claude said, "If you were mine, I would *absolument* buy for you *des bijoux."* Calculating the effect of overstepping the boundaries of good taste just a hair, his voice low and just a little too throaty, he added, "And delight in the reward after."

Bethany felt a little flutter somewhere in the region of her lower abdomen. He was a handsome man, this Jean-Claude Renoir, and his Gallic charm was definitely not lost on her. When the salesman had returned with the classic Tiffany turquoise box tied with white ribbon Jean-Claude thanked him, then turned to Bethany and kissed her hand, lingering a moment too long, lips pressing a little too hard. Bethany smiled. Tea was going to be lovely.

Petrov's was currently the hot place for high tea, and, needless to say, Bethany was known. Vladimir, the maître d', started to lead them to Bethany's usual area, somewhere in front of the door, the ideal spot for seeing and being seen. But grasping his hand and handing off a twenty-dollar bill, Jean-Claude whispered in his ear, and instead Vladimir brought them to a quiet little table in the corner. At first Bethany was miffed, thinking she was being denied her rightful arena. But one smoldering look from Jean-Claude and she made a point of stating how exhausted she was, and how nice it would be to be out of the usual melee for a change, loudly emphasizing "for a change" so that anyone within hearing distance would be aware that she was not being relegated to Siberia but choosing to go there for a respite, like a native avoiding the tourist attractions in favor of the rustic, undiscovered byways. There was still a certain amount of table-hopping necessary, and Bethany managed to introduce Jean-Claude as both a guest of the Symingtons, her fiancé's family, and a descendant of the great artist of the same last name. She knew by the little "oh's" murmured in mild reverence that she'd made the desired impression, and she settled into their alcove feeling just slightly, but quite nicely, aroused. Nothing titillated Bethany like the attentions of a man who could enhance the air of condescension that she so carefully cultivated.

Jean-Claude didn't need a weather vane to know the wind was in his favor. He made sure the champagne was ice-cold and plentiful. He scooped spoonfuls of caviar onto little triangles of toast and popped them into Bethany's open mouth. He laughed at her jokes and pressed closer to hear the little tidbits of gossip she offered about each new arrival to the room. His knee brushed hers delicately but insistently, and by the time the second bottle of champagne had arrived his hand was under her skirt, between her thighs, gloved by a moist heat that signaled all he needed to know. Bethany knew she had to be careful. There were a lot of people at Petrov's who knew and envied her. Ninety-eight percent of the single women she knew— maybe even the married ones—would gouge out her eyes with a caviar spoon if it meant getting a crack at her fiancé, so a simple stab in the back would be nothing. She wasn't about to jeopardize her position as the future Mrs. Symington for a small flirtation. Even with a little too much champagne rollicking through her bloodstream she realized that between Jean-Claude's whispering in her ear and maneuvering between her legs, she wasn't in complete control. She suggested it was time to go.

Jean-Claude would not let her drive—for her own

safety, he proclaimed ever so solicitously. He announced that he would leave his car, which was, after all, just a rental, take her home, then get a cab to come back and get his. Accustomed to having people go out of their way for her, Bethany didn't even protest. She leaned back in the passenger's seat, eyes closed, feeling Jean-Claude's hand moving up and down her thigh. Every now and then it would go away, and she'd feel a moment of profound disappointment, but then he'd shift gears and it would be back, redoubling its efforts to make up for time lost, and Bethany would sigh and feel herself stirring inside. She couldn't remember if he'd asked where she lived, but he seemed to know his way around, never hesitating, never asking directions, driving smoothly into the circular drive in front of the Regal Towers, tossing the keys to one of the doormen as she always did, with a terse "Park it for Miss Havenhurst, please."

She'd been living there for two years, since returning from a year abroad and insisting to her father that she couldn't possibly live at home anymore. The Havenhursts were well enough off, definitely up there with Woodland Cliffs society. But their simple twenty-room colonial mansion on several landscaped acres afforded none of the privacy of an estate like the Symingtons'. For a time she tried to convince her parents to find something a little grander, pointing out that if she had been able to have her own private wing, like Drew at Belvedere, she could stay indefinitely. But much as Everett Havenhurst liked to spoil his little girl, he balked at changing his own life for her. He'd bought her the small penthouse at the Regal Towers as a compromise.

She was still in Woodland Cliffs, close to home, in the bosom of all the right people. The building was secure and fully serviced, so aware of her comings and goings that the moment she left a maid scurried into the apartment to clean up after her, leaving an ever-spotless, always-tidy home for her to come back to. Having, from childhood, developed a habit of abandoning things where she dropped them, this luxury was an absolute necessity for Bethany, who might otherwise have found herself living in an extravagantly furnished pigpen.

The only thing Bethany did not take for granted was the discretion of the ever-present staff, and she'd taken care of that on the first day she moved in by withdrawing several thousand dollars from her trust account and generously passing out hundred-dollar bills to anyone in uniform, making it abundantly clear that nothing they saw or heard in her apartment was ever to be reported to her father, or to anyone else, for that matter. She'd guaranteed their commitment to protecting her privacy by repeating the procedure every holiday and each time she indulged in some little folly that might best be left unexamined. As Jean-Claude pressed close to her in the single cubicle of the revolving door she was glad she'd been exceptionally magnanimous on the Fourth of July.

In the elevator Jean-Claude backed her into the wall with his body and covered her mouth with his while he pressed the button for her floor. For a fleeting second she wondered how he knew where she lived, but all rational thought stopped as she felt him grinding into her, his tongue in her mouth, his hand on her breast, his cock, hard, between her legs. When the elevator stopped he led the way to her door, reached out his hand, and took her keys from her fumbling fingers. Inside, she thought she might protest: This is so sudden; I'm engaged; we really shouldn't. But he gave her no chance, ripping off her five-hundred-dollar Donna Karan sundress and tossing it in a heap as though it were a K-mart special. Underneath she wore only a pair of sheer lace bikinis, and, seeing the nipples of her full, round breasts already hard, Jean-Claude locked his lips on one while kneading the other with his free hand. His other hand was already inside her panties, inside her body. It would do no good to protest; her body, wet and waiting, had already betrayed her. She tried to lead him to the bedroom then, but he pushed her to the floor and took her, bringing her closer and closer to climax with his fingers while he thrust himself inside her, fast, furious, all tenderness forsaken. Bethany was more excited than she had ever been. This was how she liked her sex, a little rough and totally out of control. With Drew there always seemed to be something missing, as though in spite of all her efforts he was looking for something more, something she couldn't do with her body and didn't know how to do with her heart.

For Jean-Claude the excitement was not in the act itself, but in the knowledge that bedding Bethany brought him one step closer to fulfilling his purpose in coming to Woodland Cliffs. She begged for him to make her come, and he obliged, thinking how he'd end up screwing them all just as he was screwing Andrew Symington's fiancée, and that thought alone was enough to make him come as well.

Lying spent in a damp halo on the Aubusson rug that had set her father back a tidy sum, Bethany felt her head starting to clear, and a tiny fissure of fear began to cut an ever-widening path through her state of bliss. This was not the first time she had had a little dalliance. But she could not consider Jean-Claude Renoir, the cousin of her fiancé's very persnickety mother, a minor indiscretion to be dismissed with a peck and a check. If it hadn't been for the second bottle of champagne, she would never have allowed this to happen. Famous name, fabulous sex and all, there was no way she was going to give up being the junior Mrs. Symington. Frenchmen were known for their worldliness, and she assumed—expected—no, prayed that Jean-Claude was typical of his clan.

"That was wonderful," she sighed at last, deciding the best defense was an offense, "but it shouldn't have happened."

"Why not?" Jean-Claude asked, all phony innocence.

"Because I'm engaged to be married, and I'm faithful to my fiancé," Bethany replied sternly, ignoring the fact that lying naked on the floor beside this virtual stranger belied her every word.

"Bien sûr, of course you are." Jean-Claude smiled, stretching languorously.

"You took advantage of me."

"But I thought I gave *you* every advantage."

"That's not what I mean, and you know it."

"Did I please you?"

She was charmed by the earnestness with which he asked, as if it really mattered, but she tried not to show it.

"Well . . . that's not the point."

"You are right. It's not. The point is, can I do it again?"

"No," Bethany protested. "That's not . . ."

She gasped as her pulse quickened. His head was between her legs, and his tongue was on the exact spot, flicking and teasing, then licking wide circles around it, sensing the precise moment when too much of a good thing became an irritant, giving her swollen sex a chance to recover, then beginning again, flicking and teasing. She thought she would go mad and moved her hand between her legs, intending to bring a faster release, but he gently held it away, whispering, "We have plenty of time," and continued to work his magic until she came in waves, over and over again, and knew this was not something that would be easy to give up.

The telephone rang, and her eyes went wide with terror as Jean-Claude reached over her still-inert body and picked it up. He put his finger to his lips and passed the receiver over himself to her, brushing her breasts with his fingertips along the way. In the way that coincidences invariably happen, she knew that it would be Drew, and it was.

Acknowledging her need for privacy with a Gallic shrug, he gathered his clothes, which had somehow been discarded between thrusts and parries, and withdrew into the bathroom. He didn't need to hear what she said; he knew his name would not be mentioned. Washing himself, he looked into the mirror and was startled by the haunted eyes of a man who would never be satisfied by something as simple as sex again. He turned away, his own gaunt image a reminder of his mission. Dressing quickly, he veiled his pain with the lowered lids and crooked smile of a sated lover.

Bethany was hanging up the telephone as Jean-Claude emerged. She looked disappointed to see him dressed, and, using her nakedness to full effect, she put her arms around his neck and began to work on his buttons.

"My dinner with the family was just canceled. Father and son had a bad day at the plant. Forrest is going out of town, and Drew is going to work this evening. So I'm all alone with nothing to do," she said suggestively.

"Ah, *quel dommage.* My dinner with the family was not canceled. My cousin Mathilde will be expecting me, especially if she is alone. I must not cause suspicion by not appearing, no?" He redid his buttons and, as if to soften the rejection, placed a wet kiss on each of her nipples. "For me it doesn't matter. But for you we must be careful."

Bethany let him go, relieved that at least they were on the same wavelength.

"Our lovely secret. Forever. Agreed?"

"Only if you allow me to come back. I haven't even taken you to bed."

They both burst out laughing, and he kissed her, on the mouth this time, and left. Inside, Bethany leaned against the door, smiling. She felt good, very, very good. In spite of her engagement, or even her marriage, she wouldn't mind if this went on a long, long time. Jean-Claude appeared to be the perfect lover, discreet and undemanding. But Bethany would take no chances. He knew something about her that no one else could know. She would have to get something on him that would make him just as uncomfortable if it were revealed. Even though she knew very little about him, she knew there had to be something. A man with that kind of passion could not possibly have an uncheckered past. She'd find out his secret, she'd let him know she knew it, and then they would be playing on an even field. In the game of love, or life, Bethany allowed no handicaps.

8

Firm in his belief that his home, however humble, was his castle, Harvey Myles opened his front door after a double shift at the plant, expecting a hot meal and a cold beer. Instead he was greeted by his wife sitting tight-lipped at an empty table.

It had been a tough day, between working late and worrying about his daughter. He'd spent a good part of his afternoon and evening shifts trying to explain Sam's actions to their colleagues, although for the life of him he couldn't figure out himself what had gotten into her. He was tired and hungry and irritated, and the last thing he needed was one of Diane's snits. Her cooking wasn't great, but it was good enough, and her dinners were hot and plentiful. He looked longingly at the stove, but as he already knew, there were no pots simmering, and the oven looked cold and dark.

"What's going on?" he asked wearily.

"Melinda is going to New York with Forrest Symington," Diane spat out, as though she were announcing a trip to hell.

"It's business," chimed in Melinda cheerfully, ignoring the doomsday implications in her mother's tone of voice. She put a small suitcase and a tote bag with her office papers at the front door, ready and waiting, with time to spare.

"Catherine, his secretary, got sick, and he's got an important meeting in New York. So he asked me to come and take notes."

"Good for you, honey." Harvey smiled at his younger daughter. "At least one of our daughters still has a job. After today, I'm not so sure about Sam."

"She's okay," said Melinda.

"How do you know?" asked Harvey.

"I asked Mr. Symington. He said he wouldn't fire her."

"I give the guy credit. That was quite a stunt she pulled today. I'm not sure I would have let her off so easy."

"Actually, he wasn't going to at first. But I convinced him that it would just get him into trouble with the union and it wasn't worth it. I didn't mention she was my sister."

Harvey burst out laughing. "Well, who would have thought my little girl would go out and save the day?" He was relieved, no doubt about it. Times were tough, and though he'd never abandon his daughter, he wouldn't be able to help Sam out much if she wasn't working. He turned to Diane; maybe there was hope for dinner still. "So everything's okay. No reason to be upset."

"I'm not upset about Sam," Diane replied tersely. "She can take care of herself."

Harvey looked confused.

"It's me," Melinda informed him, looking out the window, then at her watch for the tenth time. "She doesn't think I should go to New York."

"Why not?" asked Harvey, even more confused.

Melinda shrugged and looked at her mother. Diane said nothing, but anger emanated from her body like waves of heat.

"You're getting paid, aren't you?" asked Harvey, suddenly wondering if Diane might know something he didn't. "And they're putting you up in your own room, all expenses paid?"

"Of course," said Melinda, distracted. It was five after seven. She hoped nothing had gone wrong—the trip canceled, her nepotistic intervention for Sam discovered, her mother's wish magically granted.

Harvey, ever mindful of his growling stomach, gave Diane an encouraging smile. "See? No funny business."

"How . . . do . . . you . . . know?" Diane reiterated, separating her words for emphasis.

Melinda had had it. It was seven minutes after seven. Something was going wrong, and she needed someone to blame. "Fine," she shouted at her mother. "You think you know more, you tell me. You haven't worked at DMC for over twenty years. What gives you the inside track? Huh? How come you know more about what's going to happen than I do?"

Diane got up from the table without a word, walked into the bedroom, and closed the door. Harvey gave up all hope, went to the freezer, and pulled out a Hungry Man dinner, holding it at arm's length to read the instructions. There was the sound of a car in the driveway. Relieved, Melinda was instantly repentant.

"I've got to go. Tell Mom I'm sorry for what I said. And I'm sorry about your dinner, too."

"Not your fault, honey. You didn't do anything wrong." He kissed her on the cheek. "At least you'll get dinner on the plane."

Melinda picked up her bags and opened the door. She gasped as she saw a black stretch limo taking up the whole driveway. The moment he saw her the driver leapt out and took her bags from her, opening the back door and ushering her into the car. She'd never been in a limousine before, and she lingered for a moment before she stepped in. Her eyes glittered as she saw the fully stocked bar, the television tuned to CNN, the array of magazines and newspapers displayed in the tasteful polished-wood rack. She felt like a movie star.

"Get in," Forrest said impatiently. "We're late."

She felt like a complete fool. She had been so intent on devouring the details to recount to her sister that she hadn't even seen him. He was sitting in the far corner of the seat facing the driver, his *Wall Street Journal* momentarily lowered, regarding her with not unkind eyes. She didn't know if she was expected to sit beside him or across from him on the seat opposite. She got in, hunched a little but almost able to stand, amazed at how roomy it was even on the inside. The door closed behind her, and the car started, making her choice for her as she plopped down opposite in her own corner, as far away as she could get. He gave her a small smile, and she couldn't keep herself from grinning like an idiot in return. She couldn't help it; this was exciting. Forrest laughed, aware of her disproportionate delight at what he considered a bothersome trip.

"I've never been to New York," she said, feeling the need to explain her exuberance, which she thought he might consider inappropriate. "I've never really been anywhere. This is going to be fun."

"It's going to be mostly work, you know."

"Oh, I know that, sir," Melinda said hastily, earnestly, afraid he might think she was expecting some sort of junket. "I'm prepared for that. It's just—"

"It's all right, you don't have to explain, I understand." He smiled again, this time giving her the full dazzler, and she believed that he did, indeed, understand. Everything about her. Melinda relaxed, settling into the cushy leather, looking out the tinted windows. Work or not, it would be fun. Thinking exactly the same thing, Forrest raised his newspaper again, hiding the look of benign astonishment on his face, surprised at how pleased he was by her enthusiasm.

Diane Myles stood at her bedroom window until long after the black limousine had disappeared. She had caught a glimpse of Forrest Symington inside when the door opened to swallow up her precious daughter. She'd resisted an overwhelming urge to run out and snatch Melinda back, offering herself as a sacrifice instead. She laughed bitterly, knowing instinctively, without being able to articulate the thought, that the gods of power were appeased by vestal virgins, and it had been many a moon since she qualified in that category. She smelled a combination of chicken and paper burning, but still she didn't leave the window.

Harvey came in. "Remember when the school bus came to get her on her first day of kindergarten? You followed it over to Route 22, then flagged him down at the railroad crossing. You took Melinda off the bus and brought her home, said she was too little."

"She was only four."

"No, Di, she was five. And so were all the other kids. And I just had to take her to school myself and explain what happened to the teacher. Melinda loved school."

"This is different."

"How?"

Diane looked at her husband. She was confusing him, she knew, as she had more than once before, but his eyes were still full of love. She couldn't tell him.

"You're supposed to take the cover off the TV dinner before you put it in the oven. It's burned," was all she said as she led him from the bedroom and back into the kitchen.

Bethany had not been expected, or even wanted, when she arrived at Belvedere that evening. She found Mathilde already on her third cocktail, chattering in French with Jean-Claude, whose glazed eyes belied the smiles and frowns he bestowed on his cousin at appropriate moments. It did not matter to Mathilde. She had been more or less ignored by her husband in the many years since she'd given him power of attorney over her considerable finances. For her, the mere fact of Jean-Claude's attentive presence would have been enough, even had she been sufficiently sober to notice his discreet disinterest.

Mathilde had no wish to share the engaging company of her long-lost relative with a younger woman, even her future daughter-in-law, but she kissed Bethany on each cheek in the French way and invited her to join them. Although they had parted rather intimate company just a few hours before, Bethany and Jean-Claude made it a point to greet each other as though they had no more than a passing acquaintance, gained in present company at this very place.

Bethany was relieved to see how well Jean-Claude was playing his part, and, intent on her own role, she bubbled on about missing her fiancé and absolutely longing to see him. Even in her semi-inebriated state, Mathilde wasn't foolish enough to believe that the alliance between the scion of the D'Uberville (now Symington) fortune and this paragon of polite society was based on anything remotely connected to compelling passion. But she considered it an important union, a surprisingly safe choice for her occasionally rebellious son; and coupled with the relief she felt at knowing that Bethany would not be intruding on her evening plans, which included several more drinks and much more attention from Jean-Claude, this made Mathilde entirely sympathetic to Bethany's overwhelming need. She pointed Bethany in the direction of the den, where Drew had withdrawn after an argument with his father.

In the darkened room Drew sat alone, the conversation repeating itself in his head.

"With all due respect, Dad, it's not going to fly. Things are changing. You can't exploit people, and you can't exploit the land and expect to get away with it," Drew had begun.

"Where do you get this crap? This is business, not Greenpeace. There's a goddam recession on, and people want goddam jobs, and that's what I'm giving them. What's this exploitation garbage?" When Forrest was angry he tended to lose the refined veneer his French wife had tried to cement on him.

"Find another spot."

"Why? The mill pond is perfect. The waste will be treated. We're not planning to shit in the goddam water, for Chrissake."

"You know it can't be that carefully controlled. Not if you're going to make it economically feasible. And I know you are."

Forrest had refused to continue the debate, insisting he would miss his flight. But his parting shot made Drew realize that even with all the time in the world, he'd never be able to convince his father.

"Son," Forrest had intoned, trying to sound paternal but sounding peevish instead, "this is a DMC decision, approved by the DMC board. As a vice president, not to mention my son and heir, you are expected to publicly support and approve that position. I suggest that you privately come to terms with that and forget about representing the workers. They've got their union for that. They don't need you. I do."

Bethany coughed softly, interrupting his reverie. "I've been standing here for five minutes, and you haven't even seen me. What on earth are you thinking about, darling?"

She could tell that Drew was annoyed, but he was far too polite to say so. Still, he couldn't make his greeting sound anything but perfunctory, and she saw she had her work cut out for her. She was glad she'd worn her new purchase, and she slithered out of the light cape she was wearing, casually turning away from Drew as if it didn't matter, but listening for the sharp intake of breath that would signal the expected reaction to the dress, clinging to her shapely body, unencumbered by any other interference.

She counted off the seconds, waiting for him to come to her, to put his arms around her. She lost track after thirty and turned back, knowing she'd miscalculated as she realized Drew had barely looked at her and had obviously not seen her at all. That was all right. For the fortune that would come to her with her marriage, she was willing to work harder. Cooing her concern, she put her arms around him, urging him to forget the cares of the day as she pressed her body against his.

"Beth . . . honey . . ."

"Hmmm . . ." she murmured in his ear. It was working. She moved her body just a little so he could feel every nuance.

"I'm going to send you home."

"What?" She couldn't believe it. She knew she wasn't losing her touch. Her afternoon's activities proved it.

"I'm sorry, it's me, not you," Drew confirmed. "There's a serious crisis looming at DMC, and I've got some heavy thinking to do."

She tried to jolly him out of it, but it did no good. She wheedled, she cupped her breasts and caressed her thighs, hoping to show him what he was missing. Drew resisted the desire to push her away, hard. He was aware that Bethany was being the same as she always was. Tonight he was the one who was different, and he could not blame her for that.

More than once he'd questioned the advisability of his engagement to a woman who meant so little to him, but with the way his life had been laid out for him, it didn't really seem to matter. He recognized the handiwork of his mother, who had had Bethany lying in wait the minute he'd returned from Europe. Even though he might have questioned his mother's wisdom, he never felt a real need to dispute her choice. It seemed to mean a great deal more to her than to him. He knew pop psychology would place him squarely in the category of codependent of a classic alcoholic passive-aggressive, but he felt too sorry for Mathilde, and not enough concern for himself, to act otherwise. But something was changing, and he wasn't quite sure why. All he knew for certain was that tonight, of all nights, he did not want to share his bed with Bethany Havenhurst.

She knew it, too. Taking her leave, Bethany was tempted to wonder aloud as to Drew's true sexual orientation. Nothing besides being just a little gay, she thought, could explain the lack of desire Drew displayed to someone as desirable as she knew she was. But even if it was true, it wouldn't have changed her position on their forthcoming marriage. Her ambition was to be Mrs. Andrew Symington, and she would allow nothing and no one, including a reluctant Mr. Andrew Symington himself, to stand in her way.

More than a little threatened, she kept the caustic comments to herself and showed nothing but warmth and understanding to her husband-to-be. She said good night, making certain his kiss landed on her mouth, and, to his great relief, left him alone.

Bethany was disgruntled. She wasn't used to being brushed off. She wondered if she should stop into the salon and say good night, but then they'd know that she'd been brushed off. The carved double wood doors had been left open a crack, and she could see them holding out their glasses while Robert poured. They would not notice if she left quietly. From the wobble in Mathilde's glass, Bethany suspected there was very little she'd notice at this point. And there was Jean-Claude, ever accommodating, intent on his own game, whatever it was. Seeing him move closer to Mathilde, nodding in interest while simultaneously stifling a yawn, Bethany was more certain than ever that whatever he was doing, it was for a reason.

Suddenly she was afraid. Was their fortuitous coming together, as it were, more than happenstance? Did the new player on the board intend to jeopardize her own game plan? An afternoon with Jean-Claude and an evening without Drew told her she was at risk. She needed a new strategy. She looked back at the den. Drew had roused himself enough to close the door behind her. Jean-Claude and Mathilde were enveloped in their alcoholic tête-à-tête, with Robert in attendance. Forrest had left for the airport. Holding her cape close to keep it from swishing, she slipped up the stairs to the east wing and the guest quarters.

There were several rooms for visitors in the east wing, but since only one was occupied, Bethany had little difficulty in finding what she was looking for. Jean-Claude's clothes were hung in the closet, the drawers neatly arranged, no doubt by Odile, who did the same for Bethany when she stayed over. After a cursory overview Bethany didn't even bother to go through Jean-Claude's things. Anything of interest to her would not have been unpacked by the maid. She tried the desk, under the pillow, even the mattress. Then, when she saw a Gucci saddlebag under the bed instead of in the back of the closet, where Odile usually placed her empty suitcases, she sensed she'd found her answer.

She was surprised to find the saddlebag unlocked, disappointed to find it empty. She closed it and started to put it back. Something moved. She opened it again—empty—held it open and moved it. There was definitely something inside. She felt around the lining, smiling as a corner gave way, and she was able to lift it off, uncovering a plain brown manila envelope, sliding back and forth in its hiding place.

Bethany's French was more rudimentary than she liked to admit. When called upon to converse she would do a lot of nodding and smiling, going with the form of the conversation and hoping that substance was never called for—and in her circles, it rarely was. Using the few popular phrases she kept up with, like *"c'est génial"* when approval was called for or *"c'est incroyable"* when shock was in order, she was able to give the appearance of being completely fluent, when in fact it was a bit of a struggle for her to understand the basics. Still, she had no trouble discerning the meaning of the headlines in the yellowed newspaper. A young bride had been killed on her wedding day by a hit-and-run driver on the Grande Corniche outside Monaco. The details were unintelligible to her, and Bethany could only speculate about Jean-Claude's relationship to the dead woman. If he found it necessary to carry these gruesome clippings with him on his travels, chances were he had been the groom-to-be. Was it sheer sentiment that kept him crying over the grisly details laid out on the tearstained tabloid? She leafed through the items, disturbed not so much by Jean-Claude's loss as by her own inability to figure out how he was using it, or better yet, how she could preempt it and use it herself.

She scanned for a hint, but the language was beyond her. There were several items, dated over several weeks, but she could discern very little. Until she saw the picture. It was old and blurred, but there was no mistaking the identity. Staring at her from the back pages of a French newspaper was her fiancé. She heard movement in the halls and realized the maids were making the rounds, turning down the beds. There was no way she could peruse and understand the articles, even mustering every bit of high school French she could possibly remember. But there was no guarantee she could ever get back in here and find Jean-Claude's secret files again. What if he realized someone had been in his papers and moved them? She looked at the picture of Drew, moving her lips as she tried to translate the caption.

There was laughter in the hall, doors slamming; they were getting close. Even without comprehending a word she knew that the information held in these old papers was somehow crucial to her. She could not afford to let it slip through her fingers. Folding the articles carefully to prevent them from disintegrating in her hands, she slipped them back into the envelope and put the envelope inside her purse. Then she returned the saddlebag to the exact spot, she hoped, where she had found it. With any luck, Jean-Claude might not even check; after all, he had no reason to be suspicious. And even if he did, and found his papers missing, he would never know she had been there, would never have reason to suspect her.

She waited for a momentary return of silence to the corridor, then slipped out unobserved. She would go home and get out her trusty French-English dictionary. She would work it out word by word if she had to. But she was determined to unlock the secret of the pages. She needed all the ammunition she could get to ensure that one day she would take her place as Mrs. Bethany Symington, mistress of Belvedere.

Sitting in the darkening den alone, glad that he'd been able to deflect Bethany and send her home, Drew wondered if his professional opinion on the merits of the mill pond site were being colored by his experience there. He believed that Forrest's intentions were ultimately good. The new plant was meant to be a legacy to his son, to be placed under Drew's command as a show of confidence in the next generation. At the same time, it would give an invaluable boost to an economically stricken community. Drew had approved, even taken pride in the plans, at least until he'd been to the mill pond. His own inexperience dictated that he accept his father's advice and follow the course laid out by the board of directors at DMC. But something inside him told him it was wrong.

"Am I being ridiculous?" he asked himself aloud, wondering if he had suddenly become a misguided idealist. There was one way to find out. He wasn't going to be able to concentrate on anything else anyway. He might as well make use of the time.

Sam lay in bed tossing and turning. She couldn't read, she couldn't sleep. She thought that after her event-filled day she'd be so exhausted she'd crash, and in fact she'd gone to bed early and fallen into a deep sleep. But her dreams were restless and confused, and she forced herself awake as if to protect her unconscious from getting too close to subjects better left unexplored. She sat up in bed, unable to remember the complicated plots of her nocturnal visions, but all too aware that the cast of characters had included the man she'd begun to consider her nemesis. Unwilling to chance a return journey to that proscribed territory, she got up and went for a run.

It was almost four miles to the mill pond from her house, and Sam, who frequently ran the same route, made it in record time. Panting, she collapsed against a tree, not far from where she had hidden the last time she had been in this place. There was a hint of coming autumn in the night air, and a strong breeze quickly cooled the perspiration on her skin. She felt a chill and knew she should start back, preferably at a quick trot, but the beauty of the water, the moon dancing over the ripples, kept her breathless and drained her of the will to move.

Drew parked his car and walked the last half mile, laughing at himself but unable to shake the conviction that to do otherwise would be to desecrate holy ground. Walking softly, he realized that he was seeing more in the dimness of starlight than he had the day he had zoomed to the bank out of ignorance and retreated, just as fast, out of concern. The woman who had shouted at them at the plant was right, he thought for the second time that day. It would be criminal to destroy this place. Yet, his argument continued, there were very real benefits that would accrue not just to DMC, but to the people who worked there.

Engaged in debate with himself, Drew wasn't even thinking about her when he saw her. At first he thought it was a combination of moonlight and unconscious desire creating this apparition, making him see what he wanted to see. She looked more real this time, squatting against a tree, dressed in running shorts and a torn T-shirt. But the copper hair falling around her porcelain-perfect face left no question that she was his lost Venus. He wanted to laugh, cry, pray, touch, but was afraid to move, afraid she would disappear like smoke in air. He stood still and drank in her image, not knowing, not caring if she were real or imagined. She turned then and saw him, and dream turned to nightmare as she leapt to her feet and started to run.

It was his anguished "No!" that stopped her. It was the cry of pain from a wounded animal that cannot understand what has happened, only that he has been hurt. She turned around and saw he was running toward her. She knew she should move, and quickly, but she was riveted. He stopped in front of her and put his arms out, enclosing but not touching her, prepared to trap her if she tried to bolt again. He looked into her eyes and dropped his arms. Neither one of them was going anywhere.

"I've been dreaming of seeing you again," he said simply.

She didn't ask why; she didn't need to.

"It probably would have been better if you hadn't."

"I don't believe that, and neither do you."

He was right. Standing close to him, she was suffused with bliss. For a moment she thought nothing could possibly be better than the way she felt right now. Then he kissed her, gently, testing, and she saw how foolish she had been. She was only beginning to understand the meaning of feeling good. One kiss had made her former joy seem paltry. Another and she would see that she had been kidding herself if she thought she had ever before experienced real pleasure.

He touched her face as if to reassure himself. "You know, I was almost convinced that you were a figment of my imagination."

"How do you know I'm not?" she asked, almost unsure herself.

"This is how I know."

He kissed her again, not tentative but hungry this time. Sam stopped thinking, stopped breathing. She existed only in his embrace, and she wanted it to go on forever.

Drew broke first, not because he wanted to stop kissing her, but because he needed to look at her.

"This may sound stupid, but I feel as though I've known you all my life, and I don't even know your name."

"It's not stupid. I feel the same way. Except I do know your name."

"Who are you?" he asked, stroking her hair reverently.

She wanted to tell him . . . everything. What she felt, what she thought, what she'd been doing since she was five years old. She wanted to say that she loved him, and only him, and couldn't imagine spending the rest of her life with anyone else. There was only one problem. She would have to start with her name. And then it would only be a matter of time before he found out that the woman who had sworn she loved him had spent the day denouncing him.

She looked at him. He was waiting, his eyes filled with need and desire. She forced herself to remember that he was the enemy. If she gave in to him now, he would know her weakness, and she would lose this precious place, and her self-respect, forever. She gave an involuntary shiver of distress.

"You're cold," he said, and before she could answer he had taken off his sweater and slipped it over her head. Immobilized, she just stood there. Laughing, he reached into the sleeves, found her arms, and pulled them through. She felt instantly warmed. She tried to turn into the wind, as if the cool breezes could counteract his burning presence and help her freeze her heart. But there was only his hot, sweet breath moving closer to her lips. She knew what she would have to do.

This time *she* kissed *him*. Drew was taken aback, shocked by her ardor as he opened his mouth to accommodate her tongue, which was pressing insistently against his teeth. He heard an involuntary groan coming from deep inside his throat as her body fused to his. He sank to his knees, taking her with him, wanting her more than he had ever wanted anything in his life. He forced himself to slow, not wanting to frighten her with his need.

It took an instant for him to realize what had happened. Searing pain emanated from his groin to all parts of his body. He tried to stand but could not and sank back to the ground in agony. She stood over him, watching him, a look of horror on her face, and for a moment he thought he must be mistaken. She could not have kicked him. She was there to help him. Then she turned and ran, and he knew his angel from heaven had turned into a tormentor from hell. He was furious: at her for her unconscionable attack, and even more at himself for believing in angels in the first place.

His breath came in large, aching gasps as he waited

for the pain to subside, and he cursed the stars, the night, the woman, and the place that had brought them together. As he recovered, his fury gave way to deep chagrin. He had always been a romantic, and it always got him into trouble, only the latest of which was being humiliated by a beautiful but brutal stranger. He'd get over it, he thought, but he would change. It was time to get real, let practicality rule sentiment. Extreme beauty could make you lose sight of reality— in people, in places. It had happened to him a moment ago; it wouldn't happen to him again. Gingerly he got up and hobbled to his car. He took one last look around him. Yes, the mill pond was still beautiful, but like everything else, it was expendable. Gunning the engine, he reversed his car to the highway, heedless of the flying stones and trampled brush as he veered wildly on and off the gravel path. The new, realistic Drew Symington knew it was, indeed, the perfect spot for a DMC factory. And the new, realistic Drew Symington was determined to see it built.

Sam ran all the way home, never looking back, her heart pounding in her chest louder than her feet on the pavement. With shaking hands she fished for her key in the pouch around her waist and then double-locked the door behind her, even though she knew she could not, would not, have been followed. She had acted from instinct, and she believed she had acted correctly. She knew she had hurt Drew, physically and otherwise, but she had had no choice. To stay would have been surrender; to just walk away, impossible.

She had done what she had to do. Drew Symington would have taken her tonight, the way DMC was ready to ravish the mill pond. But there was no one to fight for the mill pond if she succumbed. There were enough attacks on her integrity already without adding a little dalliance with the D'Uberville heir to her list of shortcomings. And she was certain that once he found out who she was, no matter what had happened out there in the field, he'd have no compunction about using it against her. He was, after all, the enemy.

Even without the issue of the mill pond between them, Drew Symington could never be a part of her life. Certainly she could have let him make love to her there in the field, and there were enough hormones still raging inside her to ensure it would have been spectacular. But what would it have meant? The boss's son getting a quick and easy lay from a factory worker. She could never be anything more to him, and she had too much pride to be anything less than everything to the man she loved. Of course, she corrected herself, she didn't love him; she was just attracted to him. This nocturnal meeting would teach them both a good lesson about misplaced lust.

Feeling downright righteous, she headed toward the shower, pulling off her sweater as she walked. That was when it hit her. She was wearing his sweater. She looked at it, touched it. It was a simple pullover, understated, beige, soft, most certainly cashmere. Her hands, with a will of their own, brought the sweater to her face. Feeling its softness, she remembered how his hand had felt on her face, his lips on her lips. She tried to resist, but the tears coursed down her cheeks, leaving damp, dark spots on the downy wool. Angrily she brushed them away, and with a bitter laugh she tossed the sweater onto the floor as she stepped out of the rest of her clothes.

In the shower, water streaming over her, she imagined she was washing away her weakness. She would rid herself of romantic dreams and emerge a clearer, stronger Samantha Myles, focused on her goal and ready to fight to the death for it. She toweled herself dry, rubbing hard, knowing she was being a little melodramatic but allowing it just this once. She climbed into bed naked, too exhausted even to find a T-shirt. The moon shone through the window, and she felt her eyes begin to well and her resolve to waver. Quickly she got up and shut the blinds. It was better in the dark. Somehow she felt stronger without the moon mocking her.

"I can fight it," she said to herself, not stopping to figure out if she was referring to a battle with DMC or one with her heart. "I can fight it," she repeated over and over, like a mantra, until finally she slept.

❧ 9 ❧

The flight alone was impressive enough. They sat, of course, in first class, side by side, Melinda at the window. For the first part of the trip Forrest read and paid little attention to her, which left Melinda free to marvel at the sunset above a downy carpet of darkening clouds that looked thick enough to walk on. They were served by smiling stewardesses who laid out little trays with cloth napkins and real china on their fold-up tables. Unfamiliar with protocol and afraid of doing the wrong thing, Melinda had refused a drink until Forrest, roused from his newspapers by his own order of a double scotch on the rocks, encouraged her to have some wine or champagne, at least. She asked for champagne and was surprised at how much she actually liked the taste, even though the bubbles did, as expected, tickle her nose. She was offered little hors d'oeuvres, nibbles of shrimp and cheese bits on crackers that were nothing like Velveeta on Ritz, and although Forrest refused them all, she couldn't resist trying everything, even if it was the wrong thing to do and she looked like a pig. Dinner came, and though she expected some mystery meat on a microwave tray, it was real rare roast beef, cut in front of her, with a horseradish sauce that made her cough when she used too much and made Forrest put down his *Forbes* magazine and be attentive, while she struggled to indicate she was fine and blushed with embarrassment. Dessert was an ice cream sundae with hot chocolate, and then coffee and little chocolates, and she ate them all while Forrest hardly touched his but smiled, watching her.

"Do you really like this stuff, or don't they feed you at home?" he asked, sounding slightly amazed but not unkind.

"It's really good," she said, unable to curb her enthusiasm. Then she added, in case she had made the wrong choice, "Don't you think so?"

"It's not bad for airplane food, I guess. But it's still airplane food."

"I never had airplane food before. And it's a lot better than the cafeteria at DMC, don't you think?"

Now he had the grace to be embarrassed. "I've never eaten in the cafeteria." As if in penance, he called the stewardess over and got her some more chocolates and some Courvoisier. She admitted she'd never had cognac before either, but she liked it a lot, which seemed to please him and made her happy.

After dinner Forrest gave her a rundown of his New York meetings—whom they would be seeing, when, where, and even why. Melinda thoughtfully wrote everything down in the Secretary's Essential Calendar that she'd brought with her. She enjoyed seeing the spare white pages fill up with appointments and comments, reminders requested by her boss, special assignments she'd be required to fulfill. She felt professional and in control, and after reading over her shoulder for her first notations, making sure she was getting it all right, Forrest held the same opinion. He relaxed then and closed his eyes. Melinda allowed herself the luxury of staring at him for a few moments, but even in sleep Forrest Symington was too formidable to confront, and she turned back to her window, thrilled to see a blanket of tiny lights appear beneath a break in the clouds, blinking their welcome to a brand new world.

Melinda wasn't surprised anymore when a liveried driver met them at the gate. She handed him her bag, noticing the envious eyes of the coach passengers who walked around her to go collect their own luggage and hail their own taxis. She let him open the limousine door for her and climbed in after Forrest without a second glance.

As pleasurable as she had found the first-class flight, she realized very quickly as they entered the understated elegance of the Mayfair Hotel on Park Avenue why, in a world of real luxury, air travel of any class was regarded as a nuisance, not an indulgence. She felt suave, sophisticated even. She'd learned a lot about what the world had to offer in the few short hours since she'd left her unhappy mother in Oakdale. She was certain that only now was she prepared, in a way she could not have been before, to recognize and embrace the kind of manicured life Diane had wished for her. She was certain that if Diane could see her now, she would not begrudge her the experience. She was wrong on both counts.

* * *

While Forrest was checking himself into a suite, and Melinda into a nearby room, Diane was lying awake in bed, her eyes wide open, staring at the moonshadows on her ceiling and cursing the man whose company was inextricably bound with her family, and who had, indirectly, made everything in her life possible. Harvey came in, chuckling about something he'd seen on the "Tonight Show." Diane had stopped watching after Johnny left, but Harvey was everfaithful. He started to tell her what Jay Leno had said about the president, but he could see she wasn't listening.

"Are you still worrying about Melinda?"

"You should be, too," Diane answered, eyes still on the ceiling.

"She's going to be fine."

"You said that before. I don't know how you can be so sure."

"Do you want to tell me what exactly you're worried about? Do you think Forrest Symington is going to try to use her as a party girl?"

"She's pretty enough."

Harvey guffawed. "She's young enough to be his daughter."

Diane gave him a sharp look, started to say something, thought better of it, and clenched her teeth.

"Listen, Forrest Symington has been good to our family. We bought this house on DMC money, and our kids went to school with it. DMC paid for your three months in the sanitarium when you got sick."

"That was over twenty years ago."

"Maybe, but it's still the same company, same people running it. You do your job, you get rewarded. It worked for the rest of us, it'll work for Melinda."

"Oh, Harvey," Diane sighed. "You always think everything is so simple."

"Well, it is."

"For you, maybe."

"So what's so complicated for you?"

He got into bed beside her. Except for the three months she'd been away, and the times she'd gone to the hospital to have the kids, they'd slept in the same bed for twenty-eight years. He always dropped his clothes on the floor at the foot of the bed, where Diane would pick them up in the morning. He slept in his underwear unless they made love, in which case his underwear would be on the floor, too.

Diane remembered when they were first married and used to do it every night. She never minded picking up after him in those days, even though she was working just as long hours at the plant as he was. Then, after the babies had been born, they'd stopped doing it altogether for a few years. They both explained it by saying they were tired from working all day and getting up with the kids at night. There was more to it, but neither one of them had ever talked about it, and after Diane got sick and stopped working they'd gone back to a kind of once-weekly routine, usually on Fridays because there wasn't much good on TV that night, which they'd stuck to pretty much for the past twenty years. It satisfied Harvey, who seemed to prefer staying up late watching his shows anyway.

For Diane it *was* more complicated, but she'd long since stopped trying to vocalize the problem and had taken to going to bed early, contenting herself with a romantic fantasy or two on the nights when she didn't fall asleep right away. But tonight, while her husband snored, she drifted in and out of a semiconscious limbo, her imagination stuck in a horror story with sometimes her younger daughter, sometimes herself as protagonist, and always the figure of Forrest Symington cast, rightly or not, as the villain of all time.

Bethany didn't sleep all night. Instead she poured herself another cup of strong black coffee and gulped it down between yawns. She could have waited until morning to translate her find, but the closer she got to understanding, the more she felt it was worth the trouble. It was painstaking work for someone who didn't like to think too much, writing in English every word she understood, looking up every word she didn't. At first the task seemed endless, and she almost gave up, afraid that she would never be able to piece together the essence of the article. She could take it to a translator, but something told her that this was information she didn't want to share. If Jean-Claude had gone to such pains to hide it, surely it must mean more to him than a sentimental reminder of some dead girl he was supposed to have married. Obviously, his connection to Mathilde D'Uberville was not just the happenstance of distant cousins being brought closer by meeting in a foreign land. Mathilde might not have known Jean-Claude before he had shown up at Belvedere, but he must have had a very clear idea of who she was. After all, he was carrying around an ancient clipping about her only son.

It came together all at once. She was too tired to remember which word, sentence, or paragraph had triggered her understanding, but suddenly it was glaringly clear. The struggle had yielded more treasure than she could ever have hoped for—a deep, dark family secret; the proverbial skeleton in the closet that is supposed to exist in every life, that makes a person vulnerable to anyone who knows of its presence. She started to laugh as she got to her feet, stretching aching limbs that had been folded over her wearisome task.

Dancing a little jig, she announced, "Andrew Symington, you are mine, whether you like it or not!" Humming "Here Comes the Bride," she walked to the window to shut out the dawning day and went smiling to her bed.

It was Saturday, and Sam was grateful. She woke up feeling as though she'd spent the night wrestling with demons, and her soul felt bruised. Too tired to make a proper breakfast, she found some leftover spaghetti in the refrigerator, put it on the stove to heat, and then lost herself in reliving the events of the day before in her head over and over again.

Her anger, frustration, and utter misery increased with each self-telling of the tale. She was a mass of contradictions. She hated Drew Symington and everything he stood for. She was as right to spurn him, even as violently as she had, as she was to reject exploitation by the selfish, greedy Symington empire. So why were half the citizens in Oakdale whom she thought she was defending mad at her? And why did she wish that Drew Symington was folding his arms around her now, comforting her in a way that she knew no one else could, even though she didn't know him at all? It was wrong. It was stupid. They were wrong. She was stupid. Her head ached, and her food burned. There was a knock on the door.

"Go away," she said.

"It's Jack Bader."

"Who?"

"Jack Bader. From the plant."

"Have you come to yell at me?"

"No," he said with a laugh. She opened the door, apologizing.

"That's okay," Jack started, then he stopped, sniffing. "I don't want to be rude, but what's that smell?"

"Oh, God" was all she said as she ran to the stove. She turned off the gas and opened the pot to survey the charred remnants. The odor intensified.

Jack took an involuntary step backward. "Come on, I'll take you to the diner for breakfast. It's on me."

"That's all right. I'm not really hungry."

"I don't care. We've got to talk, and I can't stay here. It stinks. So come on."

Sam didn't know Jack very well. He'd come to Oakdale about a year ago, after a stint at the DMC plant in Mexico City. There were rumors: that he'd killed a Mexican, that he'd married a Mexican, that he'd had an affair with a Mexican woman and had killed her husband. Involved as she was with her own life, Sam hadn't paid much attention. Now she took a good look at him across the table as he wolfed down four scrambled eggs and a double rasher of bacon, and she could see how they might all be true.

He wasn't a big man, but he was packed solid, and it was clear that whatever fat he was taking in with his meal was all being converted into muscle. He had a nice face, a ready smile, and large, clear blue-gray eyes, honest eyes that he knowingly used to his advantage on the rare occasion when he found it necessary to tell a little white lie. But the most striking thing about him was his hair. Sam was surprised that she had never noticed it before, but she assumed it was because she'd only seen him in the plant wearing a hard hat. It was hair that any model, male or female, would kill for, sandy-colored, highlighted with streaks of gold that were clearly too natural to come from a bottle. It was thick and shoulder-length, and even though, at the moment, it was tied in a ponytail at the nape of Jack's generous neck, it was impossible not to notice it.

"Do any of the guys at the plant ever bother you about it?" she couldn't resist asking.

He knew what she was talking about and grinned a little sheepishly. He made a fist, and his biceps bulged impressively.

"See this? No one bothers me about anything."

She laughed. "Well, it worked for Samson."

"Only to a point," he added, laughing with her. "Anyway," he went on, "it looks like you're the one intent on pulling down the pillars of the palace."

She became defensive. "Look, those bastards are lying to us. They say they haven't picked a site, but they have. It's the mill pond, and they're going to destroy it, and us with it. What the hell good will jobs do us if—"

He cut her off gently. "I'm on your side. You don't have to convince me. I didn't come to attack you, I came to see how I could help."

She was abashed. "You mean it?"

He opened his eyes just a little wider and looked straight into hers. It was the technique he had refined to indicate honesty, and he let her see that he was doing it on purpose. She laughed, but she believed him.

"Okay." She paused. "I don't know."

"What don't you know?"

"How you can help. Or how I can even help. I feel like we've got to stop them, but I don't have any idea how."

"I guess we'd better organize some sort of protest."

"Do you know how to do that? I don't. All I know how to do is build cars."

"Oh, I wouldn't say that, Sam. You know how to attract attention to yourself. You know how to get a lot of people mad."

"Yeah, but is that an advantage?"

"It is if we can get them to be mad at Forrest Symington, his asshole son, and their abusive company."

"Do you think his son is so bad?" She couldn't help herself.

"What?"

"Never mind. It doesn't matter. You're right."

It *didn't* matter what Drew Symington thought, it mattered who he was. And he was, undoubtedly, the enemy. She just wished her heart wouldn't start racing every time she thought of him. She pushed him from her mind, and immediately other, more productive thoughts rushed in to fill the vacuum.

"Let's go to the Woodland Cliffs Galleria," she said to Jack.

"What for? A simple little designer number, suitable for both auto factory and protest movement?"

"Very funny. I think we should start by circulating a petition."

"In Woodland Cliffs? Royal playground of the D'Uberville-Symington dynasty?"

"Exactly. Don't you see? If it's just the plebes from Oakdale who want the new plant moved, who's going to care? But if we can get some of their own people to support us, then maybe we have a chance of being heard."

"And she's smart, too," said Jack as he called for the bill.

The Galleria was in full flow by the time Sam and Jack got there, after spending the morning at Sam's place typing up a petition. The arrival of cool weather had sent the fashionable elite scurrying to acquire whatever was ordained for the new season, and though there might have been a recession elsewhere in the country, Woodland Cliffs was obviously feeling no pain.

"You take guys, I'll take gals," said Jack as he opened a couple of buttons on his shirt, then reached over and did the same for Sam.

"We're canvassing for signatures, not dates," Sam reminded him.

"I know that. But it can't hurt."

Jack was right. Not everyone agreed to sign, but the fact that they both looked delectable without even trying made just about everyone they approached stop to listen. Lost in a circle of Woodland Cliffs residents, ardently arguing her case, Sam didn't even notice the approaching couple.

"What's going on over there?" Drew wondered, advancing toward the cluster.

"Who cares?" answered Bethany, tugging her fiancé into Cartier. "Drew, please. I waited until Saturday just so we could do this together. We're going to have to live with this china for years and years."

Bethany had been surprised that he hadn't protested when she called him after sleeping away the morning and asked him to help her pick china patterns at Cartier. To Drew, unable to concentrate on work, unwilling to think about the she-devil at the mill pond, it had seemed the perfect mindless activity. Bethany chose to interpret it as a sign that he was more willing than ever to get married. But all the same, she was glad to have the information she had stolen from Jean-Claude as the ace up her sleeve.

"Does it have to have so much gold around it?" Drew asked when Bethany pointed out her selections. Instantly he regretted his words as the salesman proceeded to pull out catalog after catalog of pictures of plates.

"Darling, I've already been through this process. I just wanted you to pick between the Lenox and the Limoges," Bethany said, trying to hide her exasperation. She hadn't really wanted his opinion at all; she'd already decided on the Limoges, primarily based on the fact that it was $369 per place setting. She'd only insisted he come to confirm his participation in their engagement.

"You're right, darling. I'm sorry. They're both fine. Which one do you prefer?"

Drew knew he was feeding her the line she wanted, and Bethany picked up right on cue, enumerating all the advantages of Limoges. They both understood the game. Drew had seen his parents play it many times. He hadn't really anticipated becoming so adept so quickly, but circumstances had changed for him very rapidly, thanks to the copper-haired siren at the mill pond.

She had lured him to a kind of soul-death, and he'd sworn at the moment she destroyed him that he would, in turn, destroy the place and the memories with it. He needed to rededicate his life to being and doing exactly what was expected. But he couldn't think about it, because if he did, he would have had to admit it was all wrong. Building a plant at the mill pond was wrong; his engagement to Bethany was wrong; in fact, from the moment he had first laid eyes on his naked nemesis, his whole life had been wrong. Picking china was a small penance to pay for wishing, in the deepest recess of his heart, that he could break the preordained mold into which he now fit so tightly he could never get out.

It wasn't until they were leaving Cartier that Drew saw her. The bankers had left, and she was talking one-on-one with an elderly man in overalls. She saw him at the same moment, and he could see that she had stopped her conversation in midsentence. The man was looking at her quizzically, but she saw no one but Drew. She put her hand to her heart as if to still its beating, and the gesture was so open, so vulnerable, that Drew felt himself melt. Something had happened at the mill pond to make her hurt him that Drew didn't understand, but he knew at this moment that this woman did not hate him.

Bethany was still talking about the advantages of Limoges, mentally calculating the value of service for twelve, and then suggesting to Drew that perhaps they should go for twenty.

"I've got to go," Drew said.

"What? What about the Limoges? I mean, if we're going to be entertaining—"

"I've got to go," Drew said again. And he was gone.

"Dammit, what the hell is wrong with you?" Bethany asked the air. Then, storming back into

Cartier, she amended the order to twenty-four place settings, borrowed the phone, and arranged to meet Jean-Claude in her apartment in half an hour.

Sam saw him coming toward her.

"I've got to go," she said to Jack.

"Come on, babe. We've only just begun. At the rate we're going, we can have all of Woodland Cliffs signed up by five o'clock."

"I've got to go," she repeated. And she was gone.

Drew saw her get into the elevator. He saw the doors close and her face disappear. He ran toward the escalator, but as in all malls he could only find up when he wanted down. He had lost her again. Angry, frustrated, knowing something was going on here that he needed to know about, he stormed over to Jack.

"Who is she?" he shouted, grabbing Jack's arm.

"Take it easy, pal," said Jack, shaking him off.

"Who is she?"

"Who are *you?*" asked Jack, though he had recognized Drew instantly.

Drew tried to calm himself. He could see he wasn't going to get anywhere using strong-arm tactics with this bulldozer.

"I'm Andrew Symington. I need to speak to that woman who was here with you. What's her name?"

"No kidding. You're a Symington. Isn't that something? I don't suppose you'd want to sign this petition." Jack was playing dumb. There was only one reason a Symington would be looking for Sam, and it wasn't good. She'd been identified as a troublemaker. Symington junior wasn't looking to give her a medal.

"I need to talk to her. Please tell me where I can find her."

"I really don't know. She was just a volunteer helping out the cause. I never got her name."

Drew didn't believe him for a minute, but it wasn't going to do any good to quiz Mr. Universe.

"Shit" was all he could say. "Shit, shit, shit."

"I saved your ass," Jack said to Sam when he found her back at her place. "That Symington guy wanted you bad, but I pretended I had no idea who you were."

"You know something?" Sam said wearily. "Right now even I'm not sure who I am."

"What's this? A little melancholia? Battle fatigue, perhaps? Not to despair. We got over two hundred signatures today. I counted. We're doing great. And that Symington jerk is never going to get close to you."

"That's what's depressing me."

"Huh?"

"Nothing. Go on home. I'm fine. Thanks for today. We'll do more. But tomorrow."

"Okay," said Jack, kissing the top of her head as he headed out.

The sun was going down earlier these days, and even though it was already getting dark, Sam didn't bother to turn on the lights. She felt cold and reached into her drawer to pull out a sweater. She felt the softness, and even without looking she knew it was Drew's sweater. She put it on, feeling the warmth, not just of the wool, but of the man.

"Shit," she said aloud. "Shit, shit, shit."

❧ 10 ❧

Somebody ought to write a song about New York in September, thought Melinda, unless someone already had. There was definitely something to sing about. The air was clear and crisp, and the sun shone off buildings that literally gleamed with gold. Men and women alike dressed with style and walked with purpose. There was something uniquely New York about them, and it made Melinda feel like a country bumpkin just to try and dodge them on the street. She followed Forrest on their urban forays through the maze of corporate suites on Park Avenue, delighted to be there and to be with him. She was used to limousines by now. After the first day she could sense from the way Forrest spoke when the meeting was winding down, and she would call their driver on his pager so he would be pulling up to the front of the building exactly when they emerged. Forrest smiled when he realized that she'd caught on to his routine, and though he said nothing, she knew that he had noticed and was pleased.

Wherever they went she was treated well, but not with undue attention. She took notes, read them back when requested, reminded Forrest of appointments, and consulted with other secretaries over her boss's preferences in coffee and lunch. She would have liked to get to know some of the other women, but Forrest took it for granted that she would stay by his side, so she ate her lunch with the executives in their private dining rooms, awkwardly answering their mildly personal questions about where she lived and if she liked New York, until they felt they had been polite enough and returned their focus to one another and the things that really interested them, like leveraged buyouts and market analyses.

Each night, after a luxurious bubble bath, she would wrap herself in the thick terry robe provided by the hotel and order from the room-service menu. Seeing the astronomical prices attached to the simplest fare, she'd decided she'd better stick to the basics and not go overboard, so it was always a sandwich or salad. But it delighted her to see it was always rolled in on white linen, with a silver cover, looking more elegant than the fanciest meal she'd ever had in Oakdale.

After dinner she would sit for half an hour looking out her window, down on Park Avenue, lights twinkling on the trees in the boulevard, and watch the people in their elegant clothes hailing taxis, walking arm in arm, coming and going in the night. Sometimes she would imagine she was watching herself, dressed in a ball gown, a satin cape flowing behind her to protect her from the slight chill in the night air, strolling from some charity event on the arm of a handsome man in a tuxedo, who invariably turned out to be Forrest Symington.

Embarrassed at herself, she would force herself back to reality, put on the sensible pajamas that she brought from home, and prepare a review of the day's events, which she handed to Forrest, neatly typed, over breakfast in his suite the following morning. He had been right when he told her it would be mostly work. But to Melinda they were effortless chores in an enchanted world. She felt like Cinderella after the fairy godmother's visitation, before the return of the glass slipper. She was still a servant, but at least she had been to the ball.

"I won't be needing you anymore," Forrest told Melinda on their fifth day in New York as they were heading back to the conference room of the legal firm of Colton, Fairfax and Whitmore after another executive lunch.

Melinda's heart sank. As far as she knew, she hadn't done anything wrong. Perhaps she'd been so enamored of the city and the job itself that she'd missed some signals. Had she said something indiscreet in the dining room? Forrest saw her stricken face and started to laugh.

"Today. I won't be needing you today. I'm not firing you."

Melinda blushed coral and lowered her lids to hide her relief. She realized she was losing it. Five days in suspended animation, living in a luxury hotel with someone to pick up after you and serve you food and change your sheets, driving around Manhattan in a limousine—well, she thought, it did things to your head. There was no other way she could explain the sudden irrational fear she'd felt at Forrest's words. Except to admit that somehow, in something short of a week, this job and the man she worked for had become the most important things in her life.

"We're hashing out the last details of our export contract. We'll be working through dinner, and then tomorrow it's back home. So you might as well get to see a little of New York before we go. Take the car, if you want. I won't need it."

She started to stammer, "Thank you, but I don't . . . where would I . . ." But he was already gone, and she was on her own.

It was another of those perfect autumn days, crisp and clear. Melinda emerged from the building and breathed in the air in appreciative gulps. She strode to the curb, deftly avoiding a bicycle messenger who was beating the congestion on Park Avenue by detouring over the sidewalk. She laughed, priding herself on her progress in dealing with the niceties of New York traffic. But the moment she hit the corner her confidence left her. Without a meeting to go to, and Forrest to go with, she had to admit to herself she felt lost, unnecessary. Wandering around New York alone seemed pointless, maybe even dangerous. Someone grabbed her arm. She yanked herself away, clutched her purse, and screamed.

"Sorry, sorry, sorry," repeated Dave, the driver, hoping the litany would calm her down.

"Oh, God," Melinda said. "You startled me. I didn't mean to—"

"It's okay," said Dave. "I'm parked around the corner. I was just going to get some coffee when I saw you. I figured you were looking for the car. Something must be wrong with my beeper—I didn't hear it go off."

"Nothing's wrong with your beeper. I didn't call you."

"You don't want the car?"

"No. Well, yes. Uh . . . I don't know."

"Okay, that's clear enough," he kidded.

She shrugged, unable to come up with a better answer.

"Where's the boss?" Dave asked gently, seeing she was getting upset.

"In a meeting. He didn't need me, said I could have the rest of the day off and take the car."

"Why do you make that sound like a death sentence? It's *good* news."

"I guess so."

"Not a very convincing reading. Do you want to try it again? Put a little more enthusiasm into it. Say: It sure is!"

Melinda looked at Dave and smiled, seeing him really for the first time. Sitting in the back with Forrest, studying her notes and concentrating on her duties, she'd never noticed much more than Dave's uniform before. He was maybe in his late twenties, nice-looking but not in a conventionally handsome way. His nose was sharp and his eyes a little small, but his smile was perfect, and his features combined to give him a face with character and warmth.

"Are you an actor, by any chance?" she guessed.

Dave grinned, took his hat off, and ran his fingers through his straight dark hair, tossing his head back for effect as he intoned dramatically, "How did you know?"

154

Melinda laughed, as he had intended.

"It was driving cars or waiting tables, and I tend to drop things. But it's just until I get my big break, of course."

"Of course," Melinda answered with mock seriousness, glad to see that Dave had a sense of humor about himself and his situation.

"So," Dave went on, "what's it going to be? The car or *Hamlet?*"

"Neither one," said Melinda. "I think maybe I'll just stroll back to the hotel."

"What? And waste an afternoon in New York? I know I'm just the driver here, but you've got to be crazy, lady. Isn't there anything you want to do?"

"Lots. I just don't know what exactly. Or how. Or where."

"That, my dear, is why you have a driver."

Dave was as good as his word, and Melinda got the tour of New York to end all tours. Sitting up front beside Dave, Melinda got a running commentary on every sight that every seer ever visited. They did the standards—the Empire State building, the World Trade Center, the South Street Seaport—then drove through neighborhoods like Little Italy and Chinatown, stopping once or twice to sample the ethnic fare. Melinda was charmed, as much by her guide as by the city itself, and by the time the car pulled up in front of the Mayfair they were fast friends.

"This was so great," Melinda said sincerely. "I don't know how to repay you."

"I hate to break it to you, babe, but I'm already being paid. The boss gets billed for my time. You didn't think I was doing this for nothing, did you?"

Melinda knew she was being teased. "Hey, he said I

155

should take the car. I took the car. I think that's legitimate." She faltered. "Don't you?" she asked, a little worried.

"Absolutely. Anyway, don't worry about it. My services have been acquired from 8:30 A.M. to 6:30 P.M. every day. So even if we hadn't gone anywhere, he'd have been paying."

"What time is it now?"

Dave looked at his watch. "Six-thirty-seven."

"You're off duty."

"That's right."

"So I'll let you go. How can I ever thank you?" she reiterated politely.

"Have dinner with me," Dave said without hesitation.

"Oh."

"Good answer: 'Oh.' I like it. It has a nice ring. What does it mean? Yes? No? Love to? Not if you were the last person on earth? Translate 'Oh' for me."

"Oh: I haven't had dinner out once since I got here. I usually just eat in my room and do my notes for Mr. Symington."

"Aha." Dave grinned. "A virgin."

"What does that have to do with—" She broke off, confused as he burst into laughter.

"Eater. I meant you were a virgin as far as New York restaurants were concerned. I wasn't prying into your sex life."

She blushed, and he laughed again. "You know, you're very cute when you do that. I'm not used to this. Most of the women I know have been around the block a few times, as they say. Innocence is kind of refreshing. Go change."

"What?"

156

"If we're having dinner together, which we are, you won't want to wear that."

"What's the matter with it?"

"Nothing. It's just kind of serious dressing. Don't you have something that makes you look a little less stuffy?"

"Thanks a lot."

"I didn't say you weren't pretty."

"Just stuffy."

"That's right. Look, I've got to go give back the car and get out of my chauffeur costume. I'm going to come back in half an hour as the real Dave Bernbaum. Wear whatever you want. It really doesn't matter. Just be prepared to have fun."

There was nothing remotely resembling fun in Melinda's closet at the Mayfair Hotel. She'd come prepared for executive meetings, not dates with struggling actors. She took out the one dinner suit she'd brought—just in case. But even that, with its long black velvet skirt and matching jacket with mandarin collar buttoned up to her neck, made her feel like a matronly aunt at a wedding. She thought about the women she'd seen on the street. Not the ones in the suits, power-walking to work with their high heels in their briefcases. The ones put together with odds and ends, who managed to look funny and fabulous at the same time.

Trying not to think too much about what she was doing, Melinda got the complimentary sewing kit from the bathroom, checked to make sure there was enough black thread, and laid it on the desk. She held the long black skirt in front of her, staring into the mirror, measuring with her eyes. Then, grabbing the knife from the complimentary fruit basket, she ran its serrated edge into the plush fabric and pulled on the small hole she had made. There was a sickening sound of ripping, followed by a moment of panic over what she had done. She pushed it out of her mind as she threaded the needle and basted a makeshift hem around the bottom of the newly mini-ed skirt. She put it on, still not daring to look at her handiwork, then pulled out a long red V-neck cardigan from the dresser drawer. It was meant to be worn over a matching shell, which, paired with a pleated tartan skirt, made for a bright but conservative outfit. Tossing the shell aside, she slipped the cardigan over her head and then turned around, surprising herself in the mirror.

It was hard not to like what she saw. It was even harder not to change it. Melinda wasn't used to seeing herself this way. Dark hair, white skin, red sweater open over a hint of cleavage from her full breasts, short black velvet skirt sticking out no more than two or three inches from under the sweater, barely covering shapely legs that seemed to go on for a very long time. It *was* fun. And sexy. Too sexy, Melinda thought, about to take it off and start all over again.

She looked at her watch. It was seven fifteen. Dave would be waiting for her downstairs already. Even if she wanted to change, she didn't have any alternatives. She looked at herself again and realized she didn't really want to change. She liked the way she looked. It scared her a little, but she liked it. Dressed like this, she felt like she belonged in New York. And she was sure Dave would think so, too. Not giving herself time to change her mind again, she grabbed her coat and purse and hurried out, letting the door slam behind her.

Dave wasn't in the lobby. She looked outside and in

the lounges, but he wasn't there either. She wondered if maybe she was late and she'd missed him, but then she realized that didn't make sense. He would have just waited or called up to her room. She assumed he had gotten stuck in traffic, although she had no idea where he was coming from or how he was getting there. She began to feel uncomfortable sitting alone in the lobby and went outside again, trying to appear casual as she checked up and down the street, hoping to see a familiar face approaching.

"Miss Myles?" The doorman was talking to her. "There's a call for you. If you like, the operator can put it through on the house phone in the lobby."

Dave was very apologetic. When he'd gone to return the limo they'd asked him to do an emergency run to JFK because one of the other drivers had gotten sick. Truth be told, he really needed the money, so he figured that they could just make their dinner a little later. He was going to call on the car phone but then discovered it wasn't working, so he'd had to wait until he got to the airport.

Melinda was relieved. "It's okay," she said. "I'll wait until you get back. I'm not that hungry."

"Actually, it's not that simple. The plane's been delayed, and I could end up being stuck here for hours. I'm sorry, Melinda. I wouldn't have taken it if I had known it was going to turn into such a mish-mash."

"Well, don't worry about it," said Melinda. "Things happen."

"Can we do it tomorrow instead?"

"Sorry. I'm going home tomorrow."

"Shit. I forgot. Now I'm really sorry."

"Never mind, Dave. I had a great day. You really

made my trip to New York, and I'll never forget that. Thanks for everything."

"Listen, let's keep in touch," Dave began, but Melinda had already hung up.

She felt like a fool, all dressed up with nowhere to go. The doorman was holding the door, looking at her expectantly. For some reason Melinda felt obliged to smile and go out, as though this was what she'd planned all along. The night was pleasant, and she walked as though she knew where she was going. For a while she felt as though she really did belong. People looked at her with the same appreciative glance with which she had looked at others before. She felt confident, attractive, and—hungry. There were restaurants on every block, some with menus displayed outside, all inviting. She even ventured into one that seemed especially promising, but she lost her nerve when the hostess approached her.

"I'm waiting for someone, but I see he isn't here yet."

"What's the name? I'll check the reservation," the hostess offered cheerily, trying to be of help.

"Oh, that's okay. I'll just wait outside." Melinda hoped she sounded nonchalant as she backed out.

Suddenly she felt wrong. People were looking at her, but now she wasn't sure it was with approval. She walked faster, longing for the security of her hotel room. She was sorry she'd butchered her skirt. She felt stupid and dispirited and really, really hungry.

It seemed as though the elevator was taking forever, and Melinda pushed the button three or four times, as though that could make it come faster. Flushed from her walk and her frustration, she took off her coat and tapped her foot impatiently. She had been ridiculous, trying to pretend she could be comfortable in a place like New York. She wanted to get up to her room and out of her clothes. She'd order a hamburger and french fries and eat in front of the TV and feel like a normal person again. As the elevator door opened she was thinking she might even order a beer.

"Good evening, Miss Myles. Don't you look . . . different."

She thought she'd die. Forrest Symington was the last person she needed to see right now. She pasted on a smile and mumbled something in return, making room for him to get out of the elevator as she got in. She pushed the button for her floor twice, but the door wouldn't close. It was then she noticed that Forrest was holding it open with one hand and beckoning her out with the other. She wanted to protest, but other people had entered the elevator and were looking at her accusingly. Feeling utterly humiliated, she stepped out. The door closed behind her, cutting off all escape.

"I'm sorry," said Forrest, noticing the misery on her face. "Am I keeping you from something?"

"Not at all," said Melinda, trying to mask the distress in her voice with a cheery overlay that sounded thoroughly false to her ears.

"I just wanted to ask you if you enjoyed your afternoon."

"Very much," she said sincerely, appalled as her stomach added an audible footnote.

"Have you had dinner?" Forrest asked, barely missing a beat and almost hiding his smile.

Melinda blushed and knew she was blushing, which only embarrassed her and made her blush more. "I was just going up to order room service." She put her hand to her cheek, hoping to cool its fire.

Forrest looked at her and was amazed to discover how incredibly touched he was. He'd never noticed how young she was before. She looked worldly enough in her low-cut sweater and perky little skirt, but there was an innocence about her that almost glowed like a halo. He thought that this was probably the first time she'd ever been farther away from Oakdale than Woodland Cliffs, and he was surprised at himself for not realizing it before.

"No room-service dinner tonight, my dear. You're coming with me."

"Oh, of course, if there's work . . ." Melinda pressed her coat into her abdomen, trying surreptitiously to still the growl.

"There's no work, Melinda. We're having dinner. Properly. In a restaurant. Have you had dinner in a restaurant since we've been here?"

Melinda admitted that she hadn't. She was excited again. Then worried. How could she go to a restaurant with Forrest Symington wearing half a sweater set and a chopped-up velvet skirt? Forrest didn't seem to notice. He had taken her arm and was leading her across the lobby. She looked at him from the side and found that he was looking at her full-on, unabashed. If he had a problem with her clothes, he was doing a good job hiding it, because all she could discern in his eyes was a glimmer of delight. Maybe she looked all right after all.

As they neared the door Melinda paused to put on her coat, but Forrest took it from her hand. She expected him to help her on with it, but instead he folded it over his arm and informed her she wouldn't be needing it. They were eating in the hotel restaurant.

Melinda was disappointed. She was anticipating seeing something other than the inside of the Mayfair, no matter how elegant. But the minute they entered through the lobby she understood that Le Cirque was someplace special, hallowed ground for connoisseurs of the good life. Muted golden light bathed the murals on the walls and spilled onto the people seated on banquettes below. There was a hum in the room, not loud, but lively, and Melinda knew for certain that amusing anecdotes were being exchanged and appreciated. Everyone looked stylish and beautiful and faintly recognizable.

Forrest introduced her to someone named Sirio, and it took Melinda a moment to realize that she had just met the owner of this elegant place. He kissed her hand, told her she was beautiful, and led them to a small table near the bar under the watchful eye of a ceramic monkey. Melinda noticed that the motif of the murals was monkeys in period dress, and there was monkey statuary in every available niche. It made the room seem elegant and cozy at the same time, and Melinda was enchanted by the whole effect.

Forrest ordered and then had to explain as Melinda tasted and exclaimed. Sea scallops she recognized, but Forrest had to tell her about the little black specks that dotted them like dirt, regaling her with the history of truffles and how they were found by special pigs, nosing them out in the forests of France. She wasn't too excited to learn how goose liver was made into fois gras, but when she tasted it prepared with Concord grapes and cranberries she thought her taste buds would expire from ecstasy. A simple fish was transformed into ambrosia with a diaphanous blanket of potatoes roasted to a crackling golden brown. They drank a different wine with each course—sometimes red, sometimes white—with no relation to any beverage she had ever imbibed before. When she refused dessert because she was too full an assortment of tiny cookies arrived, and when she wished she could take just one bite out of each one Forrest insisted she do just that. They ended the meal with a 1986 Château d'Yquem, and just when Melinda was certain nothing more could impress her she tasted the honey-golden sauterne and looked at Forrest with wide eyes, saying solemnly, "It's like drinking liquid heaven."

He laughed then and leaned over the table and kissed her on the cheek from the sheer pleasure of sharing her joy. Melinda felt herself floating, then forced herself earthward. Forrest was being kind, and thrill was an inappropriate response.

"This has been the most wonderful meal I've ever had and probably ever will have," Melinda said honestly, and then she added simply, "Thank you."

"Thank *you,*" Forrest replied in return.

"What for?"

"For reminding me what it was like when every experience was an adventure and every adventure was a delight."

I am falling in love with my boss, thought Melinda as Forrest walked her to her room.

"This is it" was all she said as she stopped in front of her door.

Forrest took the key from her hand and opened the door. For a moment her heart raced as she thought he had read her mind and was going to sweep her into his arms and over the threshold. But even though Forrest might have been able to divine her thoughts simply by looking at her adoring eyes, he knew better than to press his advantage. He had the reputation of being a man who knew how to get what he wanted. But even more importantly, he prided himself on knowing when the time was right to get it.

"Don't forget to lock your door," he said, trying to sound avuncular as he handed her back her key and gently closed the door behind himself. He moved down the hall to his own suite, knowing sleep would come easily tonight. He always slept well when there was something to look forward to.

Sam missed Melinda. It had been a tough week, and she was feeling particularly isolated. Harvey was adamantly opposed to Sam's campaign to prevent DMC from building a new plant at the mill pond, and Diane supported his point of view, if only to keep the peace, so going to her parents for comfort was out of the question. She needed a shoulder to cry on, and she knew that no matter how Melinda felt about what Sam was doing, she'd still be sympathetic to how she was feeling. It was the one thing the sisters could always count on—their one rule, never yet broken, to support each other no matter what.

Sam still went to work every day, thanks to Melinda's intervention, but she wasn't exactly Miss Popularity. People she had once considered friends were no longer speaking to her—and those were just the good guys. Snide remarks and poison pen letters slipped into her time-card slot had become de rigueur.

Harvey spent his whole time on the line beside his eldest daughter trying to convince her to stop being a tree-hugger and abandon what he considered her not only foolish but positively damaging cause.

On the surface, knowing she could not afford to alienate any more people, Sam listened politely, offering her own articulate arguments for saving the mill pond in response to their ugly epithets. Inside she seethed with anger at their shortsightedness and feared for what was to become of her and her community if DMC did not propose an alternate plan.

Sam tried to explain her point of view to Pete, wanting him to share her special feeling for the mill pond and her concern for what an automobile factory there would do to the environment. She even convinced him to go with her to the mill pond and experience for himself what a special place it was. She knew part of her purpose was to try and transform the mill pond into *their* place and exorcise the ghost of Drew Symington.

Pete tried. "You're right. It sure is pretty," he said, walking around the fields with Sam.

Sam could see he wanted to set things right with her, that he was on his best behavior.

"Come here and kiss me," she said, longing for that simpler time, not so long ago, when they had taken each other's love for granted. Certainly her expectations had been lower then, but at least her emotions weren't on a constant roller-coaster ride from hell.

She could feel his passion rising, but it only served to remind her of the last time she had been there, sharing a passionate embrace with someone she really wanted and couldn't have, instead of someone she could have but didn't really want. She pulled away gently, not wanting to hurt him, and tried to turn his attention back to the land. But without the incentive of Sam's tender body, Pete was no longer interested in nature's handiwork.

"It's okay here, baby. But let's face it. It's just a field. There's lots of others just as good."

"That's not the point, Pete." She knew she sounded testy and he would resent it, but she couldn't help it.

"No. The point is the D'Uberville Motor Company knows what they're doing, and you should just butt out," he barked, walking away.

Knowing she'd brought it on herself, but nonetheless feeling abandoned and alone, Sam sat on the ground and began to cry. Pete came back, unable, as usual, to withstand her tears. Sam was so strong that when she did cry, he knew that things had to be really hard for her. He wasn't a mean person, and he did love her, so he returned to comfort her.

Sam took the proffered shoulder, gratefully resting her head against him. He had been there for her so many times in the years since high school, she couldn't quite believe that he wasn't going to be there for her through this. But both of them knew that the issues between them had not been resolved, and the sense of solace was just a temporary reprieve from the building conflict.

Sam had her supporters. There were citizens in Oakdale who could see beyond the immediate and understood that any gains brought by a new DMC plant would be offset by a deterioration in their quality of life that could end up harming their children and destroying their community. Even in the midst of a recession there were people who understood that the economy could recover, but the earth could not. Sam's argument that if the pollution from the new plant affected the Woodland Cliffs property values, the D'Uberville Motor Company would find an alternative site in no time at all, hit home to a lot of Oakdale residents. It was an "us against them" issue, and to Sam, though she wouldn't admit it, even to herself, it was also "me against him."

Jean-Claude Renoir let himself into Bethany Havenhurst's penthouse. He'd learned early on that Bethany was almost never home. After their first wild encounter he'd called her incessantly and developed a more intimate relationship with her answering machine than with the lady herself. At first he'd panicked, fearing he would have to abandon his chosen avenue of revenge. Then he surprised himself by realizing he wanted to see her again as much for herself as for his plan. He'd had his share of sexual escapades, and many of them had been outstanding. But there was something about the way Bethany made love, a quality of ferocity rather than abandon, that led him to believe she'd be a genuine match for his own pressing desires. Jean-Claude could be, and had been, a gentle lover. With Lisette, even at their most passionate moments, there had never been any roughness. But something had broken in him when she died, a delicate thread that seemed to unleash a cage full of savage longings. Now his most urgent need came in the extremes beyond tenderness, sometimes in domination, sometimes in being dominated, always in the unexplored. He'd recognized a kindred spirit in

Bethany, and it excited him beyond anything he'd known since his dreams of domestic bliss had been crushed under the wheels of a speeding car. There was danger with Bethany, and it intoxicated him. And in intoxication there was forgetfulness.

She'd given him a key after their first few times together, because it became apparent that they were going to continue their illicit meetings there, and that she was always going to be late. At the beginning he waited patiently in the lobby or hung out by the curb, smoking a Gauloise. The doormen said nothing, but as discreet as they were, Bethany knew she couldn't afford to raise suspicions by having a handsome Frenchman lurking outside her door at all hours. Finally she'd explained he was a visiting relative and had given him a key, which he promised never to use unless he was invited. It made her a little nervous at first, but soon she rather grew to like it. After all, there was less than zero risk that Drew would appear unannounced, or even at all, for that matter, since lately he seemed more intent on getting away from her than dropping in unexpectedly. And, especially with Drew's growing disinterest, it was reassuring to come home and find Jean-Claude waiting for her, usually naked, prepared with some new sexual scenario with which they could experiment. Drew had never really taken to the darker side of her libido, and she'd had to suppress it for fear he might come to consider her less than marriage material. But with Jean-Claude, not only did anything go, but everything was expected, and in a symbiosis of need and desire they'd come to rely on each other for satisfaction.

In the shower Jean-Claude thought about what they

would do and felt himself getting hard. He hoped
Bethany wouldn't make him wait too long today,
because he didn't want to have to start without her.
He thrust his body forward and felt the streams of
water tapping a rhythmic tattoo on his already-
growing member. With a sigh he turned off the water
and stepped out of the stall. No point in wasting it;
since Bethany had specified thirty minutes, it was
doubtful she'd be there in less than an hour. He
reached for a towel and was irritated to find that the
maid had once again furnished the bathroom with
dainty little guest towels trimmed in lace but had
forgotten to lay out a bath sheet. Heedless of the large,
wet footprints left in his wake on the marble floors, he
made his way across the corridor to the linen closet.
But marble is slippery when wet, and as he reached for
a towel he found himself sliding in his own puddle.
Reaching out automatically for something to steady
himself, he lost his balance and threw his entire
weight on a shelf in the linen closet. Both he and the
shelf came crashing to the floor in a flurry of towels
that helped somewhat in cushioning his fall but did
nothing to mitigate his injured pride. He sat up,
cursing a blue streak of gutter French, noting that
while his buttocks were bruised, his cock was shrunk-
en but intact. He heaved himself up from the floor,
angrily kicking the towels aside, having no intention
of picking up after his little accident. Then he saw it. A
worn manila envelope as familiar to him as his face in
the mirror. He reached down and picked it up,
opening it, though he didn't have to, to confirm that it
was his, and that it contained the tattered articles that
constituted a blueprint of his life.

Absently he wrapped a towel around his waist and

went to pour himself a drink, still too stunned to think. He hadn't even missed the envelope. Ensconced as he was at Belvedere, he hadn't dared, or bothered, or needed to check the secret compartment of his suitcase. There was no point in trying to figure out how and when Bethany had acquired his clippings; it was irrelevant. What mattered now was discerning what it meant and how it would change his game plan.

Firstly, he would have to acknowledge that Bethany was not stupid. If she had read the articles, which she undoubtedly had, she had to know his purpose in courting her. Still, she called him, came to him, slept with him. Why? Lost in contemplation, he didn't hear her key in the lock.

"Oh, good, you're here. And you're naked. Or not quite. I can fix that."

She was already pulling off her clothes and reaching for his towel when she saw the envelope on the sofa beside him. She stopped dead still, on her knees in front of him, the strap of her slip coming off her shoulder, revealing one rounded, heaving breast.

"Oh" was all she said.

"I had a little accident," Jean-Claude said by way of explanation. "I'm afraid your shelf is broken."

"It doesn't matter. The concierge will have it fixed." She felt foolish. Why were they talking about a broken shelf when there were pieces of their lives to put back together? She tried to think fast, choose her tactic, offense or defense. But Jean-Claude had had more preparation time. He wrapped his fist around her hair and harshly pulled her face to within inches of his own.

"What game are you playing, *ma chérie?* I don't like to play unless I know the rules."

She remembered someone once saying that the best defense is an offense.

"How dare you threaten me! You waltz into town pretending to be a relative of the D'Ubervilles, get everyone to trust you, including me, when all the time you've got this deep dark secret you're hiding. You're the one who's playing games, not me. You're using me. You're using all of us. Because you've obviously got some horrid plan to hurt us. How would you like it if I told Mathilde D'Uberville exactly who her charming cousin is?"

He pulled her hair a little tighter. "And how would you like it if I told Drew Symington exactly who, or should I say what, his charming fiancée is?"

Bethany took a breath. She could see this approach was not going to work for her. She was afraid now, not so much of what Jean-Claude might do, but of what he might say.

"You're hurting me," she said in a low voice. She jerked her shoulders, trying to pull away, and her other strap slid off her shoulder. The slip slithered to the floor, exposing both breasts now and revealing the fact that she wore no other underwear. Jean-Claude's eyes lowered, taking in her white skin, stopping on her heaving breasts, moving down to the triangle of silky hair between her legs. And in that moment she knew she had her strategy.

Bethany stopped struggling. Instead of pulling away she moved closer. It was a calculated maneuver, but that only made it more exciting, and her nipples hardened as they brushed against Jean-Claude's chest.

One hand deftly unwound the towel while the other grasped his cock, already tumescent with anticipation. He released his grip on her hair. She let her head fall into his lap and took him into her mouth, sucking, her lips closed around him while her tongue, inside, outlined the contours of his shaft.

For a moment Jean-Claude lost all capacity for conscious thought. His brain was in a state of bliss, all sensation centered on the one spot where Bethany's heavenly mouth had come to rest. He forced himself to think, if only to prolong the rapture. Bethany knew he was a fraud, that he had unpleasant designs on her fiancé's family, but here she was, on her knees, between his legs. Why? Unless . . . He hesitated, afraid to complete his thought. Because if it was true of Bethany, it was true of himself. Unless she didn't care. Unless it no longer mattered why they had come together, only that they continued to do so, in more ways than one. It wasn't being at Belvedere that had made him forgo his nightly readings of the accounts of Lisette's death. It was having sex with Bethany. Frenchman that he was, he had to admit that when the choice came down to vengeance or ecstasy, as far as he was concerned, there was no contest. Still, she had deceived him, sneaked into his room, stolen his personal belongings. Something would have to be done. Roughly he pulled her head off his swollen cock and brought her face to his.

"You know, it was very bad of you to take my things. I think you must be punished."

Bethany's breath quickened. "Yes," she whispered hoarsely. "What are you going to do?"

In answer, he pulled her off the floor and turned her

over his knee. Her buttocks, white and quivering, lay in his lap. He struck her once, then again, leaving patches of red where his palm touched her flesh. She moaned, feeling the heat from his hand go through her skin and into her very core. He hit her harder, hurting and exciting her until she couldn't separate one sensation from the other and only knew she wanted him to fuck her more than she had ever wanted anything in her life. He did then, on the floor, from behind, driving into her until they were both screaming and then crying and, in the end, laughing from the sheer euphoria of climaxing and finally being released from the tension of their shared sexual frenzy.

Later they talked. Bethany listened with tears in her eyes as Jean-Claude told her about Lisette. They had known each other since they were children and had always planned to marry. It was Lisette who had insisted that they wait until Jean-Claude finished law school. He regretted it now, feeling that somehow, if they had married earlier, she might not have been on the road that day, coming from the seamstress with her wedding gown, when Drew plowed into her. He hadn't even stopped. Jean-Claude, coming to pick her up, had found her himself, the white gown, covered with dirt and blood, wrapped in her arms, as though she had been trying to protect it. Drew had turned himself in to the gendarmerie the following day, but it was too late. Lisette was dead, and Jean-Claude had already sworn revenge on the person who killed her.

"I was part of your revenge?" Bethany asked softly, knowing the answer.

"At the beginning, yes," stated Jean-Claude, taking her hand to soften his words. "I read somewhere about your engagement, and I thought if I could take away the woman he loved and leave him as miserable as he left me, it might ease the pain."

"And now?"

"Now I want you for myself. I don't give a damn about him. Can you understand that?"

"Yes. I feel the same way. At first you were just a flirtation. But then it became something more. Drew couldn't do what you do to me. I thought about you all the time. I needed you. Then I went to your room one day, looking for you when no one else was home, and I found—"

"How? What were you looking for?"

"I don't know. Something to make me understand why I was falling so hard for you, why you had become so important to me." She gave a bitter laugh. "I didn't expect the answer to be that you planned it that way and I was such a patsy."

"What is this 'a patsy'?"

"A sucker. A dupe. A fool."

He took her in his arms. "Don't say such things. It isn't true. Maybe before we started it's what I thought. But from the first time we made love . . . *mon Dieu* . . ."

"I know. When I saw those articles and thought you were using me, I felt humiliated. I was going to stop seeing you. But I couldn't. Nobody does to me what you do, Jean-Claude." Her voice lowered to a hoarse whisper. "And I don't think I can live without it."

She turned away, as though embarrassed by her confession, crossing her hands over her breasts demurely, as if covering her nakedness could hide her emotions. He pulled her to him roughly, holding her hands behind her back, kissing her face, her breasts. She lowered her head and bit his neck. He was getting hard again. This was not the tender devotion he had felt for Lisette. It was an animal passion, compelling and consuming. And at the moment it felt like love to him.

"Come with me to France," he said. "Let's forget all this bullshit, and just come with me."

"I want that more than anything," she said, grinding her body into his. "But we have to be smart about this. The Symingtons are powerful people. They've already hurt you once. I won't let them do it again."

"If I have you, nothing can hurt me."

Bethany had to think fast. There was no way she would give up the perfect life she'd planned and run off to some mangy little cottage in France. She needed to buy time. "You don't know Drew. He can be vicious—and violent. You've seen that. He would follow us, find us, no matter where we went. We can't just run away from him."

"Yes, we can. Nothing will happen. I won't let it."

"You might not be able to stop it. Please, Jean-Claude, let's not do anything yet. Let me figure it out. I know these people. You don't. I promise you, when the time is right, I will go with you, and you will have your revenge, and we'll be safe and together forever."

By the time Jean-Claude left Bethany's penthouse it was dawn. She slept a few hours, then showered. When the hour seemed decent enough she called her future mother-in-law.

"Dear Mathilde," she cooed. "I need your help."

"What is it, Bethany?" Mathilde was genuinely concerned. She knew her husband wasn't too fond of the girl, but there was no denying she was a lovely match.

"I think your son is getting cold feet. Has he said anything to you?"

"Engagements are always difficult for men. But I'm sure everything is all right."

"You're probably right. Still, I wish we could do something to make this easier on him."

"Do you have any ideas?"

"Well, I thought maybe you could throw a little party before the wedding. Just to show support. It could be sort of a prenuptial wedding, so he won't be so afraid of the real thing."

"I would love to do that. A party is always nice."

Bethany took a breath. So far so good. "Then I was thinking, to kind of confirm our position as a couple, I could come stay at Belvedere."

"You want to live with Drew?"

"Is that so terrible? I mean, I love him so much, and June is such a long way off. He's a man, with a man's needs. I don't want to lose him before that."

Mathilde was getting the picture. "I see. You think, perhaps, he might have other interests, shall we say?"

"He's a man."

"Yes." Mathilde understood. Like his father.

"I mean, once we're married I can get around these things. But I would just hate for something to come between us now, when we're so close. That's why I think we should do it soon. Let's not give opportunity a chance to knock with something regrettable."

"Of course, my dear." Mathilde wanted this union. Bethany was one of them. She would understand how to conduct an acceptable marriage. "We will work something out. Nothing will prevent this marriage."

No, thought Bethany, hanging up the phone. *Nothing* will prevent this marriage.

~11~

The doorbell was ringing. Sam groped for her watch to see the time, but she couldn't find it. She had been up with Jack all night, stuffing envelopes with information they'd printed up, and had stumbled into bed at five in the morning to get a couple of hours of sleep before going on the afternoon shift. She felt as if she'd just fallen asleep. The doorbell was still ringing. She forced herself out of bed, and without even bothering to put on a robe, she staggered over to the door and pulled it open with a gruff sound that was more groan than greeting.

"I'm sorry, I should have called first."

Sam couldn't believe her eyes. She wanted to laugh and cry at the same time, hug him and push him out. But all she said was, "How did you find me?"

Drew brushed a stray curl away from her eyes. His touch made her skin blaze. "Did you think I would just let you go?"

179

Sam's words came out in a rush. She needed to explain before he disappeared. "That's why I did what I did. I didn't want to hurt you. I felt so awful. I love you."

"I know that. I love you, too. That's why I'm here."

He folded her in his arms and began to kiss her. She felt warm, almost smothered. Why was the doorbell still ringing?

"Oh, God, I'm dreaming. I'm not awake at all," she told herself in her sleep. Drew disappeared. The ringing wouldn't stop. Slowly she roused herself and removed the pillow from on top of her head. She no longer felt warm and smothered. The clock on her night table said 5:52. She *had* just fallen asleep. She reached for the phone, and the ringing stopped.

"What?" was all she could manage.

"We've got trouble." Jack's voice was serious.

She was instantly wide awake. "What happened?"

"I drove by the mill pond on my way home. They're starting."

"What?!"

"There are trucks and bulldozers gathering in the field. They're going to excavate."

"Shit. He's such a bastard."

"Who? Forrest Symington?"

"Yeah, and his lily-livered son. We've got to stop them."

"Agreed. How?"

"That's just what I was going to say."

"A court injunction is going to take time, and those guys looked like they were going to work as soon as the coffee wagon left. The mill pond is going to be history by nightfall."

"Over my dead body," said Sam, sounding like she meant it.

"No self-immolation for the cause, babe," said Jack.

"But it's not a bad idea," Sam went on thoughtfully.

"Suicide? It stinks."

"Don't be so literal. I'm talking bodies. Lots of them. Lying in the field. They're not going to run us over. Bad for publicity, and sales on the new D'Ubervilles have been slow enough."

"So what? They'll call in the police. You can't doubt that. And then they'll just have us removed bodily and get on with it."

"Maybe. But if there were a lot of us to remove, and I mean a *lot*, it could take all day. Long enough to get a lawyer to go to court and get an injunction."

"I'm beginning to see the picture."

"Are you home?"

"Yeah."

"Okay. Get on the horn and call every single person on every single list we have. I'm going over to the mill pond. Send over whoever will come, and I'll get them organized."

"You could get into trouble big time for this. You know that, don't you?"

"I can't just give up. Can you?"

"And have you make me look like a wimp? Guess not."

"Okay. So go make your calls. And get a lawyer."

"Uh . . . I am a lawyer."

"What?"

"I just never mentioned it before. It didn't seem relevant."

181

"Why the hell are you working in an auto factory?"

"Rebelling. My father wanted me in his firm. I didn't want to go. They made me go to school. But they couldn't make me show up for work."

"You're a weird guy, you know that?"

"Look who's talking. The girl who can't figure out if she should be Joan of Arc or John DeLorean."

"We make a good team." Sam smiled.

"Yeah. Go to the mill pond. I've got calls to make."

"Okay. Look for me under the wheels of the third bulldozer from the right."

Pete heard about it when George, the day manager, called to say he wasn't going to be able to show up at work. They'd been opening Bamboo Bernie's early for a couple of weeks, tapping into the beer-and-bacon-for-breakfast crowd. Pete still handled the afternoon and evening, reserving mornings for work on his car. Things had gotten a lot harder since Sam had stopped being his mechanic. He was even considering apologizing again and promising he would drive the way she said, just to get her to come back. He figured if he did that, and she had something she really cared about to work on, like his D'Uberville classic, she'd forget about her stupid campaign against DMC. It made no sense to him. You can't stop progress, he thought. Why would you even want to? But he knew Sam. She was really mad at him this time, and he couldn't blame her. He'd pretty much ruined her car. He was even thinking about going and talking to her that day when George called.

"Hey, Pete, will you take the morning for me?"

"Jeez, George. I had a couple of things I had to do today. Is it an emergency?"

"Sort of."

"Something happen at home?"

"Not exactly. But my wife wants us to go over to the mill pond. She says we owe it to our kids to support the protest."

"What protest?"

"Oh. I figured you'd know. Aren't you and Sam—"

Pete cut him off. "Never mind about me and Sam. What the hell's going on?"

"They're getting a whole bunch of people to go lie down on the ground at the mill pond to keep the bulldozers from working."

"Who's they?"

"Well, you know, Sam and that guy with the ponytail who's been helping her. And I guess my wife, too, because they've got her making calls now."

"Sorry, George. Can't do it," said Pete, putting on his coat while he was still talking on the phone. "Maybe you can get one of the other guys to open Bamboo Bernie's, but I can't do it."

He hung up before George could say anything and was out the door and in his car seconds later.

Pete found Sam standing in the middle of the mill pond, shouting through a bullhorn. All around her people were lying on the ground, some reading, some chatting, some just looking at the sky. The truckers were leaning against their cabs, the operators sitting in their machines. No one was moving.

"If you attempt to destroy one blade of grass in this beautiful place, you will have to drown it in our blood," Sam's voice echoed.

A chorus of "You said it," "Hear, hear," "That's right" came from around her feet.

"We will not be moved!" shouted Sam.

Someone started singing, and then the others joined

in, Sam's voice loud and distorted on the bullhorn. "We will not be, we will not be moved. We will not be, we will not be moved. Like a tree standing by the wa-a-ter, we will not be moved."

Sam saw him watching her, and relief flooded her. She knew Pete would stand by her in the end. They'd been together so long, they'd somehow lost their bearings, but in the end it was Pete she could count on, and she should have realized that. The singing continued without her as she put down the bullhorn and went over to him.

"You came. Thank you," she whispered fervently, and she kissed him on the mouth.

She was always surprising him. Here he'd expected a fight, and instead she was in his arms. He kissed her back, telling himself he should have known there was nothing to worry about. Not a lot of women turned their back on Pete Wojek.

"I missed you," he told her when they broke for air.

"Me, too," she said. "Let's not fight so much from now on. It makes me forget how much we love each other."

"Okay by me." This time he kissed her. "Come on, sweetheart, let's go."

Sam was confused. "Where to?"

"Home, where else? I want to be alone with you. It's been a long time."

Sam held her irritation in check. He was just acting out of instinct, and wanting her wasn't a bad instinct to have.

"Honey, I can't go now," she said as gently as she could. "We're in the middle of a demonstration."

He looked around at the people lying on the ground, singing, "Like a tree standing by the wa-a-ter . . ."

"Looks like this bunch of hippies is going to keep their love-in going whether you're here or not. Let's go have a love-in of our own."

"You don't understand, Pete. I organized this thing. Me and Jack. I owe it to them to be here when the police come."

"Police? Are you crazy?"

"No. It's all been worked out. We're going to let them arrest us, and then Jack is going to court—"

Pete didn't get beyond the words "arrest us."

"You've really gone and done it this time, Sam. You're going to lose your goddam job!"

Why did he come if he wasn't going to support them, Sam wondered. "It's better than losing my civil rights," she said, just as angry.

Pete had had it. He figured he should have put his foot down a long time ago. He'd let Sam get away with too much, and now she thought she could just do whatever she wanted and he'd go along with it. She wasn't even thinking about what it would do to him—to them, he amended—if she lost her job. His father had been right when he said a woman needs to be put in her place once in a while.

"That's it," said Pete, feeling forceful. "We're going."

"You go. I'm not moving."

"You are if I say you are." And with that he picked her up by the elbows, lifting her off the ground and hugging her close to his body, and started to drag her to his car. All around them the singing was getting louder. Nobody heard Sam scream at Pete to let her go.

"Leaving so soon?" asked Jack, blocking their path. He hadn't bothered to tie back his shoulder-length hair, and the wind was blowing it like a halo around his face.

"Well, if it isn't Goldilocks," Pete said, smirking. His grip relaxed, and Sam yanked herself out of his arms and out of his reach.

"Boy, am I glad to see you," said Sam, stepping beside Jack.

"What's going on?" asked Jack, never taking his eyes off Pete.

"None of your business," answered Pete.

"Forget it," said Sam. The belligerence between the two men hung in the air like a dark cloud. "Pete's leaving, and we're going back to demonstrate."

"I don't think so," said Pete. "I am leaving, and you're coming with me."

"Don't tell me what to do."

"You heard the lady," said Jack.

"This doesn't have anything to do with you, so butt out."

"Yes, it does. Sam and I are partners."

"Partners? Is that what this is about? Are you doing this because you're fucking this faggot?"

Jack made a move toward Pete, but Sam was too fast for him. It was just one punch, delivered in the region of Pete's abdomen, but—fueled by her red-hot anger and propelled by her outraged righteousness—it was enough to make him double over, gasping for breath.

"Don't call people names, Pete, especially when it shows what a bigoted asshole you are," she said in an even voice as she turned and walked away. Jack followed, choking with laughter.

When he'd caught his breath Pete looked back. Sam was lying on the ground, her head inches away from the sharklike teeth of the largest bulldozer. She was smiling.

"I'll get you for this, you bitch," Pete said aloud, kicking at the ground under his feet. As he got into his car and took off they were singing, "We Shall Overcome."

In the Mayfair Hotel Melinda was into her second chorus of "New York, New York" when there was a discreet knock at the door of her room. Her first instinct was to run, certain they were coming to tell her she was disturbing the peace. She should have known better, she thought. You don't sing at the top of your lungs in a classy hotel in New York City. But she was still in her nightgown, and there was no back door to sneak out of. She got back under the covers and tried to sound refined—maybe they would think the noise was coming from some other room—as she called out, "Who is it?"

"Room service."

"I . . . I didn't order anything."

"I have breakfast for room 1420."

Melinda gave the key on her bedside a quick glance, just to be sure. It did say 1420. Well, what the hell, she thought. Maybe it was complimentary coffee on her last morning in the hotel.

"You can bring it in," she sang out.

She patted the blankets down beside her and tried to look demure and sophisticated at the same time. But as the waiter rolled in a cart loaded with silver and crystal, a bottle of champagne cooling in an ice bucket, and strawberries the size of plums, she got so excited she jumped out of bed and ran over to inspect.

"Wow, this looks fabulous. But I'm sorry to say I really didn't order it."

"I did."

She whirled around to see Forrest Symington standing in the door, bearing a beautifully wrapped box and a broad grin. As usual, he was dressed in one of his Savile Row bespoke suits, but his shirt was open at the neck, with his tie undone, and his hair was still wet. This is what he looks like when he's just gotten out of the shower, Melinda thought. She wanted to reach up and wipe away the droplet of water that was hovering over his forehead. She stopped the thought in its tracks, going back to safer ground.

"I don't get it," she said, and she meant it.

He laughed at her honesty. "It's the last day of your first trip to New York. I wanted to make it memorable."

She watched him slip the waiter a bill and send him out. From the waiter's smile and profuse thanks as he backed out of the room, she assumed a generous tip was included. She flashed on an image of her father counting out ten percent on a restaurant check as the rest of them hurried out to avoid the inevitable snarls that followed. She knew it was unreasonable to compare them, but Forrest Symington had such style and did everything with such grace, how could she fail to be impressed?

"I could never forget this trip," she said simply, "even without breakfast. It's the most wonderful time I ever had in my life."

Something in Forrest's heart moved. She was so clear, so open, so different from the women he knew with their social games and petty subterfuge. He felt something surge in his body and was surprised a moment later when he realized it was joy. Just being with her was making him happy. Melinda felt his eyes warming her body, and she suddenly remembered that she wasn't dressed. Her pajamas weren't exactly Frederick's of Hollywood, but she was conscious that her breasts were faintly visible through the thin material.

"I'd better go get dressed," she said quietly.

"No, don't. Open this." He handed her the box. "A token of my appreciation. For managing to do your job and make this trip a lot more fun than the cold-blooded Katy."

"You call her Katy?" Melinda asked, shocked.

"Not if she can hear me," he said with mock fear. And they both started to laugh. He was still holding the box. "Go on, take it."

Melinda couldn't get over it. Even something as simple as a box looked special in this world. It was tied with silver lace and had a sprig of violets caught in its bow.

"Aren't you going to open it?"

"Oh, yes. It's just that it looks so pretty."

"I hope you like what's inside as much."

He needn't have worried. Melinda gasped as the tissue paper fell away, knowing without any experience at all that she was the recipient of an extraordinary gift. It was a pale yellow robe of the finest silk, woven with subtle shades of purple, from palest lilac to deep magenta. It looked to be of a different era, and indeed it was, having survived intact from the turn of the century.

"I hope you don't mind wearing something that's

been worn before. I'm told it used to belong to Sarah Bernhardt. Of course, there's no way of verifying that."

"It doesn't matter. Whoever it belonged to was obviously someone very special. And now I feel that way, too."

"You should. You are."

He helped her put it on, and she tried not to be aware of the warmth of his hands through the delicate fabric. "I was only doing my job. You didn't need to give me such a gorgeous present for doing what I'm already paid to do," she said, feeling compelled to dispel any illusions.

"I didn't. I gave it to you for being yourself. And not trying to pretend."

"I don't think I could pretend with you," she said, and he believed her.

Melinda looked at herself in the mirror and saw what Forrest saw. She was transformed. The pale gold of the robe, her fair skin, her dark hair spilling over her shoulders, her cheeks faintly pink with the flush of excitement. Her lips looked full and aching to be kissed. She turned to Forrest, hoping for confirmation, then chided herself for being so silly as he beckoned her over to the table, where he was already pouring out champagne.

He toasted her, and she marveled at his kindness but didn't know how to respond.

"Aren't you hungry?" he asked, but there was something in his voice that had not been there before.

"No," she whispered.

"It doesn't matter," he said. "This is not sustenance for the body, it's ambrosia for the soul." And with that he picked up a perfect hothouse strawberry, dipped it into the champagne, and brought it to her mouth. She bit into it while he held it, and the juice burst onto her lips, where he caught it with his fingertips.

"Mmmm. This is yummy," she declared with enthusiasm, then blushed as she realized her exclamation might have been inappropriate for the mood at that moment. But Forrest just laughed.

"Everything is exciting to you, isn't it?"

"When I'm with you, it is."

Again he felt the stirring. She touched him the way no one had in a long time, the way he had forgotten he could feel. He took her hand; it was warm and soft, like a fragile bird in the nest of his palm.

"It's hard to believe, but it's that way for me, too. Dinner at Le Cirque with you was an adventure. Eating strawberries for breakfast is a thrill. It's been years since I felt that way, if I ever did."

"It's all so new to me. I guess I must seem kind of dumb."

"Never. You're smart and innocent, and the combination is absolutely refreshing. More than that, it's intoxicating. I want to be the one to introduce you to newer and more wonderful things." She was overwhelmed, silent. He went on. "I'm not asking anything from you, Melinda. I have no right to. You know my situation. I would expect nothing in return. I just want to be around you, show you things, teach you things. It would give me the greatest pleasure if you could stand to spend some time with a man who is far too old to be considered anything but a mentor."

"I'm not exactly sure what a mentor does, but I don't think it's what I want you to be."

"What is it you want?"

In answer she leaned across the table and kissed

him. She had no idea where she got the courage. She just knew that he was too much of a gentleman to make the first move, and she simply couldn't imagine leaving this room without being kissed by Forrest Symington. For a fleeting moment Forrest thought to himself that he should put a stop to this. He was her boss, more than twice her age, a married man. She deserved better. But as her lips pressed his he also thought there was no one who could give her the things he could, no one else who would educate her and turn her dreary proletarian life into something majestic and beautiful. By that time she had come around to his side of the table and was sitting on his lap, her arms entwined around his neck, her body pressing into his. It's out of my control, he thought. She's started it, and I can't be held responsible. Never removing his mouth from hers, he tightened his arms around her, lifted her up, and carried her the few steps to the bed.

Melinda saw her beautiful new robe fall to the floor. For a moment she thought of picking it up and folding it gently over a chair, but Forrest was beside her, his hands slipping her pajama top off her shoulders, releasing her breasts, which he graced with tiny kisses, one after the other. This was not like the blind groping in the backseats of cars that she'd been resisting ever since high school. She felt treasured, like a cherished work of art. She wanted him to go on, to do more. Then the phone rang.

"Should we just let it ring?" she asked hopefully.

Forrest frowned, clearly as reluctant as she was to give up his current activity. But he'd already forewarned the desk not to put calls through unless they were specified urgent. He looked at Melinda, saw the desire in her eyes that matched his own. She'd wait.

"Why don't you just see what it is?"

She picked up the phone with a languid "Hello?" and then sat bolt upright, covering her breasts and automatically going into her secretarial mode, praying there was no trace of embarrassment or disappointment in her voice. "Yes, he is. May I tell him who is calling, please? . . . I see. . . . And what is the call in reference to? . . . One moment, please." Forrest smiled as he watched her work. This girl was going to do just fine. She'd understand the line no matter what the circumstances.

She held out the phone to Forrest. "It's Stan Harkin from the plant in Oakdale. He says there's an emergency situation that he needs to talk to you about."

Forrest took the phone, and Melinda got off the bed. She gently picked her robe up off the floor and put it on, feeling the dichotomy of who she was and what she was doing. Forrest was listening intently, not even watching her, and she went into the bathroom, partly out of discretion and partly because she needed a moment alone. Things were happening so quickly, she really wasn't sure what she was doing. Maybe if she splashed some cold water on her face, she'd be able to put some perspective back into the situation. But all she could think of was Forrest Symington wanting to make love to her.

Even though he was sitting on her bed, Melinda was the last thing on Forrest's mind at the moment. Every vestige of gentleness was gone as his eyes glinted steel and his voice projected ice, even though he never raised the volume.

"I don't care if Drew has called a meeting. There's no need for that. Just get the police there immediately. I want every last protester arrested and charged with criminal trespass. If Drew has a problem with that, he can talk to me about it. I'll be on the next flight out." He hung up the phone, not bothering to say good-bye, and absently started to knot his tie.

When Melinda emerged from the bathroom he didn't even look at her. "Get us on the next flight home. I seem to remember there's one at noon. Don't forget to get us a limo to the airport, and one from the airport to the office. If we don't hit traffic, we should make it."

His words, spoken like the boss he was, did more to clear her head than any amount of cold water. For a moment she wondered if she'd dreamed the last hour, but there were the strawberries and champagne, abandoned on the silver-laden cart. And she was wearing this magnificent robe. He saw her face then and realized if he ever wanted to pick up where they had left off, he had some explaining to do.

"I'm sorry." He touched her face, and the tight knot in her stomach released a little. "There's an emergency at the plant. We've got to go back. But nothing's changed. This was special. You're special. We can figure it all out when we get home, can't we? Don't be angry with me." He kissed her lightly on the lips. How could she be angry? He was the most wonderful thing that had ever happened to her, that was still happening. She returned his kiss, then broke away.

"Okay, let me get to the phone. I still have to dress and pack as well. Why don't you get your own things in order, and we can meet in the lobby in half an hour. I'll have everything taken care of."

"How did I ever live without you?" He looked back at her from the doorway and gave her a smile that was no less dazzling for being calculated.

Melinda picked up the phone and began to dial, but the minute she heard the door close behind him she put it down again. She knew she had no time to spare, but she needed to just take a minute to breathe. He had said she was special, that they'd figure it out at home, that he couldn't live without her. She'd felt herself in such a state of suspended animation, staying in a hotel in New York, spending all her time with Forrest, she hadn't even thought about what it would be like at home. If her mother objected to her working for Forrest Symington, Melinda didn't even want to imagine what she'd do if she found out there was more than business involved. And of course, he had a wife and family. It was complicated and, yes, probably wrong. But it didn't feel wrong. It felt exciting and wonderful, as if a whole new world was suddenly being opened up to her. She couldn't pass it up; she decided she'd just better not think about it too much. She dialed the phone and booked their seats, telling the agent, when asked, that they definitely had to be first class. She could get used to this, she thought. In fact, she already was. She started to pack, feeling as though she was embarking on the journey of a lifetime. And even if it ended in disaster, how could she pass up the delight she was certain to encounter along the way?

༄ 12 ༄

"I don't think it was a wise move." Drew was arguing with his father.

"It was the *only* move. Those demonstrators are just a bunch of troublemakers. They were trespassing, and they were put in jail. You don't negotiate with people who break the law."

"Look, Dad. Even though I'm not completely convinced it's the right thing to do, I'm standing behind you on the mill pond project. But those people don't owe you their allegiance the way I do. You've got to convince them that it's right before you move ahead with it."

"Bullshit. They owe me their bread and butter. Without DMC they'd be on welfare. The mill pond plant is going to give them more jobs, and they should be damn grateful."

"I'm sure they are grateful for the jobs. They're just concerned about the environment. Can't we give them some reassurances that we're going to safeguard their health? I think we owe them that much."

"We owe them shit. They get a paycheck. That's more than the fifty thousand people that GM laid off get."

"I don't want to be disrespectful, Dad, but you're being a little arrogant about this. This isn't 1930, and you're not Henry Ford. You can't expect your labor force—"

"Don't lecture me about my labor force," Forrest fumed at his son. "When you run the company and it's *your* labor force, you can do what you want. Hopefully you'll have learned something by then."

Drew shook his head. His father had always been narrow and stubborn, but usually he was right. This time Drew was convinced that the heavy-handed way they were handling the protest was going to make things even worse than they already were. In a way, he had to admit to himself, he was a little pleased. He had come into the office the morning after his painful encounter with his nasty wood nymph and thrown his full backing behind the mill pond project. It had been more reflexive than thoughtful, and he'd been leaning toward regret ever since. Even God didn't destroy Eden because its inhabitants misbehaved. Still, having taken up a position of support, he was reluctant to renege on it. But he wasn't sorry for the delay. He had ordered the research department to compile some data for him, and he was glad to have the opportunity to study it before they actually went forward. He was still hoping that some sort of compromise might be reached, some way to build at the mill pond without destroying the place and the community around it.

There was a discreet knock at the door, and Melinda entered. She didn't even make eye contact with Forrest as she told him that Stan Harkin was waiting to see him. She'd been avoiding looking at just about everybody since they got back from New York, afraid that her eyes might reveal secrets better left unspoken. The worst moment had been when they returned to the office to find Catherine Morton at her desk, fully recovered and ready to resume her duties. Forrest hadn't even taken a breath before he told her she was reassigned and Melinda would be taking her place. He was clever enough to make it sound like a promotion for Catherine, but Melinda could feel Catherine's eyes boring into her, and she had lowered her own. At that moment Melinda hadn't felt any sense of triumph, only fear. Forrest seemed so controlled, even cold. For a minute she wondered what would happen to her when he no longer wanted her around. But then Catherine had gone, and Forrest had called her in to his office on the intercom. Still sounding like the boss, he'd told her to close the door behind her. Then he'd come to her, lifted her face to his and kissed her so gently, so sweetly, that all fears fled. But she would need to protect herself—if not from Forrest, then from all the enemies she would gain from his favoritism. Even when Stan, whom she'd known all her life, had congratulated her on her new position, she'd been circumspect, playing it down, pretending she had nothing to do with it; it was just something that Catherine and Mr. Symington had arranged between the two of them. Now she led Stan into the office and quickly backed out, proper secretary that she was, wishing the day would end and all the executives and workers would go home, leaving her alone with her boss to complete their unfinished business.

Drew greeted Stan cordially, but Forrest got right to the point. "Did you get it?"

"What?" Drew asked before Stan could answer.

"I asked Stan to find out who's behind this revolt."

"It's not exactly a revolt, Dad. It was a peaceful demonstration."

"I don't give a shit what you call it. Whoever organized it is going to wish they'd never been born."

Stan hesitated. He didn't want to do this, but his job was on the line. Either he told the truth, or Forrest would get it some other way and then punish Stan as well. Stan didn't like it, but his wife was having kid number eight, and he couldn't afford to lose his job.

"Well," he started slowly, trying to think how to put a good face on it, "it seems there were a lot of people calling up a lot of other people, and it just kind of mushroomed. I don't think any of them meant any harm."

"Just tell me who made the first call."

"Well, there's a kind of Save the Mill Pond organization that works out of a storefront," Stan tried, hoping to avoid naming names.

It did no good. Forrest knew what he was after, and he wasn't going to stop until he got it. "Who?" he said peremptorily, and Stan knew he couldn't stall.

"Jack Bader and Sam Myles. They've been arrested with the others."

Drew couldn't believe his ears. He'd all but given up hope of ever finding the guy who had built Pete Wojek's car. "Is that Sam Myles a good mechanic?" he asked, just to verify.

"The best," answered Stan, hoping maybe Sam could get some kind of reprieve because of her talent.

His hopes were dashed a moment later as Forrest interrupted, "Who cares? I want the book thrown at these two guys. I want to make an example of them, so nobody else ever thinks they can get away with this kind of shit and still work in a DMC factory."

"Wait a minute, Dad. Just wait a minute." Drew was excited. This Sam Myles was a most elusive character, and he finally had him in a captive position, so to speak. He wasn't going to allow the opportunity to pass. "Let me go talk to them."

"What for?"

"Because if these two guys got the whole thing started, maybe we can get them to call the whole thing off. You put them in jail, you're just going to turn them into martyrs. You'll end up galvanizing the movement against you. But if you *use* them, get them to tell everyone the mill pond plant is a good idea, you get everyone behind you, and you don't have to keep fighting. Could save us a lot of trouble and quite a few bucks."

Forrest realized Drew had a point. But he also understood that Drew was naïve if he thought that these guys could be persuaded to change their minds —unless they used a little coercion to get their cooperation. Personal threats could work. Drew seemed willing to take it on, and he wanted his son to get more involved in the executive responsibilities of DMC.

"Fine," Forrest told his son. "Go talk to them. Tell them, as a representative of management at the very highest level, we are prepared to crucify them and their entire families if they do not cooperate. Make sure they understand the kind of power we wield. This is not a joke, son."

"I know that, Dad," said Drew, already on his way out. "One way or another, people's lives are going to change."

And as he headed to the jail, determined to finally meet a mechanic named Sam Myles, he had no idea that he was speaking about himself as much as anybody else.

When Drew said he needed to meet with Sam Myles, the chief of police had offered to let them use his office. Drew should have been used to the kowtowing that followed whenever he identified himself in the Oakdale region, but it still embarrassed him.

"Just a regular visiting room will do, but I don't want to talk on a telephone with a partition between us," Drew had said.

The chief of police smiled. "We don't have anything like that here. Your local jailhouses aren't exactly like what you see on TV. But then, I guess you wouldn't know that."

Drew knew more about prisons than he wanted to say, but he didn't elaborate as he was led into a small gray cubicle that was barren except for two folding chairs and an old metal desk. A heavy metal door on the opposite wall led to the jail, and when Drew heard the clinking of the lock he turned away, feeling it would be somehow indiscreet to look beyond it to the cells themselves, like looking into the bedroom of someone you hardly knew.

"Knock when you're ready," the guard said, withdrawing, and Drew heard the door close behind him.

Drew turned around, smiling, wanting to show how

pleased he was to finally come face-to-face with the ace mechanic. He froze in his tracks and blinked. He could not be hallucinating. It was her. His spirit soared, but then his body, remembering, drew back.

"Is this some kind of joke?" he asked icily.

"You tell me," she said. When they had come to get her they hadn't told her who her visitor was, just that someone was waiting to see her. She wanted to run but knew she could not. She hoped her voice betrayed none of the turmoil in her breast.

"This is a mistake," he said, turning to the visitors' door, ready to call for assistance.

I can't let him go again, Sam thought to herself, and then, chiding herself for her stupid romanticism, she amended it to: I can't let him go without telling him what I think.

"You're damn right this is a mistake," she said, mustering up all the righteous indignation she could summon. "I shouldn't be the one locked up. You should be. You and your father and your uncaring, unfeeling, exploitive board of directors. You have the fucking nerve to try and build a factory that will pollute our air and poison our water supply, and then you claim you're doing it for our own good. You know we need the jobs, you know we can't live without the D'Uberville Motor Company, so you figure we'll just lie down and die, making your whole goddam family richer than you already are, and we'll be grateful for it. Well, we're not that stupid, or that self-destructive, and if you came to convince me to give up the fight and kiss your ass just because you once caught me with my pants down, you can forget about it."

"That's not why I came," he said. Even though he

had promised his father to try and get the leaders to give up the fight, the truth was that it was only a secondary justification for being there. He looked at her and couldn't keep the tenderness out of his eyes. He had a host of reasons to be furious with her, but she was so damn beautiful all he could think of was how it felt when she was in his arms.

"Why did you come, then?" Sam asked, not so irately, aware that his gaze conveyed a warmth she didn't deserve.

"I came to see a mechanic named Sam Myles. Somehow the guard got mixed up and brought you here instead."

She started to laugh, and even though he didn't think it was all that funny, her glee was infectious, and he found himself grinning like a fool for no discernible reason.

"I am a mechanic named Sam Myles," she said when her mirth had worn out.

He was confused and must have looked it. "No one mentioned—"

"They must have thought you knew already. Everybody else around here does. Only my mother calls me Samantha."

"I saw your car on Superdirt Sunday, and the jerk who wrecked it told me it was built by a mechanic named Sam Myles. I just assumed . . ." He was rambling, giving himself time. How could he say all the things that needed to be said?

"Pete's a good driver." She didn't know why she felt the need to defend Pete. Maybe because she was feeling guilty about wanting Drew. Which she did. Right now. Even though he had put her in jail.

"Maybe. But he drove like a jerk that day. He pushed it into the red and destroyed your car. I don't know how you could let him get away with it."

"I didn't." Why were they talking about cars? Samantha wondered.

"Why are we talking about cars?" Drew asked.

"Because it's safe," Sam answered for them both. "Because we have to forget about everything else and just remember that as far as I'm concerned, you're the enemy. And I will do everything in my power to keep you from destroying the mill pond."

"Is that why . . . that night . . . when we both wanted . . . both knew . . ."

"I'm sorry," she whispered. "I didn't want to hurt you, but I had to remind myself that you were going to hurt me, and my people." Her voice got even softer, and he had to lean forward to hear her. He could smell the sweetness of her hair and breathed in deeper. "You had no right to make me want you so much. I have to fight so hard out there, and now it's in here, too." She pounded her heart with her fist, and there were tears in her eyes.

He caught her hand the second time and wouldn't let her do it again. "I am not the enemy," he said slowly and deliberately, as if she spoke a foreign language. "I would never, could never, hurt you."

She pulled her hand away from his. There was a ring of fire around her wrist where he had touched her. Without thinking she put it to her lips, then hastily lowered her arm when she realized what she was doing. "I'm in here, aren't I? I wouldn't call that a trip to Disneyland." She was trying to sound tough, *be* tough, but he was laughing.

"You're right. I'm getting you out of here right now. We've got a lifetime to catch up on and another lifetime to plan ahead. And this is not the place for either one."

Her heart was beating hosannas against her chest. He was talking about lifetimes. She had not been fooling herself. They had connected in some visceral way that could not be denied. She wanted to run into his arms and stay there forever.

"Wait. I won't go with you." She heard the words from her mouth with horror, as though she had not spoken them herself.

Drew was no less stunned. He couldn't have misjudged her. He knew she wanted to be with him as much as he wanted to be with her. He felt like the night at the mill pond, but this time the pain was psychic instead of physical. She saw his face and knew what he was thinking.

"I want to be with you," she told him quickly. "But there are forty-seven other people in this jail because I told them to put themselves on the line. I can't leave unless they leave."

"Wait a minute," he objected. "What's happening between us has nothing to do with the mill pond. This is personal."

"Don't you understand? The mill pond *is* personal to me. And to these people. If DMC builds a plant there, even if it gives us jobs, it's ultimately going to destroy us. If you don't care about that, you can't care about me."

He did care about her, profoundly. But he wished she wouldn't turn it into a political maneuver. "I don't have unilateral control over these things," he said diplomatically. "A research and development team selected the site after years of discussion, and a board approved it. I can't just change it."

"You could stop it if you wanted to. At least for now."

She was right, and he knew it. He did have the power to put a hold on the bulldozers, to call for a delay until the community's complaints could be examined. They deserved that much. His father would be furious, but he was a human being before he was the heir to the throne at the D'Uberville Motor Company.

"I'll make you a deal," he said.

"What?" she asked warily.

"I'll have all trespassing charges dropped on all your people . . ."

She smiled triumphantly; she knew he'd come through. She could never love someone who didn't appreciate human values more than business. And she did love him.

"If," he continued, and she stopped smiling. Maybe it was just animal attraction, infatuation.

"If," he emphasized, "you give me your personal word that you will call off the dogs. No more lie-ins, no more demonstrations. We handle this internally and don't air our dirty linen in public. DMC stock is down enough without giving investors a reason to back away even more."

She hesitated. "I can only do that if you promise me you won't start destroying the mill pond before we've had a say in what goes on there. There's got to be some kind of referendum. The community has to be informed of the disadvantages as well as the advantages in a non-biased manner, so people can make a judgment. DMC has made me out to be the villain here, as if everything would be all right and everyone would be happy and have jobs if I just kept my mouth shut. But that's not true. And you know it. And I think everybody else has a right to know it, too."

Beautiful and smart, he thought as he looked at her, and he couldn't disagree. "Come with me to my office. We'll start the process."

Gorgeous and reasonable, Sam thought as she shook his hand formally. He held it a little too long, and the current between them surged.

"There's one more condition," he said. She waited nervously. "We'll spend all the time we need to on the mill pond project. But before we do, you have to tell me everything there is to know about you, Samantha Myles." He had said her name, finally turning his wood nymph into a real person. He felt as though everything before had been prologue. The curtain was just going up on the main event.

Melinda had gone straight from the airport to the office with Forrest, and by the time she got home Harvey and Diane were too distraught about Sam to question her about her trip to New York. Melinda was just as upset about Sam's troubles as they were, but she had to admit to herself that she was also grateful that once again her big sister had provided the diversion that saved Melinda's neck. Remembering Diane's hostility toward Forrest in general, and the trip in particular, Melinda knew she wouldn't have been able to come away from an interrogation intact. Focusing on Sam, they were a family again, and

Melinda could keep her feelings and fantasies separate, secret, and safe from her mother's scrutiny.

"I don't know what I can do this time," Melinda told her parents. "Maybe Mr. Symington will listen to me if I tell him she's my sister and she didn't mean it or something." It felt funny calling him Mr. Symington now that she knew him as Forrest. But she didn't dare say it, certain that Diane would pick up on it—and on God knew what else.

"You can't do that," said Harvey, adamant. "Old man Symington might think it's a family thing, and then we'd both lose our jobs as well." Melinda frowned. She didn't like hearing him called "old man." It was totally inappropriate. She tried to concentrate on the problem at hand.

"Who gives a damn about jobs? Your daughter is in jail," Diane rebuked her husband.

"Well, it's her own damn fault. She should never have started this protest thing. Now we could all end up laid off, and she's just too damn selfish to care."

"That's not fair, Dad." Melinda felt obliged to defend Sam even though she devoutly wished her sister was not standing in opposition to the man she . . . to her boss. "Sam is doing this for everybody, not just herself."

"Well, who asked her to?"

Melinda had a thought. She could help her sister and do something she desperately wanted to do at the same time. She knew it could turn out to be a big mistake, but she had a morbid curiosity to see how the Symingtons lived.

"Uh . . . Mr. Symington sent me home early because he was still in meetings, but he's probably gone home by now. If you want, I could go to his house and make a personal appeal."

"No!" said Diane, a little too vehemently.

"I thought you wanted her to help." Harvey looked at his wife curiously.

"I . . . I do. I just don't think that's the way to do it. You're the one who said she shouldn't say Sam's her sister. What's she going to do? Show up at his doorstep and say she's representing the little people? That's going to help a lot. He'll really appreciate having his dinner interrupted."

"Forget it, bad idea," said Melinda before her parents could get into an argument over the Symingtons' eating habits. She had known it would be the wrong thing to do even as she was offering to do it. The last place Forrest Symington would want to see her was in his home. But at least he wanted to see her in the office. And even though they hadn't had more than a minute alone since they'd returned from New York, she knew he still wanted her to be more than just his secretary. She loved her sister, and she would do what she could to help Sam. But she couldn't jeopardize her relationship with Forrest Symington. It was just beginning, and she had a feeling it could end up being the most important thing in her life.

Fortunately, Melinda didn't need to make a choice. Stan Harkin called to let them know that all the charges had been dropped and the demonstrators released.

"Nice of her to let us know," said Harvey, disgruntled. But Diane was relieved that Sam was out of jail and Melinda wouldn't have to appeal to Forrest Symington. The less personal Melinda was with him, the happier she'd be. And the last thing she wanted was for their family to owe that man any favors.

"I'm talking too much," Sam said.

"Not at all," Drew answered, and from the rapt attention on his face she knew he really didn't think so.

She had gone with him from the jail to his office, not even waiting to speak to the others. True to his word, he had given the order to have all protesters released, and he was intent on making her keep hers. She had felt awkward at first, even silly, telling him about her childhood. But he had insisted, and pretty soon they were laughing together over her anecdotes of growing up car crazy in car city.

"It certainly paid off for Pete Wojek," he said, trying to keep any hint of envy out of his voice. "I wish we could do in our factory what you did with his D'Uberville."

"You can. It's a simple adaptation I figured out almost by accident in my design class. As soon as I get a patent on it I'll let you see it. You might want to go into business with me," she said, only half facetiously.

"What about Pete?" he asked, knowing she would sense his interest was more than professional.

"I'm not working on cars for Pete anymore."

He could feel himself grinning like a fool. "He didn't deserve you."

"You mean my mechanical talent?"

"That, too."

Now she was grinning. "How come we're always talking about cars when we really want to say something else?"

"I don't even want to talk," he said, and he put his

FOR RICHER, FOR POORER

hand on her silky hair. Slowly he let it wander over her face, her eyes, nose, mouth, learning it in braille, memorizing its contours. She let her cheek rest on the palm of his hand, and gently he turned her face to his and kissed her. She felt an explosion in her head. Then she heard one in the room, and they jumped apart as Forrest burst in, flinging open the door and banging it against the wall.

"What the hell's going on?" Forrest was shouting.

"Don't you knock, Dad?" If Drew was shaken, he was not letting it show. Sam wished she was anywhere but there.

"I want to know what you think you're doing."

"I don't think this concerns you."

Forrest looked at Sam and dismissed her with his eyes. "I'm not talking about your bit on the side, boy. I don't care about that. You were supposed to go down to that jail and do a job. Instead I get word that every single damn one of those terrorists has been let go."

Sam couldn't let it go by. "We are not terrorists," she said vehemently. "We are citizens who are concerned for our lives and are exercising our civil rights by protesting."

Forrest looked at her again, this time with a glint of steel that almost hurt. "We? You were one of them? I get it, Drew, but I don't like it. You let these people go free so you could get laid? That doesn't wash. I don't care about mixing business with pleasure, but business has always got to come first."

Drew said nothing. He had seen the look Forrest had directed toward Sam. Forrest could hurt her, and he would. If Drew argued with Forrest now, he couldn't trust Sam to keep her mouth shut. And if she stated her own position as vociferously as he knew she would, Forrest would crush her like a bug. Better to let his father think that she was just a bit of fluff they could ignore than to think she was a force to be reckoned with.

"Maybe you should go now," Drew said to Sam. He wanted her away from his father, out of the line of fire. He would calm Forrest down and explain to her later. "I'll call you."

"Don't bother," said Sam icily, struggling to keep the tears from her eyes. She had been such a fool, she wouldn't give him the satisfaction of showing him it mattered. She had thought that with time she could convince him of the need to save the mill pond, that he could be an ally as well as a lov— She didn't let herself complete the thought. His father understood him better than she did. She was out of jail because he wanted to get laid. And idiot that she was, he had almost gotten his wish. But she *was* out of jail, and thanks to a little crudity from Symington senior, she knew the score. Maybe the D'Uberville Motor Company was ahead right now, but they'd only reached halftime. She was going to win this game if it killed her. They were wrong when they said, "Hell hath no fury like a woman scorned." A woman who had been suckered was a lot more lethal.

❧ 13 ❧

"For they are jolly good fe-e-llows, which nobody can deny," sang the gathered crowd as they hoisted Sam and Jack to their shoulders. Sam laughed but insisted they be put down.

"Speech, speech," came the refrain.

Sam tried to defer to Jack, but he wouldn't hear of it. "No way. I did all my talking in court. Now it's your turn."

They quieted as she began, "Thank you, everyone, for being here now, and for your support in the past. But the fight is just beginning, and we're going to need your support for a long time to come. Thanks to our super attorney here, who, disguised as a not-so-mild-mannered factory worker, has been working on the line right beside us, today we won an injunction against DMC. They have been ordered to cease and desist any construction at the mill pond until a public hearing. They have sixty days to schedule the hearing, and that's how long we've got to mount our battle. And it's not just DMC we're fighting. For Oakdale, this is a civil war. Some of your friends, your neighbors, your families even, are going to tell you you're wrong. That you're standing in the way of progress and, even worse, taking away their jobs and food from the mouths of their children. But we know better. We *want* those jobs. We *want* a plant built. Just not at the mill pond, where it's going to end up killing those very children we're trying to feed."

There were cries of "You said it" and "Right on," and more applause. Sam silenced them with her hands and a smile. "Like I said, the fight is just beginning." She paused for effect. "But not tonight. Tonight we P-A-R-T-Y."

Parked in his car on the darkened street across from the Save the Mill Pond storefront, Drew watched them celebrate, raising paper cups of cheap wine to one another. There were maybe thirty people there surrounding Jack and Sam, obviously listening to their leaders hold forth on the day's events, greeting each anecdote with cheers and hoots of laughter. Drew searched the crowd for a glimpse of Pete Wojek, just in case, and was pleased to see he wasn't there. Then he looked nervously back at Sam and Jack and wondered if perhaps Pete had been displaced by a more formidable opponent. But somehow Drew didn't think Jack and Sam were romantically involved. He was certain he would have sensed something, watching them huddled together in court, whispering head to head. There was friendship, there was respect, but for some reason he didn't think there was romance.

Drew had let Forrest believe he was accompanying

their legal representatives to court out of zealousness for their cause. But the real reason was that he had wanted to see Sam. He had made no attempt to contact her since sending her away in Forrest's presence. Instead he had immersed himself in the research and learned for certain what he had already suspected to be true. The propaganda put out by DMC's public relations machinery wasn't entirely a lie. The current DMC plans for building a factory on the mill pond would be an economic boon for both the company and the community. At least for a while. But it would be an environmental disaster that had the potential of destroying Oakdale altogether.

He tried to be dispassionate when he discussed it with Forrest. "It doesn't make sense, Dad. The waste provision is completely inadequate. In ten to twenty years the surrounding area could end up being nothing but a toxic dump."

"In ten to twenty years, son," Forrest had answered evenly, "DMC can double its output and boost its bottom line tenfold."

"What good will that do future generations?"

"Don't talk like an idiot. I'm doing this for *you* and *your* future generations. Do you have any idea what your stock will be worth by the time your kids are growing up?"

"What about the kids in Oakdale? The ones who won't be able to drink the water or breathe the air?"

"Since when did you turn into a bleeding-heart liberal?" Forrest looked at his son with disdain. "If they can't live in Oakdale, they'll move somewhere else. It's not our concern. I guarantee you, wherever they live, they'll show up for work and be grateful for it."

Drew had recognized there was no point in arguing or angering Forrest any further. Forrest, backed against the wall, would simply increase his offensive, which was already formidable. A battalion of experts and attorneys was being deployed to annihilate the opposition. Drew wanted to warn Sam, but he didn't even dare try to contact her through an intermediary. They'd gone to court, and when her lawyer turned out to be an assembly-line worker with a ponytail, Drew had groaned inwardly, already certain that she had lost. But even though the judge had looked askance at the ponytail, in all other ways Jack had been a model of correct legal procedure. His statements had been forceful, his research well-documented, and his arguments for protection of community interests had been most effective. A sixty-day injunction was granted.

It had been a major blow for the company and a major victory for Sam, and when she turned triumphantly to glare at Drew, she was taken aback to find him watching her, not with animosity, but with a look she could almost have mistaken for affection. Immediately she turned away, chiding herself, reminding herself of the old saying, "Fool me once, shame on you. Fool me twice, shame on me."

Drew knew what she must be thinking: that he had used her and betrayed her. It cut him deeply when he saw her armored eyes shoot daggers toward him. He wanted to go to her and shake her for not knowing him better, for not understanding that even though it might seem they were enemies, he was already in love with her. But there was too much at stake to allow even the semblance of impropriety. All the board of directors at DMC would need to hear was that he was personally involved with the leader of the opposition, and they'd dismiss anything he had to say out of hand. He couldn't make a move until after the hearing, after DMC's casual disregard for civic concerns was exposed. To tell her how he felt now would mean risking everything she believed in. To keep silent meant risking any chance they might have of coming together. But he knew he had no choice. Forcing his eyes away from her laughing face, he turned on the ignition and let it idle for a few moments. He wanted to turn it off, to run inside and take her in his arms, to explain he was on her side and always would be. But he knew that right now his love would destroy her. If he loved her, he had to leave her alone. Pressing his foot to the accelerator, he sped off into the night before he could change his mind.

It hadn't been easy for Bethany to convince Mathilde that the engagement party should be a surprise. Mathilde kept pointing out that since Bethany was the one who had suggested it, and was half the couple involved, it hardly seemed worth the trouble it would take to keep it secret from Drew. But Bethany insisted it might be preferable if no one knew it was her idea. Drew was funny about people throwing events for themselves. But if he thought his mother had planned it for them, he would feel honored instead of annoyed.

The truth was, Bethany didn't want to take any chances. From now until her wedding night there would be no opportunity for Drew to question what was happening. Let him be carried with the current until the marriage was a fait accompli. The fact that Drew had been so distracted by business lately she actually saw as an advantage. As long as he worried about his stupid cars, he wouldn't be thinking about *them*. And instinctively Bethany knew that the less time Drew had to dwell on their relationship, the better off she was.

Working at a feverish pace, she'd managed to have her list approved by Mathilde and invitations printed before the week was out. She knew the responses would be quick and positive. Not a lot of people in Woodland Cliffs would turn down an opportunity to spend an evening at Belvedere. She would broach the subject of her moving in with Drew at the height of the party. If he accepted, she'd know that everything was fine. If he balked, she'd pull out her trump card. They'd gone to such pains to hide his secret before, there was no way they'd want it made public in their own home, with all of Woodland Cliffs society in attendance.

The problem was that for any of this to work, Drew had to show up. Bethany checked her watch for the fifth time in as many minutes. Drew should have picked her up, ostensibly to have a quiet dinner with his parents, half an hour ago. She had called the office to scold him for being late, but they had informed her that Drew had spent the morning in court and never returned to the office. From his secretary she learned that the case hadn't gone well for DMC, and it was likely that Drew was upset. Bethany had decided then that she would lure him into the bedroom when he arrived, just to put him in a good frame of mind for the party; but now it was too late for even a quickie. All the guests would have arrived at Belvedere by now.

The phone rang. She ran to it, already cursing Drew silently for his excuses.

"Whair are ze two ov you?" She recognized Mathilde's heavy French accent.

"I'm obviously here, and I don't know where the hell Drew is. He can't have forgotten. He never forgets anything. Unless he found out somehow, and he's just not going to show."

"My Andrew is not like that." Bethany didn't like the possessively maternal way Mathilde phrased her remarks about Drew, but she was right. Drew never did anything rude or hurtful. He was just so perfect, it bored her to tears. But his money and position weren't boring, and Bethany obediently agreed that Mathilde knew her son best. As if to prove it, the doorbell rang.

"He's here," Bethany said hurriedly, grabbing her coat and moving toward the door with the cordless phone still in her hand. "Get everyone ready. We're on our way. We'll be there in five minutes. And Mathilde," she added carefully, "thank you so much for this. It's going to be a very important night for us."

Mathilde hung up the phone, aware that Bethany was laying it on a little thick. She knew Bethany was a flatterer, as dishonest as they came, but that hardly mattered. She was at least a known quantity, and therefore controllable. She understood her future daughter-in-law, knew they shared a perception of what was important: position, money, correct family. Drew laughed at all that, but if he were married to Bethany, she would keep him in line. Mathilde hadn't spent the years building up her reigning station to have it all carelessly discarded by her free-thinking son. Her husband, though groomed to finesse by her own careful monitoring, was basically common. Her children and grandchildren would not be. She heard two quick beeps coming from the intercom. It was the signal prearranged with the guard at the gate.

"All right, *mes amis.*" She clapped her hands to get their attention. "*Ils sont arrivés.* They are here."

The buzz quieted, and a hush settled, waiting for the door to open.

"Surprise!" everyone shouted right on cue as Drew and Bethany stepped into the light of the chandelier in the foyer. Drew looked at Bethany. She thought she saw a hint of accusation in his eyes but reassigned it to her own guilty imagination.

"Oh, my God," she exclaimed, breathlessly going into action. "What is going on here?"

People were coming toward them with congratulations. "All this for us? Why, this is so sweet." She sought out her future mother-in-law from the crowd. "Mathilde, you are so sweet. I can't believe it."

Drew was still silent, eyes moving from her to his mother.

"Drew, darling," she encouraged. "Are you still in shock? Say something."

"What is this?"

"You silly. It's an engagement party. For us."

"This is a mistake," he said quietly. "You should have told me about this."

"Well, how could I?" Bethany blithely ignored the concern in his voice. "I didn't know myself. Isn't it a lovely surprise?" Perfectly aware that Drew did not share her opinion, but pretending otherwise, she quickly hailed some friends and melted into their circle, exhorting Drew to mingle.

Drew turned to Mathilde. He was trying not to be harsh. "Why did you do this, Maman?" he asked, using the French diminutive he'd called her when he was a boy to soften the steely disapproval in his voice.

"Because I wanted to do something nice for you and Bethany before the wedding. You are not upset, are you?" she asked plaintively, knowing full well he was and that he'd never tell her.

"You should have consulted me first" was all he could say before he was pulled away by one of Bethany's girlfriends, wanting to know how she could get someone just like him.

Bethany worked the crowd, moving from the foyer through the salon. She kept one eye on Drew, pleased to see that he was being monopolized by Deirdre Holliman, a woman she considered no threat at all. As long as Drew was occupied, he wouldn't have time to object to the proceedings. And by the time it was over Bethany would have made her pitch, and all that would be left to do would be to move in, bag and baggage. She'd have to make tonight extra special for Drew after everyone left, just to reinforce the fact that she intended to provide service for payment rendered. Men liked to know they were getting something for their money. And although Drew's demands had always been fairly regular—a little too regular for her taste—she knew that in bed she could offer satisfaction guaranteed.

"Congratulations, Bethany," came a voice from behind.

She turned, her superficial patter at the ready. "Thank you so much for com—" She stopped short. It was Jean-Claude. She had been so busy planning the party that she hadn't had time for their afternoon trysts in the past couple of weeks. He had called a few times, telling her that he had moved out of his cousin Mathilde's mansion and taken a room at a hotel, so they could be together without fear of interruption. But she had pretended she was ill, insisting that she loved him too much to subject him to her diseases when he offered to come over anyway, promising that as soon as she was better she was going to break it off with Drew and come to him. They would have a lifetime to be together in sickness and in health. Needless to say, he hadn't been on her list. He must have been invited by Mathilde. She let him lead her to the terrace, making sure no one was watching.

"This is so awful," she said as they moved out of the sight lines of the other guests. "Why didn't you tell me this was going to happen?"

"I didn't know," Jean-Claude assured her. "Mathilde just called to invite me today. It seems the hotel staff is not so efficient. They returned the invitation marked addressee unknown."

"This is too unbearable." Bethany preempted any remarks he might have. "It's awful having everyone think I'm going to marry that man when all I want is you." She moved him further into the shadows with her body and pressed herself against him. She could feel him rising to meet her.

"When will you tell him?" Jean-Claude asked plaintively, and she knew she was home free. He was easy, at least with his clothes on. She had known others like him, men who were so easily manipulated by day but could be in deliciously terrifying control at night. It worked for her, soothed that submissive part of her that wanted to be taken, but only in circumstances of her choosing.

"I've been so sick I couldn't even get out of bed. You

know that. Tonight was my first night out, and I only came because he insisted, and I thought it would be a good chance to tell him."

"Maybe it still is."

"Here? At the party?"

"Why not? You don't want to be engaged to him any longer. Why go on with this charade?"

He was getting aggravated. The last thing Bethany needed was Jean-Claude, horny and upset. "You're right, my darling. I'm going to tell him tonight. But only if you promise me you'll leave."

"With you."

"No," she answered, a little too vehemently. "I don't know what Drew's reaction is going to be. I don't want you in the line of fire. I'll come to you after, I promise."

"I'm not afraid of him."

"I know. But I am. Please, Jean-Claude. I'm begging you." She let her hand slip to his groin for emphasis. He grabbed her and kissed her hard on the mouth, pushing himself between her legs, rubbing into her. She pulled away. "I won't be able to do it if you stay."

He let her go. "Fine. But I will punish you for making me wait."

Bethany felt herself grow moist. "I look forward to it," she said, and she meant it.

Bethany watched Jean-Claude making his way through the garden to the front gate. She was pleased he hadn't bothered to go back inside and say good-bye. The less attention called to anything unusual, the better. She pulled out her lipstick from her gold evening bag, freshened her face, and entered the salon, smiling brightly.

Drew was nowhere to be seen, and Bethany spent

the next half hour cheerfully inquiring as to which of the guests had seen her fiancé, as though he might be getting her a drink or chatting with the next group. She finally found him alone in the library, brooding. Silently she approached from behind and started to massage his shoulders.

"Bad day, darling?" she asked, knowing the answer.

Startled, he pulled away brusquely, then tried to soften the curtness of his act by smiling. "Actually, it wasn't so bad."

"But you lost your case for the new plant."

"Just a delay. That might not be all bad."

He seemed a lot more cheerful about it than she would have expected. She looked at him, trying to figure out what was going on in his mind. They had never connected as viscerally in bed as she and Jean-Claude, but there had been a time when she felt she knew what he wanted. Not anymore. But it didn't matter. She knew what *she* wanted, and she just had to get him to agree to it.

"You know, darling, I've been thinking." Drew cringed inwardly. When Bethany was thinking it usually meant it cost something, monetary or otherwise.

"I hardly ever see you anymore," she went on. He said nothing, knowing she was right. He hadn't been to see her or invited her to Belvedere for weeks, using the complications with the new plant as his excuse.

"I understand you're busy, and that's okay." She rested her cheek on the top of his head. He resisted the urge to shrug her off. "But the wedding is so far away, and I miss you. So I was thinking maybe I'd just bring some of my stuff over here and stay. That way, if you came home late from the office, I'd be here. And I

could, you know, soothe you, whatever time it was."
He knew she meant "fuck you," and it was the last
thing he wanted at any hour.

But he could not be cruel. It was not in his nature.
Gently he reached over and brought her down to the
sofa beside him. She nestled into the crook of his arm,
misinterpreting his kindness for affection.

"Bethany," he began slowly, and then he decided it
might be more decent to come right out with it. "I
don't think we should get married."

Bethany refused to get alarmed. "Oh, darling Drew.
It *has* been an awful day for you. This party of your
mother's was just too much. I wish she hadn't done it.
But you know how she is."

"It's not the party, Bethany."

"I don't think we should discuss it now." Her voice
was getting just a little edge.

"I think we have to. It's a mistake. It's been a
mistake all along."

"Did I do something? Because if I did—"

"It's nothing you did," he interrupted. "It's who
you are. And who I am. Let's face it. We've never
really loved each other. Our union has been more a
social arrangement than anything else."

"It didn't feel that way the last time I came into
your room in my boots and riding jacket."

"That's in the past. I'm sure you've noticed we
haven't been together in quite a while."

"I can remedy that," she said in her most seductive
tone, cupping her breasts and pushing them over her
strapless gown so her nipples showed over the top.

Drew turned away in disgust. "Sex is not enough. It
takes more to make a marriage."

"If you're trying to say that sex with me is not

enough, I can accept that. In fact, I can even understand it, and appreciate it," she added for her own benefit. "I don't expect you to be by my side every minute. Believe me, there are plenty of wives in Woodland Cliffs who have adapted to a husband's desire for variety. The marriage still works. Look at your parents."

Drew knew she was right. He remembered the first time he had realized his parents took other lovers. He was only twelve when he had come home from boarding school on holiday to find his mother weeping and his father gone. The next day he had seen a picture of his father on the society page of a newspaper with a buxom blonde. The day after, his mother had started tennis lessons, and for the rest of his holiday she "consulted" with her tennis pro twenty-four hours a day. The pattern had been repeated with variations ever since.

"I don't want a life like my parents'," he said honestly. "Maybe that's the problem. You do. I tried to pretend it didn't matter. But suddenly it does. Very much. We're too different. We care about different things."

"Not altogether," she said. Something in her tone made him look at her sharply.

"What do you mean?"

"Well," she began carefully, "we both care about family, about values, about maintaining our moral standing in the community."

"Bethany, you're talking bullshit. If you have something to say, just come out and say it."

"Oh, Drew," she said plaintively, playing it for all she was worth. "You're getting angry, and it's just making it so much more difficult for me. No matter what you think, I do love you, and I don't want to see you hurt, or your family."

Drew controlled himself with effort. "I'm sorry. How do you think you could hurt me, or my family?"

"Not me, darling! Heaven forbid. I would never do anything to harm you. But quite by accident I've learned about a dreadful secret that would be devastating if it came out."

She shoots, she scores, thought Bethany as she saw Drew do an almost classic double take. For a minute he said nothing, but she could see the wheels turning. When he spoke his voice was quiet, his tone measured. "What exactly do you know?"

She lowered her eyes, as if it pained her to say it. "About your accident. About the fact that you killed a young bride on her wedding day and spent a year in a French prison paying for it." She reached her arms out to him, full of sympathy. "It must have been so terrible for you."

He pulled away. "Is that it?" he asked tersely.

She scrutinized his face, but he was revealing nothing. Still, it almost sounded as if he expected more. "Well," she went on a little uncertainly, "I know your parents have covered it up, telling everyone you spent the year studying D'Uberville operations in Europe."

"And now you're threatening to tell the world the real truth—that I'm a convicted murderer—if I don't marry you." His voice was tinged with sarcasm—and something else. She could have mistaken it for relief if it hadn't been so out of place.

"I told you, my sweet, it's not me. It's Jean-Claude. The woman you killed was his fiancée. He didn't

227

come here to renew acquaintance with his cousins. He came to get revenge."

"How do you know this?"

"What does it matter? I found out. And I've been spending every bit of my energy trying to keep him from ruining you."

"You shouldn't have bothered," he said harshly.

"How could I do anything else? I love you. I'm not going to let anything happen to you. Or your family. You know it would crush your mother if this came out," she added for effect. "You're getting cold feet. I understand that. It happens to all men. But don't let it ruin everything. I can help you keep things the way they are, the way they should be."

"That's just the point, Bethany. I don't want things to stay the way they are. If you want to tell your little story, go ahead. You've got quite an audience here tonight."

She was starting to panic. This was not how she had intended things to turn out. She had to rethink; she needed time. She pretended to be hurt, and tears gathered in her eyes. "How can you be so horrid, when all I've ever done is love you? Of course I'm not going to say anything. I never would. And I'm going to do my best to keep Jean-Claude from saying anything as well. Then maybe you'll believe me. I'm not giving up on this, Drew. I'm not giving up on *us.*"

"Give it up, Bethany," he said gently. "It wasn't meant to be. You're a beautiful woman. There are plenty of other eligible and correct partners out there for you. You'll do fine. Just let it go."

"I don't want anyone else," she said. "I want you."

"Alors, les amants" came Mathilde's chirping voice.

"This party is for you. You cannot hide in the garden alone. You will have time later for this."

Bethany looked at Drew. "Please," she said quietly. "Let's just get through tonight. No scene. We'll work it out later."

"Is something wrong?" Drew recognized the nervous tinge in Mathilde's voice that came just before an anxiety attack and the need for another drink.

"No, Maman, everything's fine. Let's go inside." Resigned, he took Mathilde's arm with one hand and Bethany's with the other, forcing himself to smile.

They walked back into the salon, Bethany pressed to his side, face turned up to his with doting eyes, as though her only need was to be near the man she loved. Disaster had been momentarily averted, and the situation could still be saved. With the instinct of a hyena going after prey, she knew that somewhere in their conversation she had smelled the scent of weakness. But she needed time to remember every word Drew had said, every expression on his face. She was frightened, but she was not finished.

By the time Bethany arrived at Jean-Claude's hotel room she knew what had to be done. The party had gone on past midnight, and Drew, although noticeably stiff, had acted his part, gritting his teeth and accepting congratulations, then changing the subject as quickly as possible. She'd left him as soon as the last guest was gone, suggesting that perhaps all they needed was a little time apart, and making him promise to give her two weeks before he made any public announcements. Even though Drew had insisted he wouldn't change his mind, he'd acceded. It was easier than arguing, and in fact, he thought he owed her that much. He was not blameless in having allowed a loveless liaison to go on as long as it had. With his promise in hand Bethany had kissed him tenderly on the mouth and driven straight to the Carlton Hotel, where Jean-Claude was staying.

He was waiting for her when she tapped lightly on the door, and he pulled her inside and onto the floor. He was hungry, desperate, and as much as she returned his ardor, there were things that had to be done first. It's too bad that he is nobody, Bethany thought as his kisses roused her passion, because otherwise this might be worth fighting for. Aloud she said, "I love you, Jean-Claude, and want to be with you always."

"Did you tell him?" Jean-Claude asked, still holding her.

"Yes."

"Well?"

She stayed in his arms but turned her face away. "It was terrible," she whispered. "He became violent. I really think he would have hurt me if there hadn't been a houseful of people. He told me he would never let me go, I could never be free."

"Did you tell him you did not love him?"

She gave a bitter laugh. "Love? He doesn't care about love. He cares about his image and his possessions. And I'm just something else he owns."

"The arrogant bastard. I'm going over there, and I'll—"

Jean-Claude was already moving to the door, but Bethany pulled him down beside her onto the sofa. The last thing she wanted was for Jean-Claude and Drew to have a face-to-face confrontation. In fact, it was something to be avoided at all cost. She moved into phase two of her plan.

"No, my darling. You mustn't do that. The Symingtons are incredibly powerful people. They can destroy me. They can destroy *us.*"

"Do you expect me to just sit here and—"

This was her opening. "Of course I don't. But we must be clever. We can't fight them with force. We need some leverage."

"What does this word mean, le-ve-rage?" he asked, and Bethany smiled again at the charm of his French accent. He had a lot of lovely qualities—no money or position, but a good deal of charm. If she could pull this off, she might get to have her cake and eat this bit of French pastry as well.

"It means, *mon amour,* that we have to make them more afraid of us than we are of them. What do people like the Symingtons fear most? Scandal."

"Fine. If he does not let you go, I will announce that Drew Symington is a murderer."

"Actually, I tried that already. I told him that I knew he had killed your dear Lisette, and that that was another reason I could never stay with him. It only made him angrier." She lowered her voice dramatically, wondering for a moment if she might not be taking this too far, but deciding to go for broke. "He said if I tried to leave him, he'd kill me, too."

"*Merde!* I should just shoot him, and *finis!*"

"No. You would end up going to jail for the rest of your life, and I would die without you. No. There's got to be a better way."

"Le-ve-rage?"

She smiled; he learned fast. "Exactly."

"You know something else he is hiding?"

"Not exactly. But I'm sure there is something. It's just a gut feeling, but I think there's more to what happened in France than even you know."

"What?"

"I don't know exactly. Drew just had a funny reaction when I said I knew about Lisette. As though he was waiting for the other shoe to drop."

"You took off your shoes?"

"No, that's just an expression." His charm could be annoying at times. She was going to have to spell it all out. "Drew gave me the impression that there was more to the accident than anyone knows. He wasn't afraid of people finding out he'd been convicted of negligent homicide in France. In fact, he seemed relieved that was all I knew. I think there's a deeper, darker secret there, and I've got to know . . ." She realized she was sounding a little exclusionary and deliberately softened her stance. "I mean, if you could find out what it was, maybe you could use it to free me from his terrible control. I don't know what else to do. I'm too afraid to leave him otherwise." She started to cry softly.

"Stop, *ma chérie.* Don't cry. I will find it, I swear. I will get us this leverage. I go back to France *immédiatement.* If there is something to know, I will know it. We will be together, *je promis.*"

He began to kiss away her tears, and Bethany was tempted to let one thing lead to another. But business had not yet been completed.

"Let's call the airlines," she said, gently pulling away. "You might even be able to get a flight to Nice tonight." She reached for the telephone and dialed while he began to nibble at her feet. By the time she had made the reservation he was halfway up her thigh. She pulled his head the few inches to the spot where it would have the greatest effect. As his tongue worked its magic she threw her head back in ecstasy and said hoarsely, "I'm really going to miss you." It was the first truly honest thing she'd said all evening.

❧ 14 ❧

"Mom, Dad." Melinda swallowed. This was going to be harder than she'd thought. "I'm . . . I'm getting . . . I'm moving out."

"What?" asked Harvey, as if he hadn't heard. Diane bit her lip. She'd heard perfectly well.

"I'm getting my own place. I'm twenty-four, and I really think it would be good to be on my own. And since I got a raise . . ."

"If you've got money to burn," Harvey said, "why don't you contribute something to this household? We've been keeping you long enough. Give something back instead of throwing it away."

"I'm not throwing it away. I just thought—"

"Where?" Diane interrupted. She had been having feelings for the past few weeks. Ever since Melinda had come back from New York she'd been working late, going straight to her room when she came home, never talking about her job. Something was going on. "Where's the apartment?"

"It's really nice," Melinda enthused, thinking maybe her mother was going to support her this time. "It's that new building on Fairview Road. It's a great neighborhood, but not too far from the office."

Diane knew the building. It *was* nice. Too nice. It was on the border between Woodland Cliffs and Oakdale, nicely situated halfway between two worlds without actually being in either one.

"You can't afford that," said Harvey dismissively.

"I . . . I got a really fabulous deal," Melinda lied, and she knew instantly that she'd done it badly. Her next mistake was trying to recover by taking the offensive. "Look, what's the difference? It's a great place, and I'm moving. You should be happy for me."

The slap shocked them all. Diane hadn't known she was going to do it; it had just happened. The sound stung the air. Tears sprang to Melinda's eyes, and she touched her cheek, reddened with her mother's palm print.

"What the hell?" Harvey had never seen Diane hit anyone, let alone her own child.

"She's sleeping with him," Diane said, her voice shaking but not uncertain. "It's not enough that she's his secretary. Now he wants to set her up as his whore."

"How do you know so goddam much?" Melinda was crying.

"Is it true?" Diane ignored her daughter's tears.

"You know everything. You tell me."

"Is it true? Are you sleeping with Forrest Symington?"

Melinda was sobbing. "Yes," she shouted, as though being aggressive would make it less humiliating. "Yes, it's true."

LEAH LAIMAN

"He's paying for the apartment, isn't he?"

"He loves me. He wants to be with me."

"Don't be ridiculous," Diane said, not even trying to be kind. "He's using you. You're not his first, and I'm sure you won't be his last."

"Wait a minute." Harvey was just getting his bearings. "This guy's older than me. And he's married. I can't let you—"

"Don't you see?" Diane interrupted bitterly. "You can't stop her."

But Melinda had already run into her own room, slamming the door behind her.

Lying on her bed, face buried in the pillows, she let herself cry. She had expected it to be hard, but she hadn't expected anything like this. Even though she was certain that her mother had her suspicions, she had managed to avoid a confrontation for weeks. From the time they had returned from New York the focus had been on Sam being arrested, then Sam being fired, then Sam taking her protest to court. Melinda had been grateful to have the attention off her, but she knew she couldn't go on pretending it wasn't her problem. Sam had always stuck up for her when they were growing up; how could she turn her back on her sister now? On the other hand, Sam seemed to be intent on destroying the most important person in Melinda's life right now, Forrest Symington.

To his credit, Forrest had noticed that Melinda seemed unusually tense in his presence, although she fulfilled her duties as his personal assistant without a misstep. Thinking he might have scared her with his advances in New York, he backed off a little. He wasn't about to lose his impeccable timing at this late date. With the new plant in jeopardy it had been easy to concentrate on DMC business and let the rest go. But once the injunction had been passed down and the lawyers were working on their strategy, he'd found himself restless, needing relief.

She wouldn't look him in the eye when he called her into his office, just sat in her customary chair across from his desk, pencil poised on pad, ready to take notes. Without a word he walked over to her and, standing above her, raised her chin with his fingertips until her eyes were forced to meet his. There was no mistaking his desire or her distress.

"You're upset," he said simply.

"Yes." She was shaking.

"Is it something I've done?"

"No," she answered vehemently. Then she amended, "Well, yes. I mean, not exactly."

He smiled the dazzler. Clearly, it wasn't what he'd thought he'd done, and anything else he was sure he could handle by doing more of the same.

"Tell me."

"Samantha Myles is my sister," she'd blurted out.

For a minute he didn't make the connection. He'd looked at her, waiting for more.

"Sam Myles," she corrected herself.

"Oh, I see. And you're angry at me because she's angry at me."

"No, I'm not. But I feel like maybe I should be. I mean, we've always stuck up for each other, but this time I don't know what to think."

Gently he took her by the hand and led her to the huge glove-leather sofa that dominated the conference area, sitting down beside her, but never letting go of her hand. "I don't blame you for being confused. I'm sure you've heard her side. But let me tell you my side. Is that fair?"

She nodded. There was nothing she wanted more than to hear him explain away her doubts.

"I respect your sister's concern for her community, but what I object to is her lack of regard for my responsibilities and obligations. DMC isn't just a company to me, it's a family. I hold myself accountable to every single person who works here, from the people in this office to the guys who work on the line to the salesmen in the showrooms. I have spent my life helping the whole DMC family realize the American dream. And that's what this new plant is all about. I know Sam is concerned about the environment, but dammit, don't you think I am? I have children, I hope to have grandchildren. Do I look like a monster?"

Looking into his eyes, their warmth tempered with a hint of steel, Melinda was mesmerized. What she saw was god, not devil, and if there was anger, it was the righteous anger of a good man wronged.

"The D'Uberville Motor Company is not just a business to me. It's my life," Forrest went on, seeing that he was having the desired effect. "Do you think I would threaten my own life by building a plant that would lead to disaster? A plant at the mill pond would benefit everybody. We've got the resources, and we've done the research. I know exactly how many people have been laid off since the start of the recession, and how much they've suffered. They need this plant more than I do. And that's what hurts me. Your sister is making people think that I would cavalierly risk their health just to make a buck. I've got plenty of money. I don't need any more. They're the ones who need help, and that's all I'm trying to do. Help them." He paused. "I'm sorry. I don't usually go on like this. I always have to play the cool executive. But somehow, with you . . . I'm sorry." He turned away, as if embarrassed by his show of emotion.

Melinda was more than touched. At some moment before Forrest stopped speaking she had felt her heart fly out of her chest and nestle itself comfortably into the palm of his hand. She reached out and touched his shoulder, whispering his name. He grabbed her hand and brought it to his lips, turning around to face her again. He waited, mindful of her age, his age, her position, his position. There could be no appearance of taking advantage here. She moved to him, as he knew she would, kissing him, first tentatively, then ardently. And finally he allowed himself to take her in his arms and let his passion loose.

It was late. There was no one in the office. He had taken the precaution of locking the door when she'd first walked in. She was wearing a full skirt, and it had been no problem getting underneath it. She had parted her legs for him and let him guide himself into her, her desire as compelling as his own. Then she stopped suddenly and stifled a scream. A second later he felt the warm flow of her blood and realized, in a moment of shock, that she was a virgin. He pulled out and, yanking up his pants, which he had never completely taken off, went to the bathroom and brought her a towel. She was curled on the couch, legs drawn up, trying to hold the blood inside. She looked very frightened, but still very beautiful, and annoyance gave way to a resurgence of desire. Gently he slipped the towel beneath her.

"Your couch," she said.

"It doesn't matter. I'll get a new one." He sat beside her, brushed her hair from her face, and felt her relax. "Why didn't you tell me?"

"I was afraid if I did, you wouldn't want me."

"Are you okay?"

She nodded. "I didn't expect it to hurt so much."

"If I had known, it wouldn't have. I could have made it better for you."

"It was still good."

He smiled. She had no idea what she was talking about, he realized. This could end up being even more interesting than he had anticipated. It had been a long time since he'd been confronted by such innocence.

"Does it still hurt?" he asked. She shook her head. "Take off all your clothes," he said as he started to take off his own. "I'm going to show you what good is." And he did.

By the time Melinda got to work the next morning the new couch was already in place. There had also been a turquoise box from Tiffany's on top of Melinda's steno pad. She'd opened it to find the most beautiful watch she'd ever seen. She'd giggled when Forrest had told her it was to mark her milestone, a gift for her rite of passage, like a bar mitzvah present. They'd tried the new sofa, too, more than once, but both of them realized that they were flirting with danger. It had been Forrest who had suggested the apartment on Fairview Road, conveniently located on his regular route between Belvedere and DMC headquarters. At first Melinda had resisted, hating the idea of being a kept woman. But when Forrest assured her it was a temporary measure, just so they could be alone together while they figured out what was happening to them, she relented. She knew a man in

Forrest's position couldn't just walk away from his family and his responsibilities. But she also knew, without a doubt, that they loved each other, and something had to come of that.

Lying on her bed, the feel of her mother's slap still stinging her cheek, Melinda wished there was some way she could make her understand. She loved her family, but they were provincial people who had never been more than forty miles from home, and they didn't understand that people like Forrest Symington were different. There was a tap on the door, and Melinda buried her head under the pillow, not up for another confrontation.

"It's me, Melinda. Can I come in?" asked Sam as she came in anyway.

Melinda sat up and let herself be hugged. "Did Mom call you to talk some sense into me?"

"Something like that."

"Just don't hit me, okay?" The sisters laughed, sharing a rueful dismay at their mother's hysteria.

"Don't worry," said Sam. "She's the slugger. I've brought the handcuffs."

"Great."

"Jokes aside, Melinda. Are you sure you know what you're doing? A man like Forrest Symington . . ."

Melinda didn't want to hear it. "You don't know anything about him. He's kind, he's good, he's caring."

Sam had told herself to go easy on her kid sister, but hearing Forrest Symington described as a saint was beyond her capacity for control. "Give me a break. First of all, he's old and he's married, so what the hell is he doing with you? Secondly, he's ruthless, venal, and morally corrupt. Whatever he does, whether it's

241

set you up in an apartment or build a plant at the mill pond, all he considers are his own selfish motives."

"Look who's talking. What are your motives for blocking a plant that's been found to be perfectly safe and is going to give hundreds of people jobs? Some interesting press coverage?"

"He's really got you bamboozled, hasn't he?"

"Give me some credit, Sam. I know you're supposed to be the smart one, but I can think for myself. I can see what's going on."

"No, I don't think you can. You are making a big mistake."

"Fine. Then it's my mistake to make. The way I see it, you're the one out of work, on the outs with her boyfriend, and fighting for a losing cause. I've got a job, someone I love who loves me, and a fabulous place to live. So who's making the mistake here?"

"I can see there's no talking to you anymore."

"Yeah, I guess you could say that. I'm not buying everything you say just because you're my older sister and you said it."

"I never asked you to do that."

"No, but somehow that's how it always worked out."

"I was just giving you my opinion."

"I'm not interested. I'll form my own opinions from now on."

"Fine," said Sam, and there was sadness in her voice. "If you want to talk, you call me."

She turned and left the room. Melinda wanted to call her back. She *did* want to talk. She wanted to tell her sister everything. How it had all happened. How wonderful Forrest was. How happy she was. How guilty she felt. How scared she got. But Sam wouldn't understand; none of them would. Forrest was the enemy, and if she chose to go with Forrest, she'd be the enemy, too. They couldn't see that from the moment he had shown her the possibility of another kind of life, away from the grime and the dreariness of Oakdale, she had had no choice. For the first time in her life she was taking a major step without the approval of her family. No more Myles Militia. She was on her own.

"We can't do it," Jack said vehemently. It was late, and Sam had made him leave the warm, plump arms of Teresa, his accommodating landlady, to come and meet her downstairs in the vacant storefront that Teresa allowed them to use as their headquarters.

"What do you mean *we?* Who said anything about you? I'm doing this one on my own."

"No!"

"Why not?"

"Because it's illegal, and you're going to get caught."

"Fine. As long as I get caught after I've had a chance to look at the report. Then you can bail me out, and I can hold a press conference, and maybe finally everyone will know what DMC is really up to."

"What makes you so sure there is a report and you're going to find it?"

"There has to be a report. A company the size of DMC doesn't make a move without a report, let alone build a plant. If it's anywhere, it's going to be in the CEO's office. And I've got the keys."

"How did you get them?"

"Uh . . . well, that's the not-so-nice part. From my sister. You know, she's Forrest Symington's assistant."

"Your sister gave them to you?"

"Not exactly gave."

"You stole them from your own sister?"

"Not exactly stole. Accidentally borrowed. I went over to my parents' to talk to her about . . . a family situation. Anyway, when I left I picked up her keys by mistake. We have the same key rings. Mom and Dad brought them back for us from some vacation they took. They still buy us identical stuff even though we're not kids anymore."

"Yeah, parents are like that. Isn't she going to notice her keys are missing?"

"I took them back right away. I just made copies of the office ones first. So it's not exactly stealing."

"They catch you, babe, and it's breaking and entering. No matter how you got the keys. As your lawyer, I have to advise you not to break the law."

"And as my friend and fellow traveler?" Sam asked hopefully.

"Don't do it," Jack answered unceremoniously.

Sam sighed. She had thought it was a great idea, and she had been positive Jack would agree. Maybe it was a mistake getting him out of bed. "Okay, Jack. I get the message. Why don't you go back to bed? We'll talk about it in the morning."

"What are you going to do?" he asked suspiciously.

"Close up. Go home. Sleep."

"Now that sounds like a good plan." He wasn't sure he trusted her, but he knew Teresa would still be waiting for him upstairs. One thing about older women, they were always willing to wait. Given the choice between her warm bed and body and arguing with Sam, there was no contest. "I'm out of here," he said, bussing her on the cheek. "We'll talk tomorrow, but I'm still going to tell you the same thing."

"Okay," Sam said with a laugh. "I've been warned."

She waited until she was sure he was back upstairs. Then she waited another ten minutes to make sure he would be too busy to look out the window. Then she took the keys and left.

Getting in was no trouble. There was a security guard at the desk in the lobby, and she'd greeted him as though she knew him, explaining she'd forgotten some work she needed to do at home and was just coming to pick it up. He'd given her the register to sign, and she'd cheerily penned a false name and destination. In case he was watching, she'd gotten off on the sixteenth floor, to match what she had written, then sneaked into the stairwell and climbed the four flights to the executive penthouse suite.

She was impressed. She had never seen where Melinda worked before, and she could understand how the atmosphere might have gone to her sister's head. Everything was plush, luxurious. The furniture in the waiting area was clearly more expensive than that in any living room she'd ever seen in Oakdale. Even the secretaries' desks were a burnished dark wood that gave off its own eerie glow. The door to the inner sanctum was locked, but her key fit easily. She let herself in and gasped at the majesty of the view. Windows on all sides overlooked the twinkling lights of the twin cities below. It was a clear night, and a full moon poured its pale gold rays into the room, illuminating an office that was three times the size of her entire apartment. She allowed herself a moment to explore, letting her hands brush the soft glove leather of the sofa, her breath catching at the richness beneath her fingers. If this was how the Symingtons worked, she couldn't even imagine how they lived.

Forcing herself to get to work, she went straight to the credenza behind Forrest's desk, and after trying several of the smaller keys she'd copied off Melinda's ring she found the one that fit. She silently blessed her instincts for not letting her down as she opened it to reveal a library of bound reports, standing cover to cover from one end of the cabinet to the other. Taking the penlight she had brought with her, she focused it on one title after another. There were annual reports for the past ten years; there was an analysis of design modifications in next year's models of D'Uberville SX600s, which she would have loved to read, but not now; there were published results of safety and durability tests. But there was nothing even remotely connected to the building of a new plant.

She sat on the floor, frustrated and depressed. There were other cabinets she could explore, but she had the feeling that if what she wanted wasn't here, she wasn't going to find it. She got up and went to the window, looking for inspiration from the star-studded sky.

"If you could wish on a star, is this what you'd wish for?"

She whirled. Drew Symington was standing not two feet away from her, holding a bound report. She did not need to see the title to know that it was what she was looking for. Her heart surged, and she did not know if it was from the fear of being caught or the joy of seeing him. More than anything, she didn't want to make a fool of herself.

"My turn to lose," she said, sounding more in control than she was.

He recognized the quote. It was what the infamous terrorist, Carlos, had said when he was finally captured by the authorities. It was a little melodramatic. "You sound like you're preparing for the firing squad."

He was mocking her. She was risking everything while he safely toed the corporate line and was rewarded with penthouse suites and million-dollar bonuses, and he had the nerve to trivialize what she was doing. She was furious.

"Damn you," she hissed. "This is nothing to you but a game. Stuck up here in your ivory tower—"

"This is my father's office, not mine."

"I know. Yours is on eleven. To give the impression you're working your way up, right?"

"That's not the only reason," he said a little sheepishly.

"Just the main one. You're all alike. You think—"

"Shhh," he interrupted.

But she was on a roll. "I will not shhh. I have the right—"

"Shhh," he said more insistently. "Someone's coming."

She stopped and heard the footsteps, too. It was the guard making his regular rounds. Before she could think of what to do, Drew had grabbed her and was dragging her across the room.

"Get your hands off me. What do you think—"

His hand clamped across her mouth as he lifted her

bodily and carried her into a closet, closing the door behind them. She struggled for a moment, then stopped as she heard the guard enter and saw the beam of his flashlight from under the closet door as he checked out the room. They stood very still, their chests rising and falling in rhythm as they breathed silently. Sensing she had stopped struggling, he took his hand from her mouth and just rested it on her shoulder in a gesture so reassuring that she wanted to grasp it and kiss it in gratitude. She could feel his warm breath on the back of her neck and the length of his body against hers. She closed her eyes and imagined what would happen if she turned around and faced him in this small space. And then the light from outside went off. There was the sound of the door opening and closing again, of receding footsteps. The guard was gone. Drew reached in front of her, and she thought he was going to open the door, but instead he turned her around. Their lips were inches apart, and all her imaginings came true as he drew her to him and kissed her. Her whole body remembered and welcomed him, but her mind forced her back to the reality of the moment. He was still the enemy. Or was he? Still in his arms, she threw open the door. The bracing air of the room, in contrast to the stifling space of the closet, pushed them apart.

"Why did you do that?" she asked quietly.

"Because I wanted to. Didn't you?"

She didn't want to talk about the kiss. She couldn't. "No. I mean, why did you hide me? Why didn't you just turn me in to the guard?"

"I hid myself, and you just happened to be with me."

"What?" Was he playing with her again?

"I'm not supposed to be here either. I've been studying this report for the past few nights, but I didn't want my father to know about it."

"Why?"

"Because the report confirms what you and your people are saying. That a plant at the mill pond will eventually turn out to be an environmental disaster. And I'm trying to figure out a way to stop him from doing it before he knows what I'm doing and stops me."

"But you've never said—"

"How could I? Forrest Symington is my father. DMC is my company. I'm not about to undermine either one of them. But I'm not about to let either one of them commit a grievous error either."

She felt herself grinning. He looked at her, puzzled. "Did I say something funny?"

"Oh, no," she answered hastily, but she couldn't stop smiling. "It's just that I could never quite reconcile what I *thought* about you with what I *felt* about you. Now I can."

"And what's your consolidated opinion?"

"You're an honorable man."

He felt as though he'd been knighted by the queen. "Do you trust me to help you?"

"Yes."

"Then you have to help me."

"How?"

"Call off your dogs. Stop your protests and demonstrations."

She was angry again. "Damn it, I should have known better. This is all a ploy to get me to back down. I'm vulnerable to you, I admit it. But you're not going to beat me by getting me to give in to my libido."

Now it was his turn to smile. "My God, you're a hothead. Do you ever stop to listen before you react? Do you think you're going to do any good by forcing the board to abandon plans for a new plant? Have you seen the unemployment figures for the area? Is it more important to save a plot of land than a lot of hungry people?"

"That's not fair. You know my position. We need the jobs, but not at the expense of our children's health."

"But you need the jobs. Even if the air and water are pure, children don't stay healthy if they don't have anything to eat. Can we agree on that?"

"Yes, of course."

"Good. Do you want to help me find a way to get a new plant built and keep the mill pond intact?"

"How?"

"Help me find an alternate site. So that when I stand up at the board meeting to voice my objection I have an alternative to offer. If I'm just a spoiler, they can dismiss me. If I have a plan, they will have to listen. You know this area. I don't. I've spent my life away, at school, on holidays. My mother hates it here and tried to make me believe I was really a misplaced European. But I'm not. This place is in my blood the way it's in yours. But I need someone to show me the possibilities. Someone I can trust who won't go to my father and tell him I'm in the process of betraying him."

She could see that it hurt him to do this and

remembered, absurdly, that even Attila the Hun was just plain Dad to someone.

"When do we start?" she asked, knowing he would not want to talk about it—not yet, anyway.

"Is right now too soon?"

She looked outside. The moon was high. The night was clear and bright. She already had some locations in mind to show him. They wouldn't be able to evaluate every aspect of every site, but they'd need surveyors for that anyway. They'd certainly be able to see enough to eliminate areas that were entirely inappropriate. She looked at her watch. It was three in the morning. She felt preternaturally awake.

"Let's go," she said, heading for the door.

"Just one more thing," he said, stopping her. She waited, holding her breath. It sounded serious. "Is your libido still feeling vulnerable?"

She wondered if he could see her blush in the moonlight. "Could we not talk about this now?"

He laughed, and she had to shush him as they hurried out the door and down the stairwell. When they left the building the security guard was asleep, and she didn't even bother to sign out.

"Good God, Jean-Claude. It's three o'clock in the morning!"

"I am sorry, *chérie*. Here it is nine. I am at the *préfecture de police* in Monaco. I have news. I thought you would want to know."

The connection was so good that she had forgotten for a moment that he was in France.

"I do, of course." She shook the sleep from her head and took a gulp from the champagne glass that was still on her bedside table. Ugh. Flat. Thank heaven she'd made her personal trainer leave. He was hunky, but he was stupid, and she didn't need him here to distract her right now. "I've missed you so much, my darling. Tell me what you've found out."

"You were right. There was a bigger secret."

Of course she was right. "Go on, my sweet."

"This has been very hard for me. I found witnesses, and I asked questions. Over and over I hear the story about how poor Lisette was killed. Very hard." His voice broke.

"My poor darling. At least you have me now," she said. Just get on with it, she thought.

"Merci à Dieu for you. I could not live—"

"I know, sweetheart. What did you find out?"

"Drew did not kill Lisette."

"What?" This wasn't helping. "That's not possible. It said in the newspaper that he turned himself in to the police and confessed to a hit and run."

"He confessed, yes. But he lied. He did not drive that night. Witnesses saw a woman."

"But that's not possible. The police would have uncovered such an obvious mistake."

"They did. Even the files show that fingerprints on the steering wheel did not belong to Drew. But by then they had already announced that the case was solved. They thought it would be too heartbreaking and too embarrassing to open it up again. And how do you say . . . they had their man."

"But I don't understand. Why would Drew confess if he wasn't driving?"

"Mathilde was."

"Oh, my God!" This was beyond all expectations. She had just been dealt a full house.

"It is sad, no? I think she must have been drinking. You see how she drinks still. Drew confessed *pour sa mère.* He saved his *maman.*"

"What a guy," Bethany said, dripping sarcasm.

"Pardon?"

"This is such a shock." And it was. If Drew had been willing to go to jail to spare his mother, what would he be willing to do for her this time? Marry Bethany? He might think of it as prison, but the food was better.

"To me also. For so long I have been thinking of revenge on Drew. Now, suddenly, I see he is not my enemy. He was just protecting his *maman.* I can not be angry. I think we should just put the past behind us, *n'est-ce pas?*"

"Yes, you're right. That's what we'll do." Put the past behind them? Bethany was going to push the past so far into Drew's face that it was going to guarantee her future.

"I am making a reservation to come back to you today."

"No. Don't do that," she said, faster than she should have. "I mean, I want you with me forever. But not here. Let me talk to Drew. I'm sure I can make him understand. Then I'll come to you. I want to get away from here, from these people, and start a new life with you. Can we do that?"

"Of course, *mon amour.* But you said it was so difficult for you with Drew. You said he was violent. I should be there in case you need my help."

She had said that, hadn't she? It was getting hard to keep the stories straight. Thank God it would soon be over. She didn't need to lie anymore, when the truth was a stronger weapon than she could have imagined.

"No, it will just make it worse. He isn't violent when you're not around. He just gets so jealous of you. But when I explain that we love each other and I'm going to be with you, he won't be able to stop me. And we'll be safe together in France. Don't you want me?" she added plaintively, knowing how much he did.

"More than ever, *mon amour*." He paused, mulling it over. *"Bien.* If you think it would be better for you, I will wait here. When will you come?"

Reprieve. "As soon as I can. I'll call you." She started to hang up.

"Je t'aime, ma chérie."

"Oh, yeah. I love you, too," she said, and she hung up. She let her head fall onto the pillow, but she knew sleep would be a long time coming. She was excited. Instead of counting sheep she started to go over her wardrobe item by item. She would need to shop for a trousseau, fill in the missing pieces. After all, one couldn't marry into the Symington family without the proper clothing.

❧ 15 ❧

Drew and Sam drove into the back country in Drew's D'Uberville ZSX with the top down. It was unseasonably warm for late autumn, the last of Indian summer, and Sam let her head fall back and watched the stars change position as she issued her navigational orders. At first he'd questioned her, asking if she was sure, since she wasn't even looking at the road. But then he realized she knew the terrain as she knew herself. She didn't need to think about it; it just came naturally. When to eat, when to sleep, and when to turn left.

At the fourth location she brought him to, they found what they were looking for. The property was privately owned and posted no trespassing, but it was expansive, isolated, and undeveloped. Its only link to civilization was a network of gargantuan sewage pipes that dissected the area into small segments of barren earth. It was farther from Oakdale than the mill pond, but not prohibitively so, and the desolation of its position was matched only by the ugliness of its topography. There was nothing to ruin here, no natural resources to pollute or plunder.

"What do you think?" Sam asked Drew, excited.

"Remarkable" was all he could say.

"I'd forgotten how ugly it was. I don't hang out here a lot."

"I can see why."

"I think a bunch of belching smokestacks might actually improve it, don't you?" she said, only half joking.

"Do you know who owns it? And will he sell?"

"Yes. And I think so. But he's too smart to let it go for nothing. Especially to you."

"We already own the mill pond. Building there would save a lot of money."

"There's more to life than money."

"It's easy to say when it's not your money."

"I know," she said quietly, and he could hear she was disappointed.

"Hey, I'm on your side. I'm just pointing out the drawbacks."

"Let's go to the mill pond," she said suddenly.

"Why?"

"So I can point out the drawbacks of building there."

"I know what they are."

"Maybe. But you need to feel it."

By the time they got to the mill pond the night sky had lightened from indigo to deep purple, and the stars were starting to fade. They were pulling into the clearing when the car suddenly sputtered and died.

"What happened?" Sam asked.

"I have no idea," said Drew honestly.

"It sounded like you might have bumped the drive shaft and knocked something out of whack."

Drew started to laugh. "Well, at least I can't be accused of engineering this on purpose, considering I'm out here with the best mechanic in America."

In a second she was out of the car and under the hood. "Okay, I've got it, and I can fix it. But you know," she added with a sly smile, "if you had a Mylometer, this sort of thing wouldn't happen."

"What the hell is a Mylometer?"

"It's my new invention. The one you were so interested in at the racetrack."

"Well, what are you doing about it?"

"Nothing right now. I'm saving up money to hire an attorney so I can get it patented. But at the rate I'm going, that might take a while. Okay, try it."

She bumped the hood down with a thud and stood back. He turned the key in the ignition. The engine purred, then stopped.

"What the hell? Why did that happen?" She started to open the hood again, perplexed; she knew she'd fixed it.

He stopped her. "I turned it off."

"Why?"

"I'm not ready to leave yet. We can watch the sun come up."

She gazed at the sky. Its hue had paled to lilac, and traces of pink were peeking over the horizon. She looked back at Drew, but he wasn't in the car anymore. For a minute she wondered if he'd left her there alone, and then she saw him coming toward her from the edge of the water. He had wet his handkerchief, and with the utmost gentleness he began to wipe away a little smudge of grime from her left cheek. When it was gone he kissed the spot where it had been, then kissed around it, finally making his way to her lips.

"Are you cold?" he whispered.

"No. I'm on fire." And indeed, everywhere he touched she felt her skin blazing with an intense white heat. There was an afghan on the backseat of the car, and he reached in, grabbed it, and spread it on the ground without taking his mouth from hers. He took off her clothes then, and she shivered for a moment in the cool air until he had taken off his own and covered her with himself. She floated in a cocoon of warmth, the soft wool under her, the heat of Drew's body above. Undulating gently, he made the temperature rise even further, until they were both feverish with need and desire. Sam felt herself exploding in spontaneous combustion, and as Drew melted inside her she knew his fireworks had matched her own. She opened her eyes and caught her breath, for she had never seen a more dazzling sky above a more resplendent panorama. She wanted him to see what she saw, but the possibility of separating was inconceivable. Reaching behind her, he pulled the throw around them both; then, holding her closer than she'd ever been held before, he turned her gingerly with him so that they were lying, still joined, on their sides. Together they watched the fiery ball of the sun inch its way into the flaming sky. And when it had reached its height, so had he, and they began coming together again without ever having been apart.

"I love you, Samantha Myles," Drew said when they were dressed and ready to go.

"You hardly even know me."

"I know that I love you."

"You're engaged to a socialite."

"Not anymore."

"I don't fit in your crowd."

"You fit perfectly in me."

It was true, but still she felt there were objections to be raised. "It's going to be very complicated," she said.

"It's going to be worth it," he answered.

She believed him. She had no more arguments. "I love you, too, Andrew Symington. I always have. I always will."

She wanted him to drop her off at her door.

"It's been a very long day . . . and night . . . and day. I need to be alone, to think, to sleep."

"I understand. I'll be alone with you."

She laughed. "Actually, I wouldn't mind, except that I wasn't really expecting company. My place is a horrible mess."

"I won't look."

"You won't be able not to. Please. Give me a chance to make a good first impression."

"You already have. The best."

"That's not what I mean." She blushed, knowing what he meant. He touched her cheek and smiled. For an iron maiden, she was very vulnerable. He kissed her and took her keys from her, and she did not protest.

When they got upstairs she kicked some dirty laundry under the bed and made him tea. He asked to see her Mylometer design, and she was proud to show him, knowing he would understand and appreciate it. He studied the carefully drawn diagrams that she gently took from their folder and pronounced her a genius, meaning it sincerely. They talked about cars and what could be done with a little ingenuity, and they laughed when they realized how the mental excitement could stimulate the physical. Then they made love again in her bed, slowly and tenderly, savoring every moment.

When he saw how hard it was for her to keep her eyes open he got out of bed and started to dress. "You have the day to sleep and clean up. Then I'm coming over, and I'm never letting you out of my sight again as long as you live. Is that a deal?"

"Fair enough." She laughed and kissed him five or six times before finally sending him on his way.

Sam was already asleep when the doorbell rang. Wondering what Drew had forgotten, she stumbled to the door. Pulling on her robe, she opened it, a gentle admonishment on her lips.

"What . . ."

She froze and quickly tied her robe tightly around her. Pete was standing in front of her, and he was drunk.

"Surprise, babe. Can I come in?"

"I don't really think this is a good time, Pete." But he was already inside the door, closing it behind him.

"You don't? Why not? Your new boyfriend's gone. I saw him leave. And here I thought you were too busy for me because you were fighting for a cause. Is that your new cause? Getting laid by a rich faggot?"

She knew it was important for her to stay calm, to calm him down. "Look, you're drunk, it's late. I think you should go home and sleep it off."

"I don't give a shit what you think." She could see

she had used the wrong approach. "I've been waiting for you, bitch. I was ready to apologize and work things out, maybe even back you up on the mill pond thing if that's what was important to you. But now I see that was stupid. What's important to you is dumping me so you can fuck the boss's son. A dirt-track driver couldn't get you ahead fast enough."

Now she was angry. "How dare you talk to me about what's important? You think I don't know why you're here? You don't want to apologize and support the mill pond. You want me back because you've been losing a lot of races lately and you can't get a mechanic to fix your car like I could. You thought if you could get me in bed with you, you could get me to make you another car. Well, I've got news for you. It doesn't matter what you do at the track. You're still a loser."

The minute she said it she was sorry. Something changed in Pete's face, visibly hardened. The hang-dog, pathetic look of the drunk was gone, and now his eyes were glazed with a hatred that was frightening in its intensity.

"No, baby," he said quietly, ominously, "I ain't a loser. You are. Because I'm more of a man than that faggot you're making it with now. And I'm going to prove it to you. Just one more time. So you'll know I ain't the loser."

He started moving toward her.

"Stop. Don't do this." She was backing away, but he reached out and grabbed the ties of her robe, pulling her to him with a violent tug. She fell against him, and he put his mouth on hers. She tried to turn away, feeling the scratch of his beard, smelling the sour beer being exhaled in punchy breaths into her face. He pushed her back for a moment, still holding her by her robe with one hand while he groped at his zipper with the other. It was just an inch of space, but it was all she needed. She jerked up her knee as hard as she could and connected. Pete groaned and doubled over. His breath came in rasping gasps as he slumped to the floor.

"You bitch," he moaned.

She backed away. "Get out before I call the police."

"I'll make you sorry for this," he gasped as he stumbled out the door.

"Yeah, I know," she said, dismissing him. But she was still frightened. She knew Pete well enough to take him at his word.

It took all of Drew's willpower not to call Sam. He'd come into the office after two hours' sleep and been sorely tempted every hour on the hour since then. But just because he was awake didn't mean she was. And he had promised her the day. It was the least he could give her, considering that he intended to monopolize the rest of her lifetime. He'd already ordered some surveys done on the property they'd discovered together and was having some discreet inquiries made by a realtor without obvious connections to DMC. It was hard to concentrate on anything else, and he would have welcomed almost any interruption except the one he got.

"I told the girls out front that you were expecting me," Bethany said as she sailed in. She was perfectly put together as usual, striking in a black and red Yves St. Laurent suit.

"I'm sorry, Bethany, you should have called. I'm extremely busy today."

"Surely not too busy to spend a few moments with your fiancée."

He looked at her sharply. He thought he had clarified their relationship. Why was she acting as though nothing had happened?

"Look, I agreed not to make any public announcements until you were ready, but we both agreed the engagement was off."

"I didn't exactly agree, darling."

"What is this, Bethany? Please do me the courtesy of not playing your silly games. I haven't the patience for it anymore."

"My goodness, aren't we testy?"

"I didn't get a lot of sleep last night. Do you want to get to the point?"

"Well, if you're going to insist on doing away with all the niceties, fine. The point is, I still think we should get married."

"You're delusional," Drew said shortly.

"Don't you want to know why?"

"No. It doesn't matter. I don't love you. We're not getting married."

"As the song goes, what's love got to do with it? There are so many other factors to consider——"

"No, there aren't," he interrupted.

She ignored him. "Like your mother, and how she would feel if everyone knew about her little accident on the Riviera."

"What?" She smiled. She had his attention now.

"See, that's just the thing, darling. I know your mother has a slight drinking problem, and she didn't mean to kill that girl. And I understand how sweet it was of you to cover up for her. But I don't know how other people would react to it. And she's so very fragile, your mother. And she seems to care so much what people think."

"Are you trying to blackmail me?" She heard the contempt in his voice but remained unperturbed.

"Don't be silly. I'm trying to protect you and your family from getting involved in a nasty scandal."

"If I marry you."

"Well, why would it matter to me if we weren't married?" she asked, as though her reasoning was unquestionably logical.

He shook his head. "Do you have any idea how repulsive you are to me now?"

"Do you have any idea how little I care? You don't want to play games, fine, let's not play games. I've had my spies out. I know you're infatuated with a bimbo factory worker, but so what? You think you'd be the first husband in Woodland Cliffs who diddled some nobody? I think I can provide better sex than you could possibly get from some blue-collar pussy, but if you don't think so, that's your loss. Marriages around here aren't based on that. And we both know it. Not my parents', and not yours. We're uniting dynasties, and that's what's important."

"If that's all you think it is, why don't you just pick some other dynasty to unite with? There are plenty of other men around who I'm sure would be glad to live by your rules."

"Because, silly, the Symingtons are the most important people here. And if I'm staying in this little pond, I intend to be the biggest fish. But it's not like you're not getting anything in return. Look at me. I don't see cause for complaint. And of course, your family's reputation—your mother's, really—would be safe."

He wanted to laugh, but he didn't dare. Bethany might be arrogant and misguided, but she wasn't stupid, and she was very, very dangerous. She was right about Mathilde. As shallow and petty as it was, appearance meant everything to her. And as little as it meant to him, she was still his mother. If he rebuffed Bethany now, she'd be on the phone by this afternoon. And by tonight Mathilde would be under a suicide watch.

"All right, Bethany, I see your point," he said, hiding his disgust with difficulty. "You may be right, but I need a little time to think about it, sort things out."

She smiled, triumphant. "Take all the time you want, darling." She came over and put her arms around him, kissing him lightly. He made no move, though every fiber of his being wanted to push her away in revulsion. She headed for the door, turning back for a moment before she left.

"Oh, and by the way, about that cunt on the assembly line—"

He flinched. "Don't."

She went right on as if she hadn't heard. "Don't see her anymore. Once we're married I don't care what you do. But while we're engaged it's unseemly for you to rut around the workers."

She was out the door before he could respond, and it was a good thing, too. He had never hit a woman in his life, but he would have hit her if he'd had the chance.

On the first day in her new apartment Melinda was in heaven. She took the day off from work in order to move in and get settled. Her mother had sat at the kitchen table with sad eyes, saying nothing, watching her lug her suitcases out. Melinda was glad that her father was on the early shift and wasn't around for last-minute recriminations. She couldn't really blame them for being against it; Forrest was older than her father, and married. But still, she knew that what she was doing was right for her. She wasn't naïve enough to think that Forrest would suddenly divorce his wife and marry her. She had heard Mathilde was not strong, and they were planning a June wedding for their son. Forrest had explained it might take a while to make permanent changes, and she understood that. But he was as committed to her as any man could be, and this apartment, their apartment, was the first step in proving it. And as much as the rift with her family hurt, she felt they'd come around when they saw how happy she was.

On the first day Forrest managed to leave the office early, and he showed up on her doorstep with champagne and roses. They baptized the bed with their lovemaking, and Melinda felt that now it was truly her home. She wanted to make Forrest dinner and spend an evening in domestic bliss, but he looked at his watch and remembered that Mathilde had invited some people over and he really had to get home.

The second day he surprised her by arriving just as she was getting dressed for work. Teasing, he told her he'd make allowances for her tardiness just this once and made her take her clothes off again. He only stayed for twenty minutes, and by the time she got to the office an hour after him he was all business. But she carried her secret inside her like a hidden treasure all day and felt special, knowing she'd be with him again at night. She left at five, expecting him to follow a short while later. He called at six-thirty to say he was already home. Mathilde wasn't feeling well, and he'd had to go home to her. But he promised he'd sneak out later to see her if he could. As it turned out, he couldn't that night, but it appeased her to know that now that she was in her own apartment he could see her whenever he had time.

The third day he couldn't come at all. She tried to steal a moment behind the closed door of his office as they used to, but Forrest said it was too dangerous, and now that he'd gotten her the apartment they didn't need to do that. The apartment seemed very empty when she went home, and when she opened the refrigerator there was only the salmon she had bought to make Forrest dinner, and it was smelling a little funny. She threw it out and opened some tuna, which she ate straight from the can watching television.

The fourth and fifth days he did stop in on his way home from work, and she could see a pattern was being set. If they weren't too busy, she'd leave the office about five-thirty or six; then he'd show up an hour later, stay for twenty minutes, and go home. Weekends, he explained, were out of the question. But he gave her her own credit card at Saks and told her to go shopping. She spent most of her time away from work alone now. Because of her special relationship with Forrest she couldn't very well make friends with any of the girls in the office. She missed talking to her sister and having dinner with her parents, but any reconciliation at this point seemed impossible. Still, she told herself, she had her moments with Forrest, and as brief as they were, they were wonderful and tender, and all that love should be. He never came empty-handed or left without telling her he loved her. And Melinda was convinced that the fervent quality of his love made up for the diminished quantity of his time. And when he told her that someday they would really be together and spoke about starting a new life with her, Melinda believed him with all her heart and soul.

By the third week Melinda didn't mind so much that Forrest was spending so little time with her. She was coming down with the flu, and it was all she could do to get herself through the days at work. She remained available to him when he wanted her, but the rest of the time she slept. She was grateful for her solitude now, and she waited for the bug to pass, dreaming of things the two of them would do together after Forrest's son was married and he had more time. When the general listlessness turned into active nausea she called in sick and went to the doctor—a woman named Karla Norris, recommended by the corporate health plan. It only took a urine sample and a few minutes for them to tell her she didn't have the flu. She was pregnant—about four weeks, by their estimate.

Melinda was amazed at the equanimity with which she took the news.

"What kind of birth control have you been using?" Dr. Norris asked her.

"None. I mean I just sort of started, and I meant to get something, but I didn't get around to it. I didn't think anything would happen so fast."

"I see. Didn't anyone ever tell you it only takes once?" The doctor wasn't being unkind, she was just a little incredulous.

"Of course, I know that. I just . . . " Melinda faded off. She just what? Didn't think about it? Didn't care?

"How do you feel about it? Do you want this baby?"

"Oh, yes, absolutely," Melinda answered with such certainty that she surprised even herself. But she was certain.

"Do you have a regular partner?"

"I beg your pardon?"

"A mate? Husband? Boyfriend?"

"Oh, yes, I see. I'm not married, but I have a . . . man." What was Forrest? She didn't know what to call him. But labels didn't matter. "This is definitely a child of love."

"He'll support you on this?"

"He supports me on everything."

"No financial worries?"

She laughed. "None whatsoever. The father is a wealthy, generous man, and we're planning to be together soon. We already have an apartment, and there's plenty of room for the baby. In fact, this might even make it all happen sooner." She patted her tummy, feeling wonderful. Now that she knew what was making her ill, it didn't seem to bother her as much. She couldn't wait to tell Forrest.

"In that case," said Dr. Norris, "congratulations. See the nurse at the desk. She'll set up an appointment for you. I'll want to see you in four weeks. Meanwhile, I'm giving you a prescription for vitamins. Take one a day, rest as much as you can, eat well but in moderation, and stay away from alcohol."

"Okay. Yes. Thank you. I will. Thank you, Dr. Norris." She shook the doctor's hand, grinning from ear to ear, and went out singing, "I'm having his baby."

❦ 16 ❦

Every time the phone rang Sam expected it to be Drew. Twice it had been Jack, wanting to know when she was coming to Save the Mill Pond headquarters. Once it had been Diane, wanting to know if she had talked to Melinda. Once it had been a telephone solicitor wanting to sell her a subscription to every magazine ever printed. Once the doorbell rang, and Sam ran to it, certain that Drew had come in person. But remembering her encounter with Pete the night before, she called out a quick "Who is it?" before opening the door. It was the gas company, come to check her meter, and she had opened the door to an unnervingly cheery representative who had made his notation and gone in a mercifully short time. Sam thought of calling Drew, assuming he was hesitant to call and wake her if she was still asleep. But it was already late in the afternoon, and she wasn't sure whether he'd be home or at the office. And either way, she wouldn't feel comfortable calling. By this time her name had to be known in the Symington household as well as at DMC executive offices, and in both places, no doubt, she'd be persona non grata.

Every time Drew got near a phone he wanted to call Sam. But every time he dialed the number he forced himself to hang up before the ringing began. He knew she was waiting for his call, as he knew her need could not be any less than his own. He longed to go to her, forget the phone call, just show up and sweep her away. They could disappear together into some distant paradise where they could live a simpler life, dedicated to the pursuit of nothing but their own happiness. But he knew he could not just disappear, and he knew she would not just come. Both of them were bound to this place, to its people and its industry. And until they had come to terms with their surroundings they could not come to terms with each other.

At first he considered telling her the truth, explaining Bethany's position and why he couldn't simply defy her. Then he considered Sam and her own quotient for defiance. Much as he loved her, and knew in his very essence that she loved him, he was not certain she would understand. She was prepared for public combat with her family, her colleagues, her community in pursuit of her principles. What would she make of a man who refused to take a stand against one scheming, vicious woman? Even worse, would she interfere with his course of action, which he had decided would be the most painless for all involved, because the plan was based on deceit, and Sam believed in forthrightness above all things? He laughed bitterly at the irony. Sam was too honest for him to take her into his confidence, too trustworthy for him to trust.

Not wanting to give his name to any of her environmental cronies, he'd waited until he was sure she'd be home from the protest center before he called. Her joy on hearing his voice reflected his own, but he reminded himself of his mission and tried to temper his tone.

"I've been waiting all day," she said, more as statement than scolding.

"I'm sorry," he said. At least that much was true.

"It doesn't matter now that we're talking. Where are you? Can you come over? I've cleaned my place."

More than anything, it was where he wanted to be. In her place, in her arms, in her heart. "No, I don't think I should." Bethany had already told him she had spies watching him. The last thing he wanted to do was lead them back to Sam. "Could you meet me somewhere?"

"Sure," she said, and he heard the dismay in her voice. "Where?"

He saw that his attempt at nonchalance was a complete failure. He'd have to hone his poker skills if he intended to delude her about his true feelings. "How about that all-night coffee shop on Fulton Street, just outside Woodland Cliffs? Do you know the one I mean?"

She knew it well. It was a seedy greasy spoon frequented primarily by rich high school boys from Woodland Cliffs who would stop for fries and fish tales on the way home after a night of slumming with the girls in Oakdale. Her stomach sank as she sensed without his saying that he hadn't picked the spot for its convenience. "Ten minutes" was all she said as she hung up.

Sam arrived to find Drew in a booth, his coffee cup empty, shredding a paper napkin. From the looks of the confetti on the table, she realized he must have been there for quite some time before he made the call. She leaned in to give him a kiss, but he seemed almost to recoil, and she slipped into the seat opposite him instead. She looked into his eyes, and for the second before he turned away all she saw was misery.

"Do you want something?" he asked with a feigned cheerfulness she found jarring.

"Yes. I want to know what's wrong."

He wanted to smile. She was so straight, so true to form. He was tempted for a moment to be like her, to drop the bullshit and tell her the truth. Then he could bury his head in her hair and nibble at the spot he had found the night before, in the hollow of her collar bone, where sensations seemed to coalesce and trigger passion. He was wanting and she was waiting, but tonight honesty was a luxury he could not afford. By the time he turned back his eyes were veiled with an impenetrable shield, and his voice was coated with a tone so affable that it sounded unctuous even to his own ears.

"About last night," he began.

"Yes?"

"It was wonderful, of course, but . . ."

She said nothing. She wasn't going to help him, and he didn't blame her.

He tried again. "Look, I'm sure you're as embarrassed about it as I am. After all, we did kind of get carried away by the circumstances."

"Is that what you think happened?"

"Well, yes. Don't you? After all, it's not as though we could possibly have any future together. Right?"

"Right," she answered, her eyes glistening with certainty, her heart breaking. "Right," she said again with more vehemence. Fool me twice, shame on me.

"I don't think we should let it get in the way of the progress we made on the mill pond issue. I mean, I'm still going to propose the alternative site, and I'd like to hold you to your promise not to demonstrate as long as that remains a possibility."

"By all means." She could barely speak, and he ached for the pain he was causing her.

"I do think we can win this if you just give me a little time, let me handle it my way," he said, meaning more than she could possibly understand. "It may be hard to believe right now, but everything's going to turn out all right." He wanted to give her hope, ease her through the agony, but by the anguish in his own heart he knew it could not be done. Best to end it, cut her loose and let her go. "I'll . . . I'll keep you posted."

She was being dismissed. She wanted to run, but her legs felt like lead weights. Actually, she was grateful for the betrayal of her body. It forced her to move slowly and deliberately, preventing her from further humiliating herself by racing out in a cascade of blinding tears. "Please do," she said, sounding to herself as though she was very far away, and wishing that she were.

Drew watched her go, resisting the urge to chase after her. It wouldn't do any good; there was nothing more he could say at this point. It was more important that Sam be safe than that she understand. Besides, he thought, glancing at his watch, he would be late for his date with Bethany.

In the anteroom of the D'Uberville Motor Company's executive offices Pete Wojek could feel the sweat collecting around his collar. He was tempted to loosen the tie he had borrowed and relax a little. But looking at the unsmiling receptionist, primly sitting at her desk, he had a feeling that relaxation was not a welcome attitude in this place, and he needed to make a good impression, coming, as he had, without an appointment. Originally he had called to set up a meeting, but when he'd been connected to Symington's personal assistant and realized it was Sam's sister, Melinda, he'd hung up. He couldn't risk it.

"Can I help you?" the receptionist asked as he approached the desk. Up close, he could see she was quite a babe. This might not be as hard as he had anticipated.

"Hello." He beamed a one-hundred-and-ten-watt smile in her direction. "I'm Pete Wojek," he said, and he paused as though he expected her to recognize his name. Her smile was receptive but blank. "Four-time winner of the Oakdale Fairgrounds NASCAR races," he added, as though stating the obvious.

"Yes?"

"I'm here to see Mr. Forrest Symington."

"One moment please," she said, and she picked up her phone, murmuring into the mouthpiece for a few minutes while he leaned back on his heels and tried to appear nonchalant. "I'm sorry," she said, still holding the phone to her ear, "but Mr. Symington's assistant is out sick today, and the girl who's taking her place

Pete could answer that with an emphatic no. Sam had been saving up to get a patent lawyer, but he was sure that once she got laid off, that dream had been put on the back burner.

Forrest was pleased. He'd have his staff do the research, but if it turned out to be true that there were no patents pending, he was not about to let this device slip through his fingers. He studied Pete's face, saw the earnestness and the slight air of confusion, the bravado coupled with a certain lack of intelligence in the eyes. He highly doubted that the man standing in front of him was capable of developing anything remotely as clever as the complicated mechanism he was looking at. But it didn't matter. By tomorrow his own design team would have transposed the charts and drawings into a standard DMC portfolio. By the end of the week, with a little greasing of palms, DMC could have a patent in place. The original plans would be disposed of without a trace. And no one would know anything—except Forrest and this not-too-bright race car driver, who obviously had his own agenda.

"DMC has its own design team. We don't usually go outside for our ideas."

"I bet no one has come up with anything like this," said Pete confidently.

"You'd be surprised."

Pete was sure the old guy was bluffing, but he was still holding on to his hand. "If you're not interested—"

"I didn't say that," Forrest answered a little too quickly, and Pete knew he was right. "We're always interested in research and development in the industry, even when it parallels our own. Our team might find these drawings instructive in some way."

"That's what I thought," said Pete.

"And where does your interest lie?" asked Forrest politely, as though he were offering milk or sugar. "If you're looking for some sort of participation, I don't think we could accommodate you. On the other hand, I would certainly be prepared to proffer, shall we call it a finder's fee, for bringing this to my attention."

It was the moment Pete had been waiting for. "Well, I'll tell you, Mr. Symington," he said, mustering all his good ol' boy charm. "I'm a driver, not a businessman. So I'm not looking to get involved in business. I am looking for a new car, though. My last race ended in an accident, and I've lost my regular . . . crew . . . so my car hasn't been the same since. And I know you guys here know how to make cars."

Forrest laughed companionably with Pete. This was going to be easier than he thought. "Your name is Pete Wojek, right? Pete Wojek. Yes, come to think of it, I have heard you talked about. You're a good driver. We've been thinking of doing some NASCAR sponsorship. Would that be of any interest to you?"

"Hell, yes!" shouted Pete. This was better than he had bargained for. He was hoping for a new car, maybe a payoff. But getting the D'Uberville Motor Company to back him was a dream beyond his most self-indulgent imaginings.

"We'd supply the car, of course. Regular maintenance between and during races would be no problem. And perhaps a small stipend to make it easier for you to dedicate yourself."

"Mr. Symington, this is great. Just great," Pete gushed.

"Of course, we'd expect complete confidentiality in return. *On all things,*" Forrest emphasized.

"Absolutely. Not a word. This meeting never happened."

Forrest smiled. "We don't have to carry it that far. After all, we did have to meet to talk about your DMC sponsorship. Beyond that, well, I think we understand each other."

"We sure do."

"Good. We'll be in touch." He reached out and shook Pete's hand, then turned away, making it clear the interview was over. He waited a minute to be sure the door was closed securely behind his visitor. He looked at the papers on his desk, studying them closely now that he no longer had to feign disinterest. Simple but brilliant, the modifications outlined in the few pages were clearly the work of an automotive genius. And Forrest knew that if he handled it properly, they would never see the light of day.

Melinda was in the bathtub when Forrest arrived at the apartment.

"You're early," she called out as she heard him making his way toward her.

He stood in the doorway of the bathroom and watched her. "You sound disappointed."

"I am. I was going to get all dressed up and fix my hair. I wanted to look really beautiful for you tonight."

"You already do," he said. "In fact, I don't think I've ever seen you look more lovely." It was true. Her face was scrubbed clean, and her hair piled in disarray on the top of her head. But she was glowing, with heat or health or youth he did not know. It made him catch his breath, and he knelt by the tub to kiss her wet face. Her breasts, plump and full, floated on the water. Desire overwhelmed him, and he reached beneath the bubbles and lifted her out of the tub, carrying her to the bed.

"I'm making your suit all wet," she said, laughing, pleased to see he was in such a good mood.

"It doesn't matter," he said hoarsely, "I'm taking it off anyway."

Lying naked beside her, he suddenly remembered that she had taken the day off to go to the doctor. "Are you okay?" he asked, as much to protect himself as her.

"I'm perfectly wonderful," she sighed, and she closed her legs around him. He had no more questions, at least for the time being.

When they had made love, and she had pressed the water marks from his Armani suit, he gave her a small package from Tiffany's.

"Another present?" she asked, delighted. "What's this one for?"

"Because you were sick, and I was worried about you, and I love you."

I'm the luckiest girl in the world, she thought as she tore away the white ribbon and opened the turquoise box to find an emerald and diamond ring—not large, really; just right for her finger, tasteful and exquisite.

"Oh, my God," she breathed as he slipped it on her finger and found it to be a perfect fit. She'd never seen anything so lovely. She gazed at her hand, enthralled, then at her lover. It was hard to believe that things could get better than this, but they were about to. "Now I've got a present for you," she said.

"Hey, you're not supposed to buy me things."

"I didn't."

"It's something you made?"

She laughed. "Sort of. Actually, we made it together."

He felt a warning light go on, but he chose to ignore it. She'd been so lethargic lately, and he was glad to see her back to her old self. He'd set her up here just to keep her this way. A half hour with this naive and happy girl and he could get through another evening of jaded banter with boring cosmopolites like his wife. He looked at his watch.

"Damn, I didn't realize it was so late. I've got to go, sweetheart. Did the doctor say you could come back to work tomorrow?"

"Yes. Do you want to know what else he said?"

"What?"

"Well, I don't have the flu."

She was being coy, and it made him uncomfortable, but he was compelled to respond. "That's good," he said warily, hoping to let it go at that. He started to stand, but she placed herself on his lap, her arms around his neck. She felt like a warm, plush toy, and he could have played with her forever, but recreation time was over.

"Honey, I've really got to go."

"You won't want to when I tell you the good news."

"I never want to. But I *have* to." He moved to lift her off him.

"I'm pregnant," she said, and Forrest fell back into his chair with Melinda firmly planted on his lap. She giggled. "I knew you'd want to stay." She looked at him, beaming, waiting for his corresponding joy.

"You can get an abortion."

She felt as if she'd been kicked in the stomach.

Quickly she moved to another chair, as though his body might suddenly burn her or contaminate her. "I don't want an abortion."

"Don't be ridiculous. You can't have this baby."

"Why not?"

He looked at her. She seemed genuinely bewildered, even hurt. He wondered if she was, indeed, so naïve, or playing dumb, or just plain stupid. He was amazed that he still found her desirable, but he did. There was something worth salvaging here.

"Melinda, darling, I didn't plan on this. You told me you were using birth control."

"You know you were the first. How could I have been using birth control?"

"I asked you, and you said—"

"I said I'd get some. And I was going to. But then I got sick, and then"—she was close to tears—"I was so happy. I thought you'd be happy, too. I thought you'd like to have a baby."

"I've already had babies."

"Not with me."

He didn't know whether to laugh, cry, or scream. He chose to stay in control. "I'm a married man, thirty years older than you, with grown children. Can't you see it would be impossible?"

"No, it wouldn't. Not if you were committed to me, like you said."

"I *am* committed to you. I got you this apartment, didn't I? I go out of my way to come here, to be with you, when I should be at the office or in my home."

Melinda was beginning to understand. Forrest was committed to her as a way station, not a way of life. He had never intended to leave his wife and be with her, and now that she thought of it, he'd never said he did. He said they could stay together forever, and she supposed if she remained in this apartment, pliant and available, they could. They had been lovers, but in fact, she was still his employee—providing a variety of services, to be sure, and being compensated very nicely, thank you—but an employee nonetheless. For the first time since Forrest had initiated her into the realm of sensuality, Melinda felt she had done something dirty, sinful. Not by loving a man she should have known she could never have, but by believing in him.

"I'm having this baby."

"You can't."

"I am."

"I won't allow it. I can't afford the scandal. You can't live here and work for me and be with me and have a little bastard."

Melinda felt the floor falling out from beneath her. The walls were crumbling. She knew she was going to be crushed. She wanted to fall to her knees and beg him to reconsider, not to turn her dream into a nightmare. But one remaining shred of pride held her erect and kept her from groveling. From someplace inside her—she didn't know where—she found the strength to say what she needed to say.

"Fine. I won't live here. And I won't work for you. And I won't be with you. You may choose to think of the life growing inside me as a little bastard, but it is *my* child. You may control your family and your corporation, but you don't control me. I want this baby, and I'm going to have it."

Forrest got angry then and told her she was being an idiot. He called her names and pointed out the hardships she would suffer with no one to support her or the child. He warned her he wouldn't give her a penny, and if she tried to blackmail him, or institute a paternity suit against him, he'd ruin not only her, but her family as well. She insisted she wanted nothing from him, and against his better judgment, he believed her. But still he threatened. Melinda was frightened and admitted as much. But through her tears and entreaties she never wavered. Screaming at her to be gone from his sight and his life by morning, Forrest stormed out of the apartment, Melinda's words still ringing in his ears: "I'm going to have this baby."

After Forrest was gone Melinda collapsed in tears. Somewhere in the midst of the pain and the fear and the need, the final remnant of her pride shriveled and died. Melinda picked up the phone. "Mom," she said, her voice choked with sobs, "can I come home?"

❦ 17 ❧

French toast meant reconciliation. Diane had gone all out making a full American breakfast for her family. Harvey didn't pretend to understand it. His two grown daughters were back home—one was pregnant, both were out of work—but his wife was cooking again. At least *he* still had a job to go to, and, given the dynamics of his overwhelmingly female household, he was just as glad not to linger. He kissed Diane, Sam, and Melinda in quick succession, told them not to get into any more trouble for one more day, and pointedly added that he'd see them at dinner, with the emphasis on dinner.

"He's been fixing himself a lot of Kraft Macaroni and Cheese lately," Diane said with a chuckle after he had gone.

"Poor Dad," said Melinda. "I sin, he suffers."

"I can't cook when I'm upset." Diane shrugged.

"We know," her daughters said in unison, and they all laughed.

"Actually, you're being a real trouper, Mom," Sam interjected. "Anytime you start feeling overwhelmed, just let me know. I can always go back to my place."

"No, it's fine. I like having my girls here." She could have added, and out of the clutches of the insidious Symingtons, but she didn't.

Melinda had come, as she had left, with two suitcases and her overnight bag. She had left the gifts, the designer dresses, the Tiffany jewels behind, along with the key to the apartment. All that remained of her brief foray into a fairy tale with one of the wealthiest men in America was the baby in her belly. And it was only the sight of her swelling breasts and her growing stomach that kept her from believing it was all a dream. Melinda had stayed up with her mother that night, talking about the future, but never mentioning the past.

Melinda had braced herself for a grilling, but Diane had asked no questions. The scenario seemed to hold no surprises for her. In fact, she was relieved, preferring the occurrence of the inevitable to the anxiety of anticipation. Melinda would live at home and look for another job while she could still work. After she had the baby Diane would help with child care while Melinda went back to work. It would be a financial strain, but somehow the family would manage. As for what people might think, it was too late for any of them to give a damn.

Sam had come the next day when she heard of Melinda's predicament. She had told them a little of her own heartbreak, and they had commiserated over the bitter coincidence of two sisters being undone by father and son. Diane had said little during the exchange, but her mouth had set, and she'd finally cursed all the Symingtons and told her daughters to learn a lesson and stay where they belonged. The girls agreed, and, feeling she belonged with her family, Sam had stayed one night and then another, reluctant to go back to her own apartment, void of comfort and full of memory.

While the girls did the breakfast dishes and sang two-part harmony, Diane perused the paper. The item was so small, buried in the local business section of the Oakdale *Spectator,* that she almost missed it. The headline said "DMC Patent," and the article, one paragraph, single column, stated simply that the D'Uberville Motor Company had patented a device that was said to enhance automobile performance while improving pollution controls.

"Sam, come here and look at this," she said, holding the paper out to Sam. "Isn't that kind of like the thing you were working on?"

Sam dried her hands on her jeans and took the paper, first glancing at the article, then—attention caught—studying it intensely. With a sinking certainty she knew it was her invention. It was hideously clear that Drew Symington had stolen first her heart, then her self-respect, and now her life's work. It was too late to do anything about the first, but she'd be damned if she'd let him get away with the rest of it.

"Say something, Sam," Melinda said, frightened by the mute rage in her sister's eyes.

"He stole it," said Sam, standing up and throwing down the paper. "Drew came to my place, and I showed him my plans. I was almost asleep when he left. He saw where I kept them. He must have stolen them."

"There's nothing you can do about it," said Diane,

hurting for her daughter, but fearing for her even more. "Let it go."

"No! Who the hell do these people think they are? This isn't about being seduced and abandoned. This is about criminal theft of industrial design. I refuse to sit on my hands and take it. I'm going to confront that bastard right now."

"Don't," Diane pleaded. "What good would it do? Besides, what makes you think he'll even see you? You can't just storm into the executive offices at DMC. They'll have the security guards after you, and before you know it you'll be back in jail."

"I can help you get in," said Melinda softly.

"Don't encourage her," said Diane.

"How?" asked Sam, ignoring her mother.

"Well, I know Forrest hasn't hired a new personal assistant yet. He's probably looking for someone my size so all that stuff he got me doesn't go to waste."

"Why do you even want to get involved with these people again? No good will come of it," Diane implored them.

Melinda ignored her, too. "Meanwhile, he's using one of the girls from the pool. We were kind of friendly, and she even called me to find out what happened when he gave her the job. She's been a big supporter of your Save the Mill Pond project, and I think she wouldn't mind arranging to be 'away from her desk' at the moment you show up."

Sam's original intention had been to confront Drew, but really it made more sense to go to the head of the corporation. Drew might have stolen her blueprints, but DMC would have to give the patent back to her. Besides, if she wanted to be honest with herself, she had to admit that it was far more daunting to have to face Drew than his father, no matter where the power lay.

"Call your friend. I'm on my way," Sam said as she kissed her sister and headed out the door.

"Samantha, please," Diane called after her. But it was too late. Sam was gone, and Melinda was on the phone.

Forrest didn't recognize her at first. Sam had stopped at her apartment to change into clothes that would be less conspicuous in a corporate setting. He had turned when he heard the door open and found himself face to face with a gorgeous young woman with flaming hair curling around her face and shoulders. After a quick but appreciative once-over that took in the nondescript clothes encasing a body that wouldn't quit, he assumed she'd been sent to be interviewed for the position of his personal assistant. He smiled his dazzler, hoping she could type, and thinking someone like her could go a long way in helping him forget how much he missed Melinda.

"I'm sorry," he said, all but oozing charm, "I'm not seeing people about the job until after five. Didn't my secretary—"

"She was away from her desk, so I just showed myself in."

He started having second thoughts. She was a little aggressive for an assistant. "Then you'll have to show yourself back out." She was very beautiful. Perhaps she just had to be tamed a little. The thought excited him. "Make an appointment with my secretary for after five. I'll be happy to speak to you then," he added.

"I think we should speak now." She sat down.

He was getting a little irritated. Beautiful or not, he didn't need any more aggravation from the women he employed. He picked up the phone. "Let me make myself clear. Either you leave now, or I'll call security and have you removed, Miss . . ."

"Myles. Samantha Myles."

He put down the phone. He had a full dossier on her, but he'd seen her only twice before. Once in the plant, with her hair wrapped in a bandanna and her body covered with overalls; and once with Drew, when he'd embarrassed her and she'd run out. Both times, feeling it unnecessary to acknowledge her as a human being, he hadn't really bothered to look at her face. He was interested to note that though she looked nothing like Melinda, the sisters were equally enticing.

"What is it you want, Miss Myles?"

"I want my invention back."

"I'm sorry, I don't know what you're talking about."

"The device for engine efficiency and emission control, which you patented for DMC, was stolen from me."

"We are in the business of making cars. We patent a lot of devices."

"Please, Mr. Symington. Do me the courtesy of not playing dumb. If we don't talk about it here, we'll talk about it in court. But I'm not going to sit back and let you fuck me like you fucked my sister."

Obviously, she wasn't going to be polite about it. "You're making some serious charges."

"About me, or my sister?"

"Perhaps you should extend the same courtesy to me."

"Fine. You stole my design. I want it back."

"Do you have proof?"

"The last person who saw those plans was your son. Now they are gone. And you are claiming the design is your own."

"My son?" Forrest was taken aback, and relieved. She knew less than she thought.

He seemed genuinely surprised to Sam, but she would not be deterred. They'd been fooled by the Symingtons enough not to fall for more feigned innocence.

"I have four years worth of diagrams, experiments, models, and prototypes to back me up. If you're not willing to resolve this with me here and now, I will take it all to a lawyer and see you in court."

"You're welcome to do that, Miss Myles. But you'll be wasting your money. And I know that you can't have a lot to spare, considering you've been out of work for some time, and I don't really see the trend reversing for you or your family. At least, not in the automotive industry."

"Are you threatening me?"

"No. I'm informing you that I hold the power in this area, and trying to fight me about a questionable invention or the site of my next factory is an exercise in futility. Both will end in my favor. I will not relinquish DMC's patent. I will build a plant at the mill pond. If you can't live with these realities, I suggest you move away."

"If you think I'm going to let you take credit . . ."

She stopped. Forrest was laughing. "Take credit? Is that what concerns you? Well, don't worry about it. There will be no credit taken, because no one is ever going to see this device in action. Let me explain something to you. The particular patent you're concerned with was acquired by DMC not for the purpose of producing the device, but for the purpose of suppressing it. As far as I'm concerned, automobiles in general, and the D'Uberville cars in particular, are adequately efficient and nicely profitable as they are. We will continue to build them without major modifications, as they are being built now. And by this time next year we'll be building them at our new plant at the mill pond."

Sam felt her world collapsing. Everything she'd worked for—her future, the future of the community—was going up in smoke. For a minute she thought she might cry. Then she looked at Forrest's triumphant smile. She was shocked to see how much he resembled Drew. She'd never seen the same cold, calculating hardness around Drew's eyes, but that didn't mean it wasn't there. Somehow she must have mistaken the shrewdness she saw in Forrest's face for the kindness she had imagined in Drew. She'd been blinding herself to a lot lately, but no more.

"Mr. Symington," she said, suddenly feeling the utmost calm, "I have to thank you. I came here feeling like a victim. I had a whole litany of complaints against you and your family, some of them of a highly personal nature. But you've reminded me that righteous indignation is not enough. I don't deny that you have the power. But I remind you that even though the lion may be king of the jungle, he's not immune to predators, some of whom are much smaller and weaker than himself."

She marched out of Forrest's office, head high, priding herself on her dignity, and nearly blew it all by bumping into Drew on his way in.

"What are you doing here?" he asked, looking as though he wanted to kiss her.

She pushed the observation from her mind and coated her voice in a hatred she was not sure she felt. "I'm giving you notice. No more moratoriums, no more concessions, no more personal appeals. From now on I will fight you body and soul, on every front." Drew felt a chill go through him as he watched her walk away. Her meaning was clear. His biggest fear, and his greatest hope, was that she would succeed.

"What happened?" Drew asked his father as he came into the office.

"It's not important," Forrest said.

Drew pretended to accept his father's assessment. "Are you ready to go?" he asked. "We're having people for dinner tonight. Mother will be waiting."

Bethany had dressed for dinner with painstaking care. It was the first time she'd been back to Belvedere since the ill-fated engagement party, and she needed to strike exactly the right note. She'd chosen a Valentino gown, white to convey innocence, simple to convey elegance, and strapless because she considered her breasts her most tantalizing feature, and there was no point in hiding them completely. Her blond hair was loosely arranged on her shoulders, softening her face and giving her an air of artlessness. With the attention she was getting from Drew, she knew she could congratulate herself on her choices.

There were ten for dinner, and although Mathilde generally insisted that it was more civilized to split couples, Bethany had been seated beside Drew. She had been worried at first, fearing that while Drew might keep up appearances on the surface, there would be an undercurrent of hostility that she would have to battle. Even she had to admit that maintaining a relationship through blackmail was not ideal. To her delight, he seemed to have resigned himself to his fate and simply gone back to being the model fiancé he had been before the whole ugly business about separation had been mentioned. In a way, she wasn't surprised. After all, she'd made it clear that once they were married she would not impinge on his freedom. And life with her, she thought as she leaned toward him, discreetly maneuvering her chest into his line of vision, would definitely have its compensations. He might despise her, but he couldn't not want her. That was unthinkable.

"Let's get out of here," Drew whispered, looking at his watch for the third time in as many minutes.

"Where do you want to go?" Bethany murmured, knowing the answer, knowing she had not been wrong.

"My room."

Bethany looked around the table. Forrest seemed more distracted than usual, and Mathilde had partaken even more liberally than was her habit of the several selections of wine with dinner. Drew's sister Sarah was quietly bickering with her husband James, who was chatting up the wife of some minor foreign dignitary that Mathilde had discovered at someone else's dinner party. There was nothing to be lost by abandoning this group early, and a good deal to be won by regaining her foothold in Drew's life, although her foot was not the part of her anatomy she planned to use.

"I'm with you," she whispered, and she squeezed lightly between his legs.

He stood immediately, before she could feel the familiar swell, and announced, "If you'll all excuse us . . ."

"But what about *café?* And brandy," said Mathilde, clearly more concerned about the brandy than the company.

"Please go ahead without us. We might join you later." It was sufficient encouragement for Mathilde, and no one else seemed concerned about their presence—or absence. Mumbling a few polite words, Drew took Bethany by the arm and led her out of the dining room.

Drew had prepared. His suite was lit by candles, and the scent of roses in full bloom lay heavy in the air. A bottle of Dom Pérignon cooled in a silver bucket while two crystal flutes stood at the ready nearby. Bethany almost purred with satisfaction. She had expected to have to work much, much harder.

"This is so delightful, Drew darling."

"I thought we should celebrate." He popped the cork and poured the champagne. "To my returning to my senses, and to the woman who made me do it," he toasted.

"Aren't you sweet," she said, twisting her arm through his before she sipped. "And I was so afraid you'd be angry with me."

"Angry? Well, I admit I was a little, at first. After all, it's not every day that your fiancée tries to blackmail you. But after I thought about it, I realized it was just your way of ensuring I didn't make a fool of myself."

"Absolutely. You know I would never have said anything to anyone really. I'm not out to hurt you or your mother. I love you both. You're family to me."

"I know that." He put his glass down and took her

in his arms. "What I don't know is how you ever got that information in the first place. I thought we'd covered our tracks pretty well."

"You might be able to fool the French authorities," she said, chuckling, "but you can't fool your little Bethany. And you'd do well to remember that." She kissed him to take the sting out of her words, but he seemed not to mind.

"I wouldn't dream of trying." He laughed and kissed her back.

"You're just not a very good liar, my darling. When I told you I had found out about Jean-Claude it was your face that told me I didn't know everything."

"Did Jean-Claude know?"

"Not at first. He really thought that you were the one that had hit his poor little fiancée and left her to die on the Grande Corniche. That sad little man thought he was going to get his revenge on you by stealing me away. Can you imagine?"

"But then how did you find out that it had actually been my mother driving and not me?"

"I have to admit I was a teeny bit naughty. I let Jean-Claude think maybe he would have a chance with me if he could just dig a little deeper and find the truth. Sorry little joke that he was, he believed me and ran off to France to find the truth."

"Bethany," Drew scolded mockingly, "did you lead that poor man on?"

"Maybe I tantalized him just a little. But really, Drew, how could he think for a minute that I would leave you for him? He's a nobody. It's simply ludicrous. Now are we going to stand here talking all night, or are we going to fuck?"

"What do you think? Go into the bedroom. I have a surprise for you."

"I like the sound of that." She hoped it was something just a little kinky. She hadn't had any real fun since Jean-Claude had gone back to France. She really wished she could have found a way to keep him here and keep him quiet. She opened the door to the bedroom and for a moment thought she had somehow managed to astrally project her thoughts into a corporeal image. "Jean-Claude!" she gasped. "You can't be here."

He was sitting on the edge of the bed. "But I am."

She whipped around and saw that Drew was busying himself with the champagne. "Get out of here before Drew sees you."

"But he knows I am here."

This was a nightmare. Bethany willed herself to wake up. She closed her eyes and prayed to be in her own cream carpeted room, between her cream silk sheets. She opened her eyes. Jean-Claude was still there. He seemed to have been crying.

"How . . . how long have you—"

"Long enough to have heard every word you said."

For the first time in her life Bethany was at a loss. Everything was registering, but nothing was computing. None of this was part of her plan. "I don't understand," she said plaintively.

"Let me explain." Drew was behind her now. In one hand he carried the champagne, in the other, three glasses. Somehow she didn't think it was a good sign. "I brought Jean-Claude back so that he and I could have a long-overdue talk. Having learned what love is, I know what he lost, and I needed to tell him how sorry I was. I've explained to him that Mathilde was drunk when she hit his lovely bride, and the year I spent in jail, she spent in a rehabilitation center. Unfortunately, as you both know, it did no good. I was able to spare my mother the horror of a year in prison, but not the horror of being a lifelong prisoner of her disease. She doesn't drive, Jean-Claude. She hasn't been behind the wheel of a car since that day. I know it doesn't help you. But I want you to know that now she only hurts herself."

"You shit," Bethany screamed at Drew. "You set me up."

Drew smiled. "What was that you were saying about my not being able to fool little Bethany?"

"Okay. I take it back. You fooled me. What is the point of this stupid trick? So now Jean-Claude knows that I don't intend to leave you. Nothing changes."

"Pas vrai," said Jean-Claude. "Nothing is the same."

"Listen to me, both of you." Bethany was not going to let them gang up on her. "Just because you two have done some macho bonding doesn't mean this story's over."

"Arrête, Bethany." Jean-Claude stopped her. "It *is* over. I have closed the book. I cannot get Lisette back. Drew cannot get back his year. Mathilde cannot get back her health. We are all victims. You are the only villain," he said to Bethany. "You have tried to gain from our tragedy." He pronounced it in the French way, "tra-je-dee." "But now *c'est finis."*

"It may be *finis* for you, babe, but it's not *finis* for me." Bethany realized she was shouting. She struggled to regain control. "I am warning you"—she turned to Drew—"if you want to protect your mother's name—"

"No, *I'm* warning *you*. The tracks were covered once. They only needed a few more judicious payments to be covered again. As you know, and as you like to remind me, money can buy almost anything. And I have more than you. Bottom line is, you breathe one word of this to anyone—and I mean anyone—at any time—and I mean anytime—and everyone in Woodland Cliffs will think that you are a delusionary paranoid who cannot tell truth from her own ugly fictions. And I think Jean-Claude will back me up on that. Am I right, Jean-Claude?"

"Sorry, Drew, I don't exactly understand what you said. But I will tell everyone she is a liar."

"That's what I said."

"You're both bastards."

"A case of pot calling kettles black? Look at it this way, Bethy baby. Keep your mouth shut and you're free to ply your trade on some other eligible member of the country club elite. That way you might even get someone you deserve."

She knew he didn't mean it as a compliment, but it didn't matter. She also knew it was her only recourse.

"I'm keeping the ring."

"Be my guest."

"Are you pouring?" she asked Drew coolly. "I think I'd like one for the road. I'm not driving," she added with heavy sarcasm.

"By all means."

They clinked glasses, looking for all the world like three patrician pals ending an amiable evening in a civilized fashion. She would not let Drew Symington see that he had undone her. Someday she would find a way to return the favor.

❧ 18 ❧

"He's here," Melinda said softly, waking Sam from her nap. Sam had been up all night planning protest strategy with Jack, and she was still groggy, but she didn't have to ask to whom Melinda was referring.

"What do you mean he's here? Where?"

"In the kitchen."

"What's he doing in the kitchen?"

"Waiting for you. Mom didn't want to let him in. But Dad said he still works at DMC, and Drew's the boss's son, so she had to."

"I don't want to see him."

"Actually, I told him that already."

"What did he say?"

"That he'd just sit there and wait until you changed your mind."

Sam started to smile, and then she stopped herself, remembering she'd promised not to let herself get suckered again.

"What does he want?"

"He's not going to tell *me,* Sam. Why don't you just go out there and find out?"

"I can't."

"I know." Melinda was in complete sympathy. "If it was his father, I wouldn't be able to face him either."

"God, can you believe it? The two of us getting fucked over by the chip and the block."

"In more ways than one."

There was a soft knock on the door.

"I'm going out the window," said Sam in a panic. But a moment later the door opened and Diane came in.

"What's going on here? You can't just leave me out there with him."

"Tell him to go," said Sam.

"I did. He won't."

"Where's Dad?"

"He was on late shift. He's gone to work."

"Well, what do we do?" asked Melinda. "We can't all move in here until he decides to leave."

"Wait a minute," said Sam, jumping up from the bed. "Will you look at us? No wonder people like the Symingtons turn people like us into victims. We let them do it. Why are we cowering in here like three fugitives? We didn't do anything wrong. We should be after them, not vice versa. No more. Drew Symington is a shit and his father is worse, and I'm going to tell him so."

Drew was standing by the window when Sam walked into the kitchen, and he turned at the sound of her footsteps. His eyes told her all she needed to know, but she refused to see.

"Staying away from you has been the hardest thing

I've ever had to do in my life," he said without pride and without ceremony. It was the truth, but she refused to listen. She was standing in the room before him, but inside she had locked herself away, eyes shut tight, ears blocked. She would not let him penetrate her armor; not this time. Because this time she knew that if he so much as touched her heart, it would be a mortal wound from which she would never recover.

"Who do you think you are?" Sam began, revving up her righteous indignation. "You and your father act like feudal lords, seducing the peasant girls, then discarding them when you've had your pleasure. Then, to add insult to injury, you steal what little we have and expect us to kiss your feet for it. You think because you've got the power you're above the law. Because you're in control, you don't need compassion."

Drew had expected Sam to be angry, but he was a little confused about the particulars. "The only thing I ever wanted to steal from you was your heart. But I didn't think you'd mind since I'd already given you mine."

Sam felt her engine faltering. Why was he saying these things, and with such conviction? She needed to give it some gas, accelerate her rage. "What a load of shit! And the fact that the D'Uberville Motor Company now has a patent on an invention of mine has nothing to do with it."

This conversation was not going the way Drew had imagined it would. "My father said you sold it to him."

"I would never sell it."

"Someone did."

"You're the only person I ever showed it to. No one

else knew about it, except you and me and . . ." She stopped short.

"And?" he prompted.

"And Pete." She was almost whispering. "He came to my place the night . . . after you left. He . . . he wanted . . . he tried to rape me."

Drew felt as if he'd been punched in the stomach. "Christ. I shouldn't have left you."

"It's all right. Nothing happened. I got him off me, made him leave. But he swore he'd get even. He knew where I kept the plans. He had a key to my place. Pete must have taken them."

"My father just said they were sold to him. I assumed it was you. If he had known they were stolen—"

"He knew."

"How could he?"

"I told him."

"What?"

"That day you saw me coming out of his office I told him. I went to see him because I was afraid to see you, afraid I'd lose my nerve. He told me that I'd never be able to prove the designs were mine, and that he intended to suppress the invention anyway."

"I can't believe this. My father?"

"Well, it's true. The crowning touch was that he told me that DMC was going ahead with the plant at the mill pond. It all made sense. You never called me after that night because you got what you were looking for."

"I never called you because I had to deal with Bethany first. Once I resolved that problem and she was out of my life, I never stopped calling you. When I couldn't get you at home I tried you at your Save the Mill Pond storefront. I almost got into a fight with Mr.

Ponytail because he wouldn't tell me where you were."

"Jack?" She laughed.

"Yeah. What exactly is your relationship with him anyway?"

"You sound jealous."

"No. I just can't figure out what he is. A lawyer? An assembly-line worker? A male model? He's too smart and too good-looking. Okay, I'm jealous."

"You don't need to be. You're the only . . ." She stopped herself. "What am I saying?"

"Say it."

"No! I'm not doing this to myself again. And I'm not going to let you do it to me. I'm not going to end up like my sister. Seduced and abandoned, with a baby to remind me I was never good enough to be a Symington." Her eyes welled with tears, threatening to wash away her resolve. If he took one step toward her, brushed one fingertip against her, everything she was determined to avoid could and would happen.

But Drew wasn't moving. He was sitting down, pale and dizzy. "What are you telling me?"

"Oh, God, you don't know, do you? Why should you? He wouldn't tell you."

"Then you tell me." His voice came from somewhere inside, the voice of a little boy who's afraid to hear that his father isn't perfect but can't rest until his fear is confirmed.

"It's not my story to tell. I'll get Melinda."

At first Melinda had been reluctant to say anything. She felt humiliated enough without having to discuss her condition with the son of her tormentor. But Drew had patiently drawn her out, his concern so genuine, his compassion so heartfelt that eventually

Melinda told him everything. Even Diane, who sat at the opposite end of the kitchen table, eyes hard, jaw set, had felt compelled to say that he was nothing like his father. It wasn't an easy compliment to take, and it hung in the air as the four of them avoided each other's eyes, each with a private wound in need of healing.

"There's a board meeting at DMC tomorrow at noon." Drew broke the silence first. "Do you think you could be there?"

The three women were taken aback. "Why?" Sam asked for all of them.

"I'm supposed to propose the alternate site for the plant."

"What good will it do? Your father already told me that they were building on the mill pond, and that was final."

"It might not be if you come."

"Maybe Sam should go," said Melinda. "But why do you want me there? I've had nothing to do with the mill pond protests."

"Just trust me. I need you all. Will you come?"

Melinda and Diane looked to Sam. It was her call. I must be an idiot, Sam said to herself. But aloud she said, "We'll be there."

The board of directors, including Mathilde D'Uberville Symington as majority stockholder, was already assembled in the D'Uberville Motor Company conference room when Drew Symington entered. There was a murmur of greeting as he made his way to the head of the table, where Forrest waited and whispered urgently in his ear. Forrest's face remained smiling and impassive as he listened to his son and quietly answered, "This is not a good time. We can't impose on these good people to keep them here longer than necessary."

"I'm sorry, Father," Drew insisted. "It's the only time. They'll either wait and have an orderly meeting, or you can start now, and I guarantee you they'll be here a lot longer than you had planned."

Forrest never flinched, but there was a rigidity in his bearing as he stood and addressed the group. "Gentlemen and ladies, you'll have to excuse us for the delay. An urgent matter requires attention from the top. Please help yourselves to coffee or cocktails and indulge us with your patience."

Forrest smiled; Drew smiled. The assembled members of the board smiled back, priding themselves on being a part of a team headed by such a dazzling duo. DMC *was* the Symington family, with all their attendant wealth and position. As the Symingtons went, so went the corporation, and it was encouraging to see them looking so fit, so efficient, and ever so appropriate. Mathilde considered following her husband and son to find out what was going on, but someone was already pouring the scotch, and she thought perhaps she'd do just as well to wait until they returned.

"This is outrageous," said Forrest through gritted teeth as he followed Drew to his office. "You had better have a damn good explanation."

"I do," said Drew as he opened the door and ushered his father ahead of him.

Forrest had to admit they made quite a sight. The mother, gray now but still beautiful, her face a little lined, but her body holding up remarkably well; the two daughters, one copper, one chestnut, both endowed with enough attributes to fulfill any reasonable man's sexual fantasy.

"If this is about poontang," he said with calculated coldness, "you are wasting my time."

"This is about attitude," said Drew, affronted by his father's vulgarity. "And that remark typifies what we're talking about."

"There is a board of directors worth several million dollars between them waiting in the conference room. If you don't mind, I'll forgo the morality lecture and get back to business."

Forrest turned on his heels and headed toward the door.

"If you leave now, you won't have a business to get back to," said Drew, and the tone of his voice made Forrest stop.

"Are you threatening me?"

"Yes."

"With what?"

"With exposure," said Drew. "I'm prepared to go in there and introduce Melinda Myles as the woman who is carrying your child."

"Are you crazy?" Forrest was apoplectic. "Your mother is in there."

"I know that. That's why I'd prefer not to do it."

"What is it you want?"

"Several things. Return of the patent of the invention that was stolen from Samantha Myles. Full support for Melinda Myles and her—your—child. An assurance that DMC's new plant will be built on an alternate site and not at the mill pond."

Forrest was furious. "You're my son, but you're a fucking idiot. You fuck some piece of ass from off the line, and suddenly you want to be a working-class hero. This is bullshit!"

If Forrest had not been his father, Drew would have struck him. But even with all the respect drained from their relationship there was a primal regard for the man who had given him life that forced Drew's fist back to his side. "Don't ever—I mean *ever*—speak of the woman I'm going to marry in those terms again. Do you understand me?" His words were edged with ice and froze the air between them.

"I understand you," said Forrest, "but I don't believe you. You want to go in there and cause a scandal, go ahead. But it's not going to bring me down. I'm still the one in control. I'll put such a spin on it that they'll be convinced that I've been victimized by a little whore and an ungrateful heir."

Melinda gasped. She had borne a lot from Forrest, but she hadn't expected to hear herself described that way. She was amazed at how much it hurt, even now. Sam took her hand and squeezed it. They'd agreed to let Drew speak for them, but seeing the blood drain from her daughter's face, Diane had had enough.

"I don't think so, Forrest." They all looked at her, shocked to hear a woman's voice. It wasn't just that she had spoken; her tone was so familiar somehow.

"Don't get mixed up in this, Diane," Forrest said. Melinda and Sam looked at each other and then at Drew. Something was going on that they knew nothing about.

"I am mixed up in it, Forrest. You should never have gone after my daughter."

"I couldn't help myself. She reminded me of you."

"Mom"—Melinda sounded desperate—"what are you talking about?"

"I'm sorry, Melinda. I tried to warn you, but I couldn't tell you. I guess I should have. But no one knew. Not even your father."

"You and Forrest?" Melinda was in a state of shock.

"It's why I've always hated DMC. He used me the way he used you, and when he was done with me I was fired."

"This is preposterous," blustered Forrest. "Do you expect anyone to believe—"

"I still have the letters," said Diane quietly. "You were still young then, not so careful. I have all those little gifts from Tiffany's, and the notes that say 'I love you.'"

Melinda was pale. "He gave me things from Tiffany's. He wrote me notes. This is so sick."

Forrest sensed defeat. "This was all a very long time ago. It's an unfortunate coincidence, perhaps, but I don't see the significance in rehashing—"

"I think your board might think it's significant," said Diane. "If they were to find out it wasn't just Melinda, it was her mother, too. It kind of makes it look like a pattern. I think some of your board members might find it downright disgusting."

"Are you going to jeopardize your own marriage, Diane? Your husband still works at DMC. Maybe we could find a better spot for him, give him a raise."

"You can't blackmail me anymore, Forrest. I was too scared for too long, and my daughter is in deep trouble because of it. You want to ruin my life, go ahead. There's not much worth saving anyway. But I'm not going to let you destroy my children."

There was a long silence in which the air seemed to move as the balance of power shifted.

Finally Forrest spoke. His voice sounded old, its

vibrancy replaced by weariness. He talked to Drew, and it was as though there was no one else in the room. "I'll accede to your demands, but I have some conditions of my own."

"What are they?" asked Drew, frightened by the change he had wrought.

"We will go into the meeting. I will approve your preferred site for the new plant. And then you will announce your resignation, effective immediately, from DMC and all its subsidiaries. You will leave my house. You will leave my family. You can live with your new friends on child support and the proceeds of that cockamamy invention for all I care. But you are no son of mine. Do you agree?"

"With pleasure," said Drew. His voice was dry, his face devoid of emotion. But bonded to him at last, Sam could feel his pain as though it were her own.

Sam found Drew later at the mill pond. Diane had taken her daughters home after Forrest had signed a document that Drew had already prepared, promising to negotiate a settlement in good faith for the support of Melinda's child and transferring to Sam the patent for her invention. Then Forrest and Drew had gone into the board meeting to complete the final phase of their agreement. When two hours had passed and there was no word from Drew, Sam knew where to look for him. He wasn't surprised to see her, and when he pulled her into his arms, folding himself around her like a vine around a tree, she felt as though they were intertwined for life.

"Has this been the worst day of your life?" she asked him.

"Yes," he said, thinking of his father's eyes following him with an icy chill as he left the boardroom. "And no," he added, kissing the top of her head.

"How did your mother take your resignation and . . . the rest?" She didn't know what name to put on the finality of the agreement he had made with his father. Banishment seemed too Shakespearean, yet that was what it was.

"Truthfully, I don't think she quite grasped it. We'd been out for quite a while. She'd had several cocktails."

"Anyway, once he's had a chance to think about it, he could change his mind. At least as far as the family is concerned."

Drew gave a bitter laugh. "Forrest? I don't think so. I'm not sure which he regards as a greater betrayal— my exposing his offenses or my willingness to abdicate the throne of Woodland Cliffs society by marrying outside its self-appointed aristocracy. Which reminds me, I owe you an apology."

"What for?"

"For saying you were going to be my wife before I even asked you. I had no right to do that, but he was really pissing me off."

"Listen," Sam said hesitantly. "I know you were very angry, and you probably said a lot of things you didn't necessarily mean. I mean, I'm not going to hold you to . . . if you don't want . . ."

He silenced her with a finger to her lips.

"Do you see where we are?"

"Under a tree."

"Good answer," he said. "But not the right one. Under which tree? Do you recognize it?"

Sam looked around her. With the bushes turned crimson, the trees all bare, it looked a very different place from the lush, green, floral-scented mill pond of spring. Still, she knew where they stood.

"I consider this hallowed ground," said Drew.

She laughed. "A naked girl hiding behind a weeping willow is not exactly God in a burning bush."

"Don't scoff," said Drew, half joking himself. "I knew from the minute I saw you here that I could never have a life without you. So it's appropriate that we make it official in this very place." The gold and brown carpet of leaves crinkled as he got down on his knees. "Samantha Myles, I love you. Will you marry me?" It was a simple, heartfelt declaration that moved her almost to tears, and for a moment she couldn't speak. "Don't do this to me, Sam," Drew said. "I have nothing left in this world but you."

Sam saw that he was serious and got down on her knees in front of him. "Yes," she said. "If you want me, I will marry you. But are you sure it's worth it? If you marry me, you'll have nothing."

"I'll have you. That's all I need. And maybe a tent," he added as afterthought. "Because after today I've got nowhere to live."

"There's always my place. If you don't get nose-bleeds leaving the high altitude of Woodland Cliffs for the humble streets of Oakdale."

"I thought you'd never ask. You know," he said, talking as much to himself as to her, "my father started with nothing."

"Yes, but he married your mother, who had more money than God. I've got about one hundred and thirty-two dollars, not counting the fortune I've accumulated in my penny jar."

"Okay, neither one of us has money. But you know how to build cars, and I know how to build companies. My father had money and ambition, but we've got love and knowledge. Which do you think will get you further?"

They both pretended to think for a minute, then answered in unison, "Money and ambition," and they started laughing.

"Sam," said Drew after a while. "Can we go home now?"

"Yes, my darling," said Sam, liking the sound of it. And she knew they were both thinking the same thing. Home. Not a gated estate with tennis court and swimming pool. Not even a simple one-bedroom apartment with no view and not enough closets. Home. A place where they would always dwell together, richer or poorer, with just enough space for two hearts and two souls to share forever after.

Pocket Books
Proudly Presents

The Second Title in Our
Summer of Love Trilogy

FOR BETTER, FOR WORSE

Leah Laiman

The following is a preview of
For Better, For Worse . . .

It was going to be the wedding to end all weddings. A huge snow-white tent, its poles wrapped in white satin, had been set up on the estate grounds. Knots of white freesia tied with satin bows trimmed the seams and perfumed the air with a heavenly scent that could have been the essence of paradise itself. More freesia adorned the tables, purple this time, surrounding a profusion of white and purple orchids that rose from silver chalices in the center of each table. The guests were just beginning to arrive, and the caterers had finished laying out crystal and silver, linen napkins, and plates of the finest china.

Each table had its own champagne fountain, and an oversized bowl of beluga caviar, cushioned in a silver tureen of cracked ice, with a tiny, sterling, long-handled spoon nestled in its inky center. No expense had been spared, but then, why should it be? This was to be the wedding of Andrew Symington, only son and heir to the D'Uberville Motor Company fortune, and he was marrying the woman of his dreams.

The fact that Samantha Myles, his bride-to-be, came from a working-class family, so far below the D'Uberville-Symington station at the apex of Woodland Cliffs society as to give some of the dowagers headaches just thinking about the change in altitude, made no difference to Drew. Sam was beautiful, with copper hair, green eyes, creamy skin, and a gorgeous figure that defied her appetite for everything. And she was smart. A natural-born automotive genius, Sam had invented a device that could change the production of automobiles into a more cost-conscious, environmentally sound industry. Though everyone knew it was a love match, merging her genius with the fortunes of the scion of DMC could prove to be profitable all around.

When she'd accepted his proposal, Sam hadn't even considered her fiancé's family business. It had been his patrician face, with his straight black hair and startlingly blue eyes, rather than his formidable lineage that had attracted her at first. In fact, knowing he was a Symington only made her more determined to forget all about him, after their first inauspicious meeting at the Millpond. He had been in the company of his then-fiancée, an idiotic social climber named Bethany Havenhurst, when he had found Sam, naked and shivering behind a tree, after an interrupted skinny-dip. If ever Cupid's arrow had played havoc with the lives of inappropriate targets, this was such a case. But the more they had determined to splinter the instantaneous link that had been forged between them, the tighter the bond had become. Until, unable to fight Eros' charge, they had finally accepted what they had known from that first moment. They loved each other. They could not live without each other. They would marry.

There had been complications. Ugly personal business between Sam's sister and Drew's father, when Melinda Myles had worked for Forrest Symington as his executive assistant. The antagonism of Drew's mother, the formidable Mathilde D'Uberville Symington, whose family fortune and aristocratic lineage had made possible both the Symington's financial and social positions. But the particulars of the reception made it clear that all objections had been laid aside. Everything was being handled with the kind of elegance and good taste that only lots and lots of money— D'Uberville money—could buy.

It would have been understandable if the Myles

family had felt out of their element. They were simple people who had lived in Oakdale all their lives, and at one time or another all of them had worked for Forrest Symington or his father, and soon his son, at the D'Uberville Motor Company. Their friends were men and women who worked on the line, who came to the wedding in their Sunday best, but with car grease permanently embedded under their fingernails and in the creases of their hands. They were an odd mix with the elite of neighboring Woodland Cliffs society, who sported designer gowns that they would wear just this once and cost more than Harvey Myles made in six months. But, somehow, it worked. The warmth of simplicity mingling with the air of elegance created an atmosphere both genial and gracious, so that everyone felt welcomed and welcoming. The bride's side marvelled at how down-to-earth the boss could be. The groom's side couldn't get over how interesting the workers were. And both sides agreed that inasmuch as it was the wedding of the year, it was, after all, going to be a lot of fun.

For the bride, it was all too good to be true. Samantha Myles looked at herself in the mirror and couldn't believe the image that confronted her. She felt like Cinderella, in her white gown, with a sweetheart neckline that showed off her long neck and smooth, full bosom to perfection. Made by the House of Chanel of the finest peau de soie, with tiny swirls of seed pearls embroidered at the hem and on little cap sleeves, it hugged her body before bursting into a full cascade of train in back. Her hair had been piled on her head in a crown of copper curls, by Alexandre, flown in from Paris by her future mother-in-law, especially for the occasion. A sheer veil fell from the ingenious cluster of pearl-studded silk and fresh flowers all the way to the floor. And even Sam, modest about her appearance and dismissive of her beauty, had to acknowledge the radiance, ascribing it to inner joy rather than to the plain fact that she was absolutely gorgeous.

Stepping out onto the terrace of the guest wing at Belvedere, the Symington's estate, Sam gazed down at the white tent that covered the lush, green-grass carpet of the grounds. The sun was shining, and the air was cool and fragrant. She searched the throng for a glimpse of Drew, desperate to see him, but hoping she wouldn't. Things were too good to give the fates any excuse to administer a portion of bad luck.

"Don't worry, he's here," said her sister, Melinda, joining her.

"Have you seen him?"

"Yup. He looks good in tails."

"He looks good in anything. Even better without anything."

"I don't think I need to hear this," Melinda laughed.

Sam looked at her maid-of-honor. No puffed-sleeve, empire-waisted special, Melinda's gown was a sophisticated swirl of chiffon that fell like a Grecian column from an embroidered bodice that accentuated her full breasts and narrow waist and hips. A spray of tiny purple orchids, the same color as her gown, was pinned into her chestnut hair, which tumbled loosely over her shoulders.

"You look beautiful," Sam told her sister.

"Look who's talking," Melinda said, smiling back.

They hugged each other then, careful not to muss themselves, but needing to feel the closeness, needing to know that no matter what fate befell them, good or bad, they'd still be the "Myles Militia," standing together against the world.

"I'm dreaming, aren't I?" asked Sam, closing her eyes.

"Yes," said Melinda simply.

"Pinch me."

Melinda did as she was told.

"Ouch," said Sam, opening her eyes, rubbing her arm. "What did you do that for?"

"You told me to," said Melinda, sitting on the edge of the bed.

"No I didn't. I was sleeping."

"Well, you must have been dreaming, because I distinctly heard you say, 'Pinch me.'"

Sam sat up and looked around. She was in her old bed in her old room at her parents' house on Thayer Street.

"Oh God," she groaned. "I *was* dreaming."

"It couldn't have been that bad. I've been trying to wake you up for ten minutes and you just kept turning over and smiling a lot."

"I dreamt I was getting married today."

"You *are* getting married today. If you get out of bed, that is."

Sam hoisted herself out of the bed and went to the open window. The sun was shining and the air was cool and fragrant. An awning had been raised over part of the backyard where folding chairs had been set around a dozen bridge tables. Since none of Drew's friends or family were expected to show up, they had figured they wouldn't need much more. Diane had gathered pansies and anemones from the garden and was bunching them into little vases in the center of each table. Sam smiled. It wasn't elegant, but it was sweet.

"How are you feeling?" Sam asked her sister.

Melinda patted her tummy. "A little sick when I got up, but I'm okay now. Let's hope the little monster stays quiet today."

"How's your dress?"

"It's fine. Don't worry. Mom let it out enough so no one will know your maid of honor is five months pregnant."

"Everybody here probably knows already."

"That's true. Does it bother you?"

"Of course not. At least, it doesn't bother me what other people think. The question is, does it bother *you?*"

"Not as much as it should. I mean, I wish things weren't so complicated. For your sake as well as mine."

"Well, don't worry about it. Since Drew has been disowned, and I'm obviously never going to have anything to do with my father-in-law, I'm free to hate him for what he did to you."

"You don't have to hate him, you know. I don't. I should have known better. And I really want this baby."

"I know. We all do."

"Good. Because I'm going to need all the help I can get."

"Drew and I can practice on it, until we get one of our own."

"Okay. But first we've got to get you married. So how about getting dressed?"

Sam walked over to the bedroom door, where her wedding gown hung on a wire hanger, still in its plastic dry-cleaner's bag. She had borrowed it from a friend at the plant who had gotten married the year before. It was a classic white gown, full and lacy, not necessarily a style she would have chosen for herself. But it fit, and her mother had helped her open the bodice into a sweetheart neckline that showed off her long neck and smooth bosom and reaffirmed the old adage that all brides are beautiful. It wasn't going to be the wedding of her dreams, but it was going to be her dream come true. Andrew Symington had chosen Samantha Myles over his family and his fortune. They loved each other. They could not live without each other. They would marry.

"You're sure he's here?" Sam nervously asked her mother.

"Of course I am," Diane laughed, hugging her anxious daughter. "He's by the back door, waiting for his cue." They were in the kitchen, getting themselves lined up for the procession. Mrs. Voskovic, their next-door neighbor, had offered to be the wedding coordinator, but her constant chatter got on Diane's nerves, and with fuses already short, she'd sent her out into the backyard to sit under the awning and watch with the other guests. A string quartet from the music department of the community college had agreed to play for twenty-five bucks a head.

"He doesn't look sorry, does he?" Sam pursued her fears.

"Not a bit. He's a little nervous . . ."

"Nervous? Why?"

". . . Like you. But he seems happy."

"I should have seen him."

"You said you didn't want to. It's bad luck."

"I know. But then I could tell—"

"What's the hold up?" asked Melinda. She looked beautiful in the peach dress she hated; a single peach rose, large and in full blossom, was nestled in her chestnut hair. Anyone who didn't know would not have thought she was pregnant, or even overweight.

"We're waiting for Jack. He had to wait for the rest of us to get done so he could change," said Diane.

Sam felt more misgivings. "Do you think it was wrong for me to ask him to be best man? I mean, I've got Melinda, but Drew didn't have anybody. . . . I've done that to him, haven't I? Made it so he couldn't even have his own best man."

Melinda looked at Sam's apprehensive face and hugged her sister, careful to leave some space between them to keep their dresses from crushing.

"Hey, what happened to the girl who's motto was 'I think, therefore I'm right'?"

Sam shrugged. "You always said I was wrong."

"Since when did you listen to anything I had to say. Come on, Sam. You're my big sister. You're not supposed to get scared."

'Well, I am."

"Don't be. This is right for you and you know it."

Diane gave Melinda a grateful look. When they wanted to, the sisters knew how to take care of each other. Everything was going to be fine.

Hearing a door open, Diane and Sam both turned. "Jack," sang out Sam, opening her arms. "Just in time. I was getting ready to call the whole thing off, but since you've already got your tux on, we may as well go ahead."

"You're Jack?" Melinda asked, incredulous. He looked better than he had when she had first seen him. He had shaved and was cleaned up, wearing a tuxedo instead of jeans and a ratty, torn sweater. For the first time, she noticed the long, blond hair, which he had tied into an inconspicuous ponytail for the occasion.

"And you must be the lovely Melinda," he said, with a trace of irony so faint that only Melinda could hear it.

"I forgot you two have never met. You're both such a big part of my life, it seems like you should know each other."

"Actually, we have met once, but only briefly." said Jack, grinning broadly.

"Come on, kids," said Diane as she signaled the quartet to start the processional. "It's time to do it."

Jack proffered his arm to Melinda. She almost refused it, but she saw Sam's face, happy and hopeful again. She placed her hand on his arm, but there was no warmth in the gesture.

"Have you no sense of decency?" she whispered as, still smiling, he locked her hand in his and forced it into the crook of his arm.

"Have you no sense of humor?" he whispered in return as he led her down the makeshift aisle to the strains of Pachelbel's Canon.

Sam wasn't quite sure how she got there, but suddenly it was her turn. For a moment, she stood and surveyed the scene. More folding chairs had been arranged in rows, away from the tables, crowding around an improvised altar. There were about sixty people, all dressed in their Sunday best, a gap forced between them, down the middle, to allow for an aisle. She saw Drew standing, his back toward her, and she wondered if he was thinking of the grounds of Belvedere, so far removed from her parents' backyard. But then the strings began their sweet version of Wagner's *Lohengrin* "Wedding March," and he turned toward her and all her questions and fears became irrelevant.

Everything Sam needed to know, she saw in Drew's face. He did not see the crowded yard with its patches of brown grass. He didn't even notice the rickety chairs or, in the background, the reception's haphazard tables. He paid no attention to the guests, dressed in K-mart instead of couturier. His entire focus was on his bride as she moved slowly and deliberately toward him, and his eyes told her that there could be no mistake.

Sam smiled, and a cloud moved away from the sun and lit them all with a heavenly glow. Anyone who saw knew that it was right. Sam and Drew loved each other, they belonged together.

And in a radiant light that transformed a shabby backyard into a Shangri-la, they became husband and wife.

Look for

For Better, For Worse

**Wherever Paperback Books Are Sold
mid-June 1994**

THE SUMMER OF L♥VE TRILOGY

by Leah Laiman

FOR RICHER, FOR POORER
(available)

FOR BETTER, FOR WORSE
(coming mid-June)

TO LOVE AND TO CHERISH
(coming mid-July)

POCKET BOOKS

982